BLOND BABE IN THE WASHINGTON JUNGLE

She had come into town fresh and innocent, with her big blue eyes, her lovely blond hair—and a number of other very visible assets.

But now she was in a spot the charm school back home had never told her about.

That's when Grace Latham, and her old friend, the redoubtable Colonel Primrose, decided to lend her a hand—too late to prevent one murder, but perhaps in time to stop the mysterious killer from striking again . . .

"The latest and probably the best Col. Primrose-Grace Latham set-to . . . This is high tension stuff"
—The Washington Star

ABOUT THE AUTHOR

LESLIE FORD has become one of the most widely read mystery writers in America. Her first novel was published in 1928 and since then she has written around forty others.

Miss Ford lives in Annapolis, Maryland.

Among her books are *False To Any Man, Old Lover's Ghost, The Town Cried Murder, The Woman in Black, Trial By Ambush, Ill Met By Moonlight, The Simple Way of Poison, The Clue of the Judas Tree* and *Three Bright Pebbles,* all published in Popular Library editions.

Washington Whispers Murder

BY LESLIE FORD

WILDSIDE PRESS

Washington Whispers Murder

Published by Wildside Press LLC
www.wildsidepress.com

I

The man with the traveling bag and briefcase waited quietly on the service stairs of Mrs. Sybil Thorn's handsome house on Woodley Road in Washington, D. C. When the coast was clear he crossed the hall to the small room second floor back, and stood listening to the cocktail party going on in the rooms below. If he hadn't caught a quick glimpse of Congressman Hamilton (Call Me Ham) Vair's heavy blond figure through the pantry door as the maid discreetly slipped his note into Vair's hand, he'd have thought he'd come to the wrong place to find the man whose private undercover investigator he'd now been for several months. Normally, you didn't have to look for Ham Vair, much less listen.

He closed the door of the small room and took off his seedy grey overcoat. The glamorous Mrs. Thorn must have been giving Ham Vair lessons in deportment.—Forget that a dizzy columnist ever called you the youthful and handsome Hot Rod from the Marsh Marigold State. Don't boom, and don't burst out laughing, and don't clap people on the back, she'd probably told him . . . or not these people anyway. He remembered the string of shiny limousines parked on both sides of Woodley Road. Because the party was obviously one more step in the master plan to groom Ham Vair for bigger and better things. It took dough, of course, but Sybil Thorn, twice divorced and as cynically ambitious in her way as Vair was in his, had plenty of that, and friends to kick in more when his campaign got rolling.

The man took his briefcase over to the desk. Parties to meet the right people were just frosting . . . for a wedding cake, Sybil Thorn was no doubt figuring, when dime-a-dozen Congressman Ham Vair became Senator Hamilton Vair, one of the prestige-and-power laden Ninety-Six. The real stuff was right here in the mahogany file by the desk, kept in Mrs. Thorn's back room because Vair was too cagey to keep it in his apartment or in his office on Capitol Hill.—If you called it a file, the man thought dispassionately. A monument, was more like it. A monument to a vindictive personal hatred that circumstances had suddenly converted into the political opportunity of a lifetime. It was a file on a man named Rufus Brent. Rufus Brent's appointment to head up the new Industrial Techniques Commission had given Congressman Vair, the thirty-one year old representative from Taber City, center of the Ninth District out in the Marsh Marigold State, a target that would make him front page news from coast to coast. And Vair had hated the guts out of Rufus Brent before the Industrial Techniques Commission was ever thought of.

He started to open the file when he saw the ball of crumpled paper lying by the baseboard, as if someone had crushed it up and hurled it at the wastebasket. He picked it up and smoothed it out. It was a page from a weekly news digest that had hit the stands that day. Half-way down the savagely crumpled page he saw why Vair was neither booming nor laughing at the party down there. A single paragraph had jerked the Senate seat out from under his eager posterior.

"Look for an indefinite delay," it said, "in setting up the new Industrial Techniques Commission. Reason is, nobody to head it. Congressional approval for an agency with unprecedented peacetime power to cut red tape and expedite vitally necessary retooling for late model military and commercial aircraft was based on a strictly bi-partisan agreement to keep the Commission clear of politics. Rufus Brent, able but little-publicized Western industrialist, was unanimously accepted as the Commission czar before the Bill could be submitted to the Congress. He has since been forced to refuse the job, for what are authoritatively stated to be purely personal and private reasons. It is unlikely that anybody else of his calibre that both parties can agree on can be found at this time."

The man's face was expressionless as he read it through a second time and put it down on the desk, glancing at the door. Vair barged into the room, his florid handsomely heavy face flushed, his jaw thrust out the way he thrust it out on the hustings, a campaign natural. His blue eyes were glittering.

"Look, you——" He shut the door and lowered his voice to a savage whisper. "You know better than to come here when there are people around. What the hell do you think you're doing? You're fired. Get out."

The glitter in his eyes hardened as he looked at the man behind the desk—crisp brown caplike haircut, shaggy at the edges, smooth impassive face, not handsome but casually attractive except for the eyes that were too small, too flat, and too cold-grey, the one flaw in an otherwise perfect counterfeit. The flush on Vair's face deepened as he saw the man shrug and reach calmly out to pick up his briefcase.

"And wipe that superior smirk off your wellbred mug or I'll knock it off." He swung his arm back. "——Investigator. Undercover expert! I knew you were nothing but a high-class shake-down artist, but I didn't know you were a lousy heel. Four months you've been bleeding me white, investigating Rufus Brent, and I have to go buy a twenty-cent magazine to find out the great Western industrialist's not taking the job." His voice rose, brutal and mocking. "For purely personal and private reasons. And where the hell have you been? You're supposed to be hot stuff at personal and private reasons. What the hell have you been doing? Why didn't you tell me six weeks ago that old devil wasn't coming to Washington? You let me beat my brains, figuring out my whole campaign to make hash out of Mister Rufus Brent . . . and Mister Rufus Brent's not coming to Washington. You dirty double-crossing——"

The man went across the room and picked up his coat. "If you'd kept your pants up and your blood pressure down," he said coolly, "I'd have been glad to tell you . . ."

"Tell me what?"

The man shrugged again. He moved slowly, putting on his coat. With the really big shakedown of his career just in front of him, he couldn't afford to let Vair fire him now. Congressman Vair had become too important a factor in it.

"I just got fired, remember?" he said casually.

Vair's blue eyes stabbed him, bright and hard as dagger points. The flush on his face receded. "You're hired. Stuff it. What's on your mind? What have you got?"

"Rufus Brent is coming to Washington." *And you could go to hell if he wasn't. I wouldn't need you if the old fool had stayed home.*

He let his overcoat drop back on the chair. "I didn't phone because I didn't want to risk a leak. I flew back. They've persuaded him to come—long enough to get ITC organized and rolling anyway. Your senior Senator—the old goat you're trying to unseat—spent the weekend with him. Devotion to duty is what they call it, I believe."

Vair's eyes were bright, his jaw and hands working. "Oh, man!" he said softly. "Oh, brother! That's what I wanted to hear. I'm going to crucify him. I'm going to make the Toolmaker wish he'd never come into my state and my district to build one of his damned plants. He's going to rue the day he walked in there and rooked me out of thirty-five thousand fast and easy bucks on the scrap deal I worked like a hog to get going. I'd be a rich man right now if it hadn't been for Mister Rufus Brent. He'll see." He laughed shortly. "We don't like foreigners in my state. They'll run him out of there on a rail before I get through with him. He'll wish he'd made the measly contribution I crawled to ask him for. He'll wish he'd let me take his red-haired daughter to the Brentool Village square dance when I offered to. He can snap his fingers at Congressman Ham Vair, but Senator Vair. . . . He'll crawl, damn him. Mister Rufus Brent'll crawl till his knees bleed. And the red-head'll crawl too."

He crossed the room to the panelled cupboard by the fire-place, reached up to open it and jerked his head back. "What about that girl?" he demanded abruptly. "Where is she? Where is Miss Molly Brent? Have you found her yet?"

"Not her. I've found a couple of pictures of her. I don't know whether you'll want to use them. They may be too hot to handle. I don't know just how far you want to go."

He opened his briefcase slowly, delaying as he'd delayed putting on his overcoat. The heavier Vair laid it on the Brents, the more the Brents were going to need a friend when the time came.

Vair's face flushed again. "You don't? Well, I'll tell you. All the way. Do you get that? I said I was going to crucify Rufus Brent and I meant crucify him. Nothing's too hot to handle. Let him blow his brains out if he wants to. That I'd like to see."

The man took two glossy-print photographs out of the briefcase. "The Madisonburg *Times* doesn't know these are gone yet," he said easily. "They never published this one."

It was a flashlight shot taken at night in a pelting rain. A girl running wildly, her head down, her forearm raised shielding her face. She was bareheaded, slender and as fragile as the long filmy white skirt she was clutching as she ran, toward a car parked with other cars in a curving driveway. At the other side of the photograph, startled people in dinner clothes were rushing out after her from the white-columned portico of a substantial fieldstone house with lighted windows.

"You can't see her face."

"You can see the license number on her car." The man put his hand out and blocked off the house and the people running out of it, leaving only the girl running wildly through the pouring rain.

Vair laughed. "Somebody ought to be able to do a swell job with that one. Is that when it happened?"

"That's right after she got the news. That's what she's running from."

They both knew what the news had been. Neither of them needed to say it.

"Here's when it happened." He handed Vair the second photograph. "You can't see her face in this one either."

It was the same girl and the same car. The only part of the sodden white dress that showed was what a man's raincoat did not cover as she lay in a small inert heap on the side of the wet road. A state trooper stood in the rain, arms out, holding back invisible spectators. Skid marks showed on the shiny asphalt. The car was a tangled wreck against a tree trunk, barren branches dripping down on the huddled girl under the raincoat.

"I haven't found out whether she can walk yet," the man said, in his dispassionate monotone. "Or where they've got her. She's left the hospital. She wasn't at their house in Madisonburg.—If you still want to know."

"You're damn right I want to know." Vair turned to the cupboard and took out a stained green oiled silk pouch. "Here," he said. "Maybe you'll get a lead out of these. A lot of leads, for all I know. That's your job. They're just a batch of personal letters, but you can't tell. Get 'em back— I don't want the Marine Corps on my neck."

There was a flicker of light in the grey eyes. He tightened his fingers on the pouch to keep the quick tremor of excite-ment that ran through them from revealing itself to Vair. "What are they?"

"I said personal letters," Vair answered roughly. "If you don't want to be bothered with them, give 'em back. A buddy of one of the Brent boys picked 'em up out in Korea after the kid's company moved on. He brought them home and left them at my office to forward to the Brents—he thought they lived in my district because there's a Brentool Plant there. He didn't know they lived out West. I'll return 'em, but you comb 'em first."

Vair closed the cupboard door. "You know how to use that kind of stuff. Why don't you try moving right in with the Rufus Brents? You'd have plenty then—if you could work it."

He looked at his investigator critically, his eyes sweeping from the crisp caplike haircut down his pin-stripe flannel suit, shiny at the elbows and knees, to his shoes, good once but old and newly soled. "Better get a new outfit. You look mighty ragtag and bobtail to me. Draw what you need." He still eyed him. "You don't look as Harvard and Princeton—or was it Williams, I forget—as Sybil said you did when she knew you."

The man's eyes flattened for an instant at the barbed con-tempt in Vair's eyes and voice. He caught himself. "I don't use my props unless I need them," he said easily. He reached in his inside coat pocket, took a pair of narrow steel-rimmed spectacles out of a battered tin case, put them on and looked at Vair with a faint smile.

"Ha!" Vair clapped him on the shoulder, laughing. "I wish a pair of two-dollar specs was all I needed to look like I just walked out of the State Department. What is it Sybil says?—Civilized. That's it. I'd even trust you with my daughter. Why don't you try the pulpit when you get through with the Rufus Brents?"

He laughed again. "I got to beat it back now. Sybil'll be screaming her head off. Keep your mouth shut about the letters."

The man waited until he heard Vair's booming voice and rocketing laughter downstairs . . . the Hot Rod of the Marsh Marigold State top of the world again, on his way again. He took off the steel-rimmed spectacles that magnified his eyes just enough to make them match the rest of his face and made him look Ivy League and to the manor born, and put them back in his pocket. He untied the olive-drab tape around the stained silk pouch, took out the thick packet of airmail letters and began to read them. Half-way through the fourth he stopped, his hand shaking with excitement. This was it. This was all he needed.

He gathered the letters quickly together, slipped them into his briefcase and opened the file behind him. When they called Rufus Brent the little-publicized Western industrialist, they weren't kidding. The only other picture of Molly Brent besides those he had stolen from the morgue of their small-town newspaper was a picture of the whole family in a slick-paper magazine article in the file. He opened it on the desk. It was a double-spread entitled "The Toolmaker Sticks To His Lathe." There were pictures of the abandoned emergency defense plant in Vair's Ninth District, and the gleaming white concrete and glass structure of the Brentool Plant, Tabor City, that had taken its place, and set Ham Vair back thirty-five thousand dollars on his junk deal with Surplus Property. There was a picture of Rufus Brent and his wife, in rocking chairs on the front porch of their frame house in their own home town. On the steps in front of them were three children, two boys, seventeen or eighteen, and between them their kid sister, about fourteen, with braces on her teeth, hanging on to the collar of a dog as big as she was. They were all laughing. The dog's wagging tail was a white blur.

He glanced at the pictures of Molly Brent, four years older, that Vair had left on the desk. The girl running through the rain was a graphic statement of the personal and private reasons that had forced Rufus Brent to refuse to come to Washington. His coming in spite of them was the Toolmaker sticking to a bigger lathe. But with the Toolmaker in Washington, and Ham Vair in there cutting the Toolmaker's throat, the letters in the green stained pouch gave him the one thing he needed and had searched for . . . a character and a name for the slickest shakedown he'd ever dreamed up.

It was a good thing he'd waited. He could have sold Vair

out to Rufus Brent for a few paltry thousand any time since the idea first began to grow on him. But the dream that had been born the night of the girl's accident wasn't a matter of thousands. It was millions—if he married her . . . or if he got rid of her, and stuck to the old lady. . . . Son-in-law or adopted son, it was millions either way.

II

The day the Rufus Brent-Hamilton Vair dogfight became more to me than just another irritating headline in the morning paper is very vivid in my mind.

I'd had a long lunch with Colonel John Primrose (92nd Engineers, U. S. Army, Retired) in the Mayflower Lounge and left him there to go on up Connecticut Avenue to the hairdressers'. They have glassed-in cubicles that are divided, so I was only half conscious of the woman I was sharing one with. She'd got a fresh dye job and still had a brick-red streak behind her left ear. We each had a newspaper, and it had a story in flaunting type in a double column at the bottom.

COLOSSUS OF GREED WITH A WART ON HIS NOSE, VAIR CALLS BRENT IN TODAY'S BITTER ATTACK ON ITC HEAD.

"Today's bitter attack" was right. There'd been one the day before and the day before that and there'd no doubt be another. I was aware of the woman in my compartment dropping her paper on the floor and closing her eyes, when I heard the operator ask if she'd like a glass of water. She shook her head. I didn't finish reading the piece, because I was startled at the sound of a familiar voice in another double cubicle across the narrow room.

". . . Having lunch today with John Primrose?" It was that that startled me rather than the voice itself. "Oh, my dear, that's Grace Latham."

Why women think frosted glass booths are soundproof, or try to talk when they have that instrument of torture known as the dryer whirling in their ears, deafening them so their voices are ten times louder and higher than normal, I'll never know. The girl doing my hair stopped. "Shall I tell her to shut up, Mrs. Latham?" she asked anxiously.

I shook my head. The woman was an old friend and my

life's a fairly open book. But I was surprised at the red-haired woman next to me. She'd opened her eyes and turned her head. She was listening too.

"You must meet her." My friend went happily on. "There are enormous advantages in knowing Grace Latham. She has two perfectly enchanting sons. They always come home for the holidays, which is when you need attractive young men the most. And then, she's got Colonel Primrose. You've no idea what that means if you should ever get into trouble of any kind. He's a sort of super-intelligence agent of some kind, but he'll do anything for Grace. My husband's niece . . . my dear, you remember the perfectly foul mess she got into when somebody murdered that miserable husband of hers. She was a friend of Grace's and the Colonel really saved her life. My husband sent him a whopping check, but he sent it back. He said he'd just done it for Grace. So you see, my dear . . ."

She laughed pleasantly. "Of course, I'm devoted to Grace," she said, and I took a deep breath, waiting for the "But . . ." that I knew was bound to come. "But she's an awful fool, really."

The hairdresser and I looked at each other, and we both laughed.

"I'm sure she could have married John Primrose a dozen times if she'd just make up her silly mind. I've told her so a dozen times."

It was nearer fifty, as I recalled it.

"Her husband was killed in an air accident when the two boys were small. She was terribly brave, I thought, but frightfully stubborn. Life can be very disillusioning for a young widow in Washington. But the boys aren't children any more, and Colonel Primrose would make them a wonderful stepfather. Just hostages to fortune is all that stops her."

What hostages to fortune I had I couldn't think, but she went on to count them.

"It's that barn of an old house of hers, and that dreadful old savage that cooks for her. Lilac's been with her so long, I don't know what either of them would do without the other. And the Colonel's got an old house, just down the block from hers on P Street in Georgetown. Her ancestors built hers and his ancestors built his and they're just like Chinese, my dear, they're stuck, they just can't get rid of their damned ancestors. And John Primrose has that dreadful sergeant he brought back from some war with him."

That was Sergeant Phineas T. Buck (also 92nd Engineers, U. S. Army, Retired), Colonel Primrose's guard, philosopher and friend, also self-styled "functotum," she was talking about then.

"The Sergeant saved his life, or something, and I know he kept that old house going through the depression, because John Primrose didn't have a bean except his retired pay and the Sergeant had a sockful. And that old cook of theirs, Lafayette, he must be a hundred, and he and Lilac don't even speak. It's just a conspiracy, my dear, of sticks and stones, and sons, and cooks, and sergeants. It's so irritating. If Grace didn't have what money she needs, she'd have to marry, and she'd get over this quixotic idea she's got that it wouldn't be fair to disrupt that military menage of theirs.

"And my dear, she lives right across P Street from me, and every time John Primrose comes to see her, that Sergeant of his marches right along behind him, and sits in the basement kitchen till time to take him home. It's perfectly absurd, you've never known two people chaperoned the way they are. I doubt if John Primrose has ever even kissed her. And she's not getting any younger, and how she keeps that figure of hers is a mystery to me, there's not that much difference in our ages."

I was playing hop-scotch on P Street in Georgetown when she married if it makes any real difference.

"And people think she's attractive, as she is, but she's not the beauty her mother——"

She broke off. "Oh, my dear, did you see this? 'Colossus of greed with a wart on his nose.' Ham Vair's shocking, really." She laughed, not shocked at all. "But I must say he's getting himself tremendous publicity. When you think nobody ever heard of him up to a month or so ago. . . . My husband says you won't be able to get a good man to come to Washington . . . but I say where there's smoke, my dear, and it's very peculiar that nobody's been able to answer any of Vair's charges. Not that I approve of Vair or the way he's going at it, but really . . . And you'll notice the Brents haven't brought that daughter of theirs to Washington."

"—I'll get you a glass of water."

I heard the operator say that to the red-haired woman next to me. She was sitting there, her eyes closed again, her face pale and splotched, tugging at the tie of the pink salon coat swaddling her. She was trying to get up, but she was so shaken she slumped back in the chair. The voice across the room was going on.

"—Have you seen that picture of the girl the night she was caught in a raid on some gangster. . . . *Oh!*"

I could feel that breathless gasp. The red-haired woman had got up. The girl doing my hair stopped, her hands suspended, her own face white as her starched uniform. There was a discreet flurry of operators, and the soft-voiced manager was there outside and they were taking the woman somewhere.

My operator leaned down. "That was Mrs. Rufus Brent, poor thing," she whispered.

But apart from the painful embarrassment of seeing a woman so acutely distressed, I didn't think too much about Mrs. Rufus Brent. You tend to get case-hardened, in Washington. If an important man comes to do a job and nobody talks about him, you take it for granted he's not so important, and you automatically assume that if a man's clay feet haven't shown by the second week it's because he hasn't had time to take his shoes off. Then the whispering innuendo about his home life begins to creep its scurrilous rounds. If you live here, you just assume it's a calculated risk.

I do remember thinking it was too bad the Brents' daughter should be caught in a gangster's raid, but actually I was more concerned with what I'd heard about myself than the Rufus Brents. I hadn't known about that whopping check Colonel Primrose had sent back, and I was a little staggered, because he's helped a lot of my friends. I've even thought of myself as an unpaid five percenter that people run to when they're in a jam. It's never occurred to me that anything else was involved. Whenever I've seen Sergeant Buck's lantern-jawed, rock-ribbed dead pan congeal forty degrees and the viscid glaze come over his fish-grey eyes, which is whenever my presence is forced upon him, I've assumed it was purely in the interest of his Colonel's matrimonial unentanglement and that Buck unwaveringly viewed me as a termite doggedly chewing away at the foundations of their masculine independence. I hadn't realized I was also chewing at their financial structure.

So I was a little appalled at the whole thing, realizing too that they don't normally do private stuff. It's the Treasury they work for, mostly, sometimes Justice or State, and always in really superior criminal echelons. And it may be quixotic, of course, to feel it would be a shame to separate the Colonel's substance from his long-time and devoted non-commissioned shadow, but obviously that's what would happen if I married Colonel Primrose. Buck finds me difficult enough to take living up in the next block and across P Street. The glacial immobility that would permanently paralyze him if worse came to worst is something no woman in her right mind would care to contemplate—or not me, anyway. And as for the rest of the conspiracy of sticks and stones, sons, cooks and sergeants, there's one simple fact, at any rate: it's that Colonel Primrose has never actually asked me to marry him, and I'm sure we'd both be very much embarrassed if I suggested it.

Other people constantly do, though, and I doubt if I go anywhere without the man when some wag doesn't at least ask me where he is. I wasn't surprised, therefore, when Tom Seaton asked it, when I went over to dinner on Massachusetts Avenue that night, except that the Seatons are old enough friends of mine to know I do have a pallid existence of my own.

He was hovering at the top of the handsome marble staircase with its blue velvet carpet when I came up.

"Where is he, Grace?"

There was nothing waggish in his weatherbeaten face, which seemed drawn in spite of the healthy overlay of wind-and-sunburn that comes from being a farmer as well as one of Washington's leading younger lawyers. He and Marjorie and their three youngsters move down to their six hundred submarginal acres on West River in Maryland as early as they can in the spring and stay as late as possible in the fall. They'd even gone down at the end of January, this year, and it was the first time I'd seen them together in town all spring.

"You've got to get Colonel Primrose to help us out, Grace. We——"

He glanced past me down the staircase and managed a frigid bow at whoever was behind me. I turned and understood perfectly. Tom Seaton is Mr. Rufus Brent's legal representative in Washington. The man who'd come up was Edson Field, the gangly greying columnist who'd first christened Congressman Hamilton (Call Me Ham) Vair the Hot Rod from the Marsh Marigold State, and was more responsible for his initial rise to fame, or whatever, than any other single individual including Ham Vair.

"——And that's one of the reasons," Tom Seaton said as Field went on into the drawing room. "Something's got to be done, Grace, about all this back-alley stuff about Rufus Brent. Tell the Colonel, won't you?"

"Not me," I said. "I've gone out of business, as of today."

We were interrupted then, and it wasn't till we were at dinner that I saw it was no accident that had brought Rufus Brent's attorney and Ham Vair's columnist together. They were seated directly across from each other. Field's long nose was quivering with enjoyment.

"Perhaps you could tell us, Seaton," he remarked as he took his first spoonful of clear turtle soup. "What are Mr. Brent's plans? There's a good deal of anxiety about whether he's going to stay on as head of the Industrial Techniques Commission. There's some feeling that the facts Vair's bringing out may . . . er . . . impair, let's say, Mr. Brent's usefulness in ITC."

"I hadn't realized Mr. Vair had brought out any facts," Tom Seaton said. "He's made charges . . . on the floor of the House, where he's immune from legal action."

"Rufus Brent wangled the Brentool Plant—right in Vair's own district, Seaton—from the War Assets Board for two dollars a thousand of the taxpayers' money. That means Surplus Property sold him the people's farm land the plant was built on for one cent an acre. That's shrewd business even on Mr. Brent's level, isn't it? Funny business, Vair calls it. He's demanding an investigation of that deal."

I saw Marjorie Seaton's eyes smoulder as she shook her head at her husband from across the table.

"The Army paid fifty dollars an acre for the land, originally," Tom Seaton said. "I imagine the farmers didn't get more than about a cent an acre, after they'd paid off the mortgages Vair's father held, for farm machinery he'd sold them. I've never blamed Vair for being sore about Mr. Brent's deal. He had a deal of his own—no capital required —with the Gulf States Scrap Company that fell through, because of Brent, to the tune of thirty-five or forty thousand bucks. The fact that the Brent plant had raised the per capita income there till it's the richest county in the state doesn't concern Mr. Vair, I suppose. But I'd rather not speak for Mr. Brent. He knows as well as you do Vair's just trying to make him quit and go home. It certainly wouldn't do the people of Taber County any good if Mr. Brent closed Brentool Taber City down—which Vair's also trying to make him do. The place would be a sinkhole of poverty again in nothing flat, if——"

"But, Tom!" It was a woman who broke in. "If Mr. Brent wants people to be on his side, why doesn't he do something? *Nobody* knows them, here in Washington . . . they might as well be buried alive."

"Oh, my dear, it's that daughter of theirs, haven't you heard?" Another woman hurried in. "She's tragic, a complete alcoholic——"

"That's false! That's utterly false!" Marjorie Seaton's eyes were blazing. "It's more than false, it's a——"

"Shut up, Marge." Tom Seaton didn't raise his voice, but she stopped short. "—I apologize for my wife. We'll be as civilized and malicious as everybody else when we get back to town. Living with steers and tobacco distorts your point of view."

"But Marjorie, you can't *say* it's a lie, dear." That was a determined dame at the other end of the table. "The camera doesn't lie. There may be a good reason why the Brents' daughter should be running out of a place where there's just been a mob killing——"

"What are you talking about?" Marjorie Seaton demanded hotly.

"Just what everybody else in Washington's talking about, darling. If you prefer your steers and tobacco you can't hope to know, can you, dear? I've seen the picture."

"I'm afraid it's nothing you can laugh off, Marjorie," Edson Field said. "They're very rigid, out in the Marsh Marigold State, you know. That sort of conduct might be corrupting for their own youngsters."

It was the picture I'd heard about at the hairdressers', of course, and I tried to recall Mrs. Rufus Brent's face as she struggled up out of her chair. It was clear that Marjorie Seaton had never heard of it. Her face was as pale as the lilacs, and she sat in stunned silence in the babbling sea that broke around her.

"Of course, I don't approve of Vair's tactics, but—" It was a man contributing that now current Washington cliché. I heard something else whispered sharply to my left. "—It isn't the daughter, from what I heard, it's Mrs. Brent. They say she's completely gaga, my dear. They say she's a——"

I put my goblet down quickly. "Kleptomaniac" was what I thought I'd heard. Then a man laughed maliciously as he said, "Oh, really? How interesting," . . . and if you don't think men can be as malicious as women you've never lived in Washington, D.C.

"Of course, I don't really believe it," the woman who'd said it remarked pleasantly. "But it might explain why he never lets her go out without him. I asked her to lunch and she told me so herself. I told Lucy . . . she was trying to capture them and I thought a garden party might be the safest. . . ."

Bright laughter bounced like a shower of pingpong balls back and forth across the table. Marjorie Seaton's eyes were burning again, her cheeks patched with scarlet, and when we left the table and she caught up with me, her hand on my arm was trembling and icy-cold.

"Come on, Grace," she whispered. "I've got to talk to you."

A woman ahead of us with a pile of bright blue hair and so bony that a shroud would have looked better on her than the glittering backless frontless job she wore raised her voice so Marjorie would have had to be stone deaf not to hear her. "I'm told Mrs. Brent isn't a recluse at all, really, only it's men she likes . . . all very young and very handsome. And of course, the Seatons are in rather a spot, aren't they? I hear it's not any five or ten percent they have with the Brent connection, it's something fabulous, that's why Tom can afford to throw away all that money farming. I mean, they've really got to be on the Brents' side. . . ."

I felt Marjorie stiffen taut as an arrow, and when she dropped my arm I took hers, though I didn't suppose she was really going to strike one of her mother's oldest friends.

"Listen, Grace." She closed the powder-room door. "You've *got* to get Colonel Primrose to do something. That poor woman . . . you don't know what she's going through. They're driving her out of her mind. That's why she doesn't go out. She's terrified at what she'll run into. And she's an angel, Grace. She's fey as hell, but my God, she's got a right to be fey. And poor little Molly Brent . . . I don't know what the picture is they're talking about, but I don't believe it. She's really sweet, Grace. You've got to persuade Colonel Primrose to do something. It's foul, it's murder, really."

She broke off as we heard the other women coming into the bedroom outside. They were like a flock of penned-up ducks quacking about an exciting secret millpond. There was a sudden burst of laughter. "Oh, no!" somebody said. "Oh, I can't believe it, I really can't!"

"But she can and she will and she'll tell everybody else she sees," Marjorie said bitterly. "It's hideous, Grace— it's *evil*. Tell Colonel Primrose, won't you? And go see that poor woman. Just talk to her. You can't believe how horrible it all is. Something's got to happen. Ham Vair oughtn't to be allowed to live, Grace. I swear I'll . . . I'll kill him myself, if something doesn't happen."

But I didn't go see Mrs. Brent, and I didn't tell Colonel Primrose he had to do something about it. I don't know whether I was deterred by the idea that I'd cost him and Sergeant Buck too much already, or whether I unconsciously thought Marjorie was a special pleader for her husband's chief client. There was no reason why the Seatons couldn't call Colonel Primrose themselves . . . and if Rufus Brent couldn't look out for himself, who in America could?

Even then, I'd probably have told Colonel Primrose about it, except that my younger son came home for a week, and as he thinks about the Colonel a little the way Sergeant Buck thinks about me, I hardly saw the man. And then, the Monday morning after my child had gone back to New Haven, such an extraordinary thing happened in my house that I forgot the Rufus Brents. Sergeant Phineas T. Buck paid me a personal and private call.

III

No doubt the day will come when either mutation of the species or atomic science applied to gadgetry will develop some kind of Geiger counter for use in the home. Having avoided Marjorie Seaton's appeal to get mixed up in the Rufus Brent mess, I should have had some sort of instrument, that china-blue morning in May, to warn me that if I listened to Sergeant Buck I was going to be in it up to my shoulder-blades in nothing flat . . . and in reverse, which was the awful thing about it. I wouldn't speak to Colonel Primrose or go to see Mrs. Rufus Brent, but I would be so flattered by a visit from Buck that I'd turn my own home into an underground headquarters for Hamilton Vair without batting an eyelash. Still, even if there'd been a Geiger counter there, I'd have assumed it was jumping because of the headlines in the paper I put down when I heard the Sergeant's heavy footsteps coming, grimly dogged, up the stairs from my basement kitchen.

VAIR DEMANDS INVESTIGATION OF BRENTOOL
CONTRACTS. SAYS TOOLMAKER USES ITC TO
LINE OWN POCKETS.

And it had taken Vair's apologist, Edson Field, a whole week to get around to reporting the dinner party he and Tom Seaton had been to.

"A shocking sidelight on the lengths that private interests will go to silence Congressional criticism can now be told," he said in his column called *Washington Business Is Your Business.* "Rufus Brent, too sensitive to rising public indignation to threaten Mr. Vair openly, uses his astronomically-salaried Washington mouthpiece to do it for him.

"The threat to close down the Brentool Plant in Vair's Congressional district, where Brent has a stranglehold on local industry, and force the entire population of the county into unemployment and starvation, unless Vair withdraws his charges, was carefully veiled, and will be, as usual, promptly denied. It is a deplorable but well-known fact that serious business in the Capital is frequently conducted at swank dinner parties as well as in bar lounges and at cocktail parties. It is the first time, however, that this column has ever been handed a take-it-or-leave-it ultimatum to transmit to a member of the United States Congress along with his plate of green-turtle soup.

"The courageous young representative of the Ninth District has flatly refused to be coerced, bribed or intimidated. If the Brentool Plant in Taber City develops so-called labor troubles which force it to close down in the near future, do not be either surprised or misled. The fact that Rufus Brent's handy man is prepared to starve an entire community in order to silence one man is a staggering blow worthy of Darker Ages than those we live in."

It would teach Mr. Brent's astronomically-salaried mouth-piece to keep it resolutely shut hereafter, I thought as I put the paper down. I was having lunch, if that's what I could call the lettuce leaf, black coffee and melba toast I was stuck with to pay for the week of spoonbread, fried chicken and apple crisp that's our staple diet when one of the kids is home. I was having it at my end of the long polished expanse of dining-room table. Lilac still has her standards, a dinner table is made to eat at, there I eat come hell or high water, and there I sat, in lonely dignity, wondering why Buck was coming to see me.

He came through the door, ducking the low bridge so he looked like a bull squared off to charge, and brought his massive hulk to a dead stop just inside—the *Missouri* grounded and as red of face. He was in his teal blue Sunday suit and what Lilac calls his Sunday laundry, a stiff white collar on a pale pink shirt, with a hand-painted necktie some woman must have given him, it was so debonair and so awful, his hair still damp and plastered over his bald spot, his lantern jaw the color of a tarnished hog kettle, his fish-grey eyes lighted with the affectionate warmth of half-thawed oysters. As he cleared his throat the lustres on the mantel set up a musical jingle like miniature elephant bells.

"We got a favor to ast you, ma'am."

His voice comes out of one side of the fissure in his granite dead pan, so that it sounded as sinister as it in fact was . . . if the Geiger counter had only been there to tell me. But again I wouldn't have heeded it, I was so pleased to have Sergeant Buck asking a favor of me. It not only looked as if he'd declared a truce in the cold war we conduct across the P Street parallel, it gave me a chance to make a payment on the just debt I'd so recently become aware I owed him.

"These personal friends of mine, they're very high-class people, ma'am. Their little girl won a contest, and she's coming to D.C. It's my appreciation they want a respectable home she can stay a couple of days till she looks around permanent. I and the Colonel are taking the 4.00 P.M. plane out West on business, ma'am. What the Colonel said was, I was to ast you, ma'am, could you keep her for us till we get back?"

Beads of perspiration popped out on Sergeant Buck's forehead and the tarnish went deeper brass, as he waited for my answer. The only thing that delayed it was the "respectable." That Sergeant Buck thought my home was respectable, and to the extent of commiting the child of a high-class personal friend of his to it, was overwhelming.

"Why, of course, Sergeant," I said. Nobody can say I'm not gracious to a sweating foe. "I'd love to have her. When's she coming?"

The breath of relief he took must have strained even his iron ribcage. "Friday, it says here, ma'am." He took a dog-eared letter out of his teal-blue pocket. "Virginia Dolan's her name. Her daddy was with us in France."

That startled me. It was the other war when Colonel Primrose and his Sergeant were in France. I'd figured the child was ten or twelve, and I'd been wondering who I'd get to climb the Monument with her if I took the day at the Zoo and maybe the Congressional Library. "How old is she, Sergeant Buck?"

"Eighteen, going on nineteen, ma'am."

"Oh, well," I said, the Zoo and Monument both happily dissolving in my mind. "She's old enough to look after herself, then."

That was a mistake.

"She's a very high-class little lady, ma'am." You could see he already regretted letting his Colonel high-pressure him into putting this tender shoot into my callous hands. "Her daddy says she ain't never been out of Taber City more than once or twice. They're very high-class people, ma'am."

"We'll do our best, Sergeant," I said. "You tell Lilac. I'm sure everything'll be all right."

"Thank you, ma'am." He started to back out of the room, and stopped. I'd picked up my coffee cup again, but I didn't get it more than half-way to my lips, because something very odd indeed seemed to have happened to that battered, congealed stonework he's facially equipped with. He was looking at my table, his dead pan sort of going to pieces in the oddest possible fashion. "—It just don't look right, ma'am," he said suddenly.

I glanced quickly down the polished bare expanse. It looked all right to me. I'd just paid some fabulous amount to get it refinished. "What doesn't, Sergeant Buck?"

"You sittin' by yourself at this bare old table, and the Colonel down the street sittin' by himself at his bare old table."

I expect I set my coffee cup down. It was on the bare old mahogany, six inches from the saucer, when I noticed it. I was so staggered I wouldn't have known if I'd put it on the floor. But no more staggered than Sergeant Buck, I think. He came to a sort of semi-attention, his cast-iron jaw the color it must have been when they first took it out of the furnace.

"No offense meant, ma'am," he said hastily.

"And none taken, Sergeant," is what I should have answered, and what I've always answered, ever since that exchange became the password of our mutual forbearance. But this time I couldn't say anything at all.

He cleared his throat again. "But if you'd let the Colonel be, till he gets back, ma'am. . . . He's mighty busy. He ain't got himself packed yet. You'd do him a personal favor if he calls up to come over, if you'd say no dice, ma'am."

As both he and I knew well that Colonel Primrose has never packed himself since he left West Point, I saw he'd already regretted his momentary dissolving. But I nodded. I was still too touched, even then, to be articulate. And when Lilac, my cook for twenty years, waddled her two hundred pounds of sometimes sulphur and sometimes molasses, I never know which, up the stairs, I was still half-dazed.

"What you done to Mister Buck?" she demanded, her black moon face hovering between perplexity and righteous indignation. "What you say got him all outside himself?"

I shook my head. I couldn't tell her it was what Sergeant Buck had said, not me. Never could I have foreseen him as a concrete-mixer-like Salome handing me on a silver charger the head of his St. John Primrose. "Nothing," I said.

"You goin' to take that girl in here for Mister Buck?" she inquired dubiously.

"*We're* going to take her." I was clear-headed enough to underline our joint responsibility. "It'll only be for a few days."

"Hm" she said. "Govamen' Girl, Troublemen' Girl. . . ."

That startled me too. I hadn't got the idea the high-class little lady was in Washington for a job. Not that it would have mattered, however, and not that I'd have heard Sergeant Buck really if he'd told me in so many words. He did tell me where it was she'd never been away from more than once or twice, and I wasn't bright enough to catch that.

I'd just left the bare board that had moved Sergeant Buck

so incredibly when Colonel Primrose did call up, quite innocent of the recent disposal operation and merely wanting to drop in for a few minutes before their plane left.

"No," I said, keeping faith with Sergeant Buck. "I'm doing you a personal favor. No dice. You've got to pack."

He laughed, not too amused, I thought. "I'm sorry we're saddling you with this girl of Buck's," he said.

"It's a pleasure. There's nothing we wouldn't do for Mister Buck."

"Mister Buck's a damn fool," he said. "Clucking around like an old hen with a yellow chick to hide. He's been combing the town for the last three days."

Of course, I should have known, when Buck came, that a favor from me was an avenue when all other avenues were closed. But I was still too touched to remember that leopards don't really change their spots, and delighted for him to hide his yellow chick in my respectable precincts. In a burst of predawn goodwill I even decided to take her to a garden party I was going to on Friday. Depending, of course . . . I'd seen only one other female friend of the Sergeant's and she was fully feathered and the moulting season well advanced. But I suppose it was fate, really, and nothing else, stacking the cards against the Rufus Brents, that decided that. I can only think now how different things would have been if Sergeant Buck's little lady had walked into that garden party with me. It seems incredible that Miss Virginia Dolan's train being held up two hours by a flash flood in West Virginia could have made such a fantastic difference in the lives of the famous industrialist and his wife, who'd never seen or heard of Miss Virginia Dolan, and in the life of little Molly Brent, which in the long run was by far the most important.

It was Thursday, the day before the garden party and the little lady's arrival, that I met Mrs. Rufus Brent the second time. I was having some people in to lunch, so I left the Red Cross early to get home and make the cocktails. Lilac belongs to the "Whoso Never Will" Society, and touching liquor is one of the things they chiefly won't. Even her friend Mister Buck has to get the bourbon bottle out of the cupboard downstairs for himself. When I saw her moon face peer up out of the area window at me, obviously disconcerted about something, I hurried, thinking I was late, until I got along the hall to the living room that opens on the walled garden and saw the woman I'd seen at the beauty shop, sitting there patiently waiting for me.

The bright red hair was dry now, gathered on the back of her neck in a bun that was magnetized, I judged from the way her flowered pink straw hat kept slipping back, giving her a dizzy off-center look. She had on a white print dress with purple, red and green splotches that looked like a colored plate from a textbook on visceral diseases in a final stage. Her face was heavy and looked as if she'd been crying, and her pale blue eyes searched my face with a tremulous pathetic uncertainty and no sign of recognition at all.

"Are . . . are you Mrs. Latham?" She wavered a moment. "I'm Lena Brent . . . Mrs. Rufus Brent. I'm a friend of Tom and Marjorie Seaton's." Her eyes moved down to the framed photograph of my two boys on the pembroke table. "You look so much . . . younger than I'd expected," she said. "Are these your sons? You really. . . ."

("Don't let 'em feed you that, Ma, it's because we've had a hard life, withered before our time. . . ." I could see it in the two engaging faces.)

As she looked back at me then, her face lighted incredibly with the most lovely smile I think I've ever seen. It transformed her utterly. If some kind of magic wand had touched her or my eyes that were seeing her she couldn't have been so totally another being. All the uncertainty and the heaviness, even the splotchy print, had dissolved in a warm soft radiance. She had an almost other-worldly quality of simplicity and kindliness that was really beautiful. It hadn't been her smile entirely. Her voice was so sweet, and so clear and gentle in an almost childlike way that the smile was only the completing of the whole illusion of youth and loveliness—if it was illusory, if it wasn't the flesh that was the illusion and the spirit the true reality.

"I'm very fond of boys," she said. "I have a picture of our two. Would you like to. . . ."

"I'd like to very much, Mrs. Brent," I said.

She undid the catch of her green straw bag. "It was a Mother's Day present. They went down together and had it taken for me."

She opened the folder she'd taken out, her face shining with the tenderness mothers are supposed to have and often don't, or conceal because it isn't very fashionable any more. "That's Rufie Jr. on the left, and Robbie."

And fine looking lads they were, clean-cut, alert and intelligent. You could see they were having their pictures taken as a labor of love and having fun while they were at it. But it was the middle picture I was most absorbed in, and utterly astonished by.

"They're wonderful," I said. "And is this your daughter?"

It would be less than the truth to pretend I wasn't curious about the picture I'd heard of, at the beauty shop and again at dinner. Between the two boys was a girl, seventeen, I'd say, no lipstick, her hair, lightish in the picture and probably red as her mother's had no doubt once been and indeed still was, slicked back and tied with a ribbon, and about as weedy and unglamorous as the dreary school uniform she wore. She was holding her lips pressed together, to keep from laughing or to cover up the braces on her teeth perhaps, or maybe both. Her eyes had a scared half-twinkle in them, as if her brothers were also invisibly on the sidelines there trying to make her laugh, as do or die she kept her eyes resolutely glued on the camera. But it was not the face of a girl who'd be around gangster hangouts. It was a lovely young face, sweet and very sensitive, but with a firm little chin half-tilted, determined not to let her brothers make her grin and spoil the picture.

"She's sweet," I said.

"That's . . . that's Molly. She's all—" She bent her head, the radiant joy gone from her face. "Oh, I don't know what happens to people!" she said suddenly, and with such naked poignancy that it made my spine quiver. "You do everything you can for your children, but there's nothing you can do to help them. They still have to suffer, you can't ever do anything to save them!"

She took the folder quickly from my hand. "Oh, forgive me, please!" she said. "I didn't mean to distress you, talking about my children. That's not why I came. Marjorie Seaton's been begging me to come, but I . . . I was afraid. Then I heard some people talking about you, and I saw your name on the list they sent us of the garden party tomorrow. It's being given for us, you know."

I didn't know, and what's more I didn't know there was anybody left in Washington who could keep that kind of secret, with all the people who'd give their right arm to meet the head man of the Industrial Techniques Commission.

"—Gate crashers," she added, no doubt at the look on my face. It sounded so strange in that incredibly gentle voice of hers that I blinked as if she'd used one of Sergeant Buck's favorite outdoor words. "We haven't been going out," she said. "But they thought we should, just to . . . to let people see we aren't really peculiar. And I thought you wouldn't mind, perhaps, if I came before I met you." Her look was an appeal as well as an apology. "I thought perhaps you wouldn't mind. . . ."

"Not at all, Mrs. Brent," I said. It was difficult for me too.

"You see, Marjorie says you know a Colonel Primrose she thinks you could persuade to . . . to help me, Mrs. Latham. And I do need help. I need it desperately."

She didn't have to tell me, though I didn't know how

desperately she did need it, even then, when I could see what she was going through, trying to control herself.

"You can't know what it's been like, these last months," she said. "I didn't want my husband to come to Washington, and he didn't want to come. They persuaded him it was his duty. He knew he'd be attacked, of course. But he didn't expect all the personal vilification Mr. Vair is heaping on him—But it isn't only that."

She said that hurriedly, as if I'd get up and ask her to leave if she didn't explain.

"It's the time it wastes, and the lack of confidence that other men in the industrial fields who don't know him are bound to have, whether they realize it or not. And my husband's a hard man, Mrs. Latham, but he can be hurt. He doesn't mind about the wart on his nose." The little smile she gave me lasted only for that instant. "He is upset when Mr. Vair says his father died alone in a state institution. It wasn't an insane hospital, as Mr. Vair implies. It was consumption he had, and the family paid everything they could, when he was moved there for special care. My husband was just eleven years old then . . . and everybody dies alone, Mrs. Latham.

"And he's terribly upset about the Brentool Plant out in Taber City. I don't know whether you know that's where Mr. Vair comes from. You see, my husband didn't want to take that plant either, but friends in the Air Force were terribly worried, the way the Congress was closing everything down. They knew the war wasn't really over. When Mr. Vair attacks them as well as him, as thieves and traitors, it's not easy. And the men at the plant stop work, and their children throw rocks and mud at the superintendent's car."

She fumbled at her bag to get her handkerchief out.

"But it's not even that that frightens me Mrs. Latham," she said simply. "It's. . . . Molly, our daughter, that I'm frightened about." She hesitated painfully. "She had a . . . a very serious accident, a terrible accident, really, and she hasn't got over it. That's why she isn't here with us. And you can't know what it's like, Mrs. Latham, having people around, prying and snooping. It's been worse since we've been here. My husband doesn't know . . . about all that, and about the anonymous letters. I burn them so he won't see them. And the telephone calls. I try to keep all that away from him. Because . . . that's what terrifies me. My husband adores Molly. He worships her. She's all he lives for, really. And now, there's some photograph of her. . . ."

That, I remembered, had been the final unbearable thing, at

the beauty shop, and I'd wondered whether she'd even be able to bring it up.

"I can't imagine Molly being in any . . . dreadful place, but she may have been out with other people, when her brothers weren't at home. I don't know what it was, and I can't ask her, now. But you see, if they're passing such a photograph around, they're just doing it to hurt my husband, they're hurting Molly to hurt him. I know Mr. Vair's trying to make it look as if my husband is an enemy of the people, and I thought at first it was just to help get himself elected to the Senate. But I think now he really hates my husband and enjoys trying to destroy him. And if he's trying to do it by hurting Molly . . . my husband has great patience, too, Mrs. Latham—but that's the one thing he wouldn't stand."

She got up and stood opening and closing her hands on the green straw bag. "That's why I hoped you . . . you'd get Colonel Primrose to help me. I hoped, some way, he could make them let Molly alone. Because, if they don't. . . . Will you get him, Mrs. Latham?"

"I'll try, Mrs. Brent," I said. I forgot all about never going to try to get him for anybody ever again. "But . . . I don't know what he could do. To stop Vair from saying these things would be a miracle, and even Colonel Primrose—"

"Oh, but I believe in miracles, Mrs. Latham." Her blue eyes widened like a child's. "I believe they do happen," she said, and I knew she meant it, and literally meant it. "I see them constantly in other people's lives. I couldn't go on if I didn't know that."

I got up too. "I can see what he says, Mrs. Brent. But he's out of town right now."

Her face and body seemed to sag with such utter hopelessness that it startled me. I hadn't realized how much hope she'd built up, in Colonel Primrose's ability really to perform some miracle for her.

"I wish I weren't so . . . so desperately afraid." She steadied herself against the chair. "I'm so frightened I can't bear to think about it. Surely there . . . there must be somebody who can save him."

I wasn't quite sure I'd heard what she said. I hadn't realized that fear was such a part of what she was suffering. I saw it then, so naked and real it was almost tangible.

"You don't believe Mr. Brent is . . ." I stopped, too confused to go on. She couldn't really mean she thought her husband's life was threatened. But still the idea was there . . . of death, in the room, pallid fingers tapping their frightening code. It was unmistakable, what was there in her mind.

"Mrs. Brent," I said, "it's . . . it's not . . . murder, you're talking about, is it? You're surely not afraid——"

She raised her head and looked at me, not startled, and not shocked at all. Her face cleared and the normal color came slowly back into it.

"Murder?" It was the word she seemed to question as she repeated it. Then she shook her head. "Oh, no," she said quietly. "I don't believe he'd ever think of it that way, Mrs. Latham. You don't call it murder when you kill a rattlesnake that's striking someone you love very dearly, do you? That's the way he'd look at it, Mrs. Latham. That's the way my husband would think about it. And that's why I've got to have somebody to help me. Somebody's got to save him from killing Hamilton Vair."

IV

But this is Washington. What made my spine stiffen, in that appalled instant, had nothing to do with the proposed murder —or call it killing—of Congressman Hamilton Vair. What appalled me was Mrs. Rufus Brent's making, out loud and in words nobody would have to misquote or distort, the deliberate statement that her husband Rufus Brent was going to kill Hamilton Vair, and with no more compunction than he'd have if he killed a rattlesnake. Maybe knowing Colonel Primrose has conditioned me to murder, but nothing I've ever known has conditioned me to the incredible speed with which the merest and most private whisper leaks into public amplifiers these last few years in Washington. There's a sonic osmosis in Washington walls that makes a paralyzed deaf mute the only absolute security risk here any more. And what Ham Vair could do with a calm statement that Rufus Brent was going to kill him, I shuddered to think.

But there was no time for me to tell Mrs. Brent what a ghastly thing she'd done. My luncheon guests were arriving and the man who helps Lilac when we have people in was already on his way up the basement stairs to answer the doorbell. I only hoped he was as blank as he looked, because there's a great deal of loose money around Washington for loose-tongued servants. I think even Mrs. Brent was startled at seeing him. She was certainly startled at the idea of meeting other people in the hall, and anybody who knew who she was must have been very startled a minute later, if they'd seen her plodding up the area steps among the garbage cans, to get out without having to speak to the front door arrivals.

All through cocktails and lunch I found myself quaking all over again at the monstrous indiscretion I'd just been a party to. Fortunately the guests were friends of friends from out of town, and one of them was a man who had a simple if long-winded solution for the world's bumble-headed ills. Just drop a load of atomic bombs, he said, with infinite variation. All I had to do was sit with a fixed smile, thinking of the one Mrs. Brent had dropped, that the slightest leak would detonate to the lasting glory of Hamilton Vair and the ruinous embarrassment of her husband, who might just as well resign from ITC and close Brentool, Taber City, that instant for all the Chinaman's chance he had to survive it. In a city where the Capitol Dome, perforated like a kitchen colander, is the symbol of how secrets are kept, it was a shocking piece of information she'd made me responsible for. Creeping out through the garbage cans wasn't going to help anything if Vair's spies were on P Street at the moment.

It was the only meal I'd eaten for some time that Rufus Brent's name wasn't even mentioned at, except as it kept shouting itself in my own inner ear. I'd have called Colonel Primrose when my guests left, except that it was some kind of hush-hush job he was on and I'd have to work an involved relay system through the Treasury. I also didn't dare risk a leak of my own. So I did nothing, except keep my mouth shut. I didn't mention the Brents' name to anyone, and I even shut my eyes when I saw in the next morning's paper that Ham Vair had made a rip-roaring speech on the floor of the House daring Rufus Brent to make good his dastardly threat to close down Brentool, Taber City and starve the women and children—I don't know why they're always the ones to starve, but presumably their husbands and fathers eat out on those occasions. I wanted nothing at all to do with any dastardly threat Rufus Brent might make, even to speaking the five letters of his name. Until I went over to Wisconsin Avenue to go to the bank the next morning.

I was passing the service station on the corner of Beall Street when I heard a rap on the window glass of the flower shop next door to it. Inside, her white-gloved gyrations indicating she'd come out and would I wait, was the friend who was giving the garden party.

"—You're coming this afternoon, darling, aren't you?"

"Why didn't you say it was for the Rufus Brents?" My tongue got out before I could stop it.

"Oh, sssh . . . sssh, my dear!" She looked hastily around at the baskets of daffodils and lilacs banking the steps behind her. "Whoever told you? But it must have been

Marge Seaton, I've only told her and one other. And I only told her so she'd get that wretched brother-in-law of hers back in town today. Is he back, do you know? I've promised at least half a dozen girls I'd have him there. What they see in him I've no idea, except his money, and he's not as rich as all that."

It is a problem. Sandy-red-haired, with a face nobody could call handsome except a chimpanzee interested in the evolutionary process in reverse, Tom Seaton's younger brother Archie certainly has something the young female of the species can't resist. His own resistance approaches the magnificent. He has a finesse in evading natural and social consequences that makes Sergeant Buck's efforts on his Colonel's behalf look like mere inept blundering. He's an older friend of my older son—he's twenty-eight—and I've been putting up with his engaging deviltries for a long time now.

"I don't know whether he's back or not," I said. I didn't know he was out of town for that matter, and since he also has a real gift for finding the most likely girls in the most unlikely places, he was the last person I knew to hurry back to a party anywhere. "And it wasn't Marge who told me anyway," I said.

"Well, don't breathe it. And that woman, my dear . . . have you seen her? She's ominous, truly. Every prominent man who married the girl next door ought to be allowed one tablet of cyanide in case he comes to Washington some day. And Rufus Brent's *ravishing*."

"I thought she was nice," I said.

"I've never heard you so malicious, Grace. I'm ashamed of you."

"Are her sons coming?" I asked. "They look better than Archie Seaton to me."

That was deliberate. You may recall from the beauty shop what a couple of presentable sons will do to make their mother worth knowing in Washington.

She brightened instantly. "Darling, I didn't know they had any sons. The daughter's all I've heard about." She raised her brows. No doubt she'd seen the picture too. "Ham Vair says she's really quite shocking."

"*Ham Vair?*"

She looked at me quickly. "Grace, you *know* I wouldn't have asked him if I hadn't had to. I just couldn't leave him out, dear. And he's the only other person I told the party was for the Brents . . . so it has to be him or Marge or the Brents themselves who told you. I told him so he wouldn't have to be embarrassed——"

"Did you tell the Brents? Or is it all right to embarrass them?"

She did have the grace to laugh a little. "How could I, darling? No, I'm afraid his name never got on the list I sent them." She looked worried nevertheless. "Do help me, won't you? I'm afraid he's coming, . . . he really hasn't any manners, you know. I do hope he wears a coat and tie—you should have seen him in the newsreel the other day. But he'll be in the Senate next year as sure as you're born. That's why I had to ask him. My husband's livid, he thinks Ham's a real menace."

"So do I," I said.

"So does everybody, darling, but it's better to have a menace for a friend than for a menace." She laughed at that, as she'd done before, I gathered. "It's simply a fact of life, dear. You'd be surprised the people who think he's going a lot farther than the Senate. You'd be appalled at the support he's gathering even among the kind of people *we* know.—Do help me, won't you? Old Washington impresses the pants off him, just now. Unless he decides to be homespun and very rude. . . ."

I hadn't realized up to that point what a successful menace Ham Vair had become so quick. Congressmen are socially a dime a dozen in Washington. A senator is something else again, especially a young and handsome senator who isn't married. If this woman, with the ex-Wall Street husband she had, felt Vair had to be stayed with flagons of Scotch and placated with martinis and shrimp on toothpicks, it meant a great deal. Especially if after the jockeying she must have done to snare the Brents for their first social appearance, she'd risk offending them not to offend Ham Vair. It was disturbing. I wondered whether I shouldn't call Mrs. Brent up and warn her Vair was going to be there, or get Marjorie Seaton to do it for me. Still, Mr. Brent would hardly choose a garden party to kill off a rattlesnake—or would he?—and anyway, I decided there was no use for Mrs. Brent to worry herself into a state of collapse before the ordeal began. It was going to be ordeal enough even without Vair. Too many people feel that way about cyanide and great men's wives in Washington.

And if Congressman Vair felt any embarrassment about coming to the party for the man he'd accused in that morning's paper of "battening on defense contracts while our sons are being killed in Korea," he was managing to conceal it, when I saw him. And he hadn't come in homespun. In comparison with him, all the men there, from the justices and the Cabinet straight down the Capital hierarchy, looked like fugitives from the Try-It-On-And-Take-It Barrel at the Jostle Mart on Wisconsin Avenue. He had on a white raw silk suit, gleaming like mother-of-pearl in the late afternoon sunshine, that must have cost three times the price of the decent banker's-grey worn by his host, whom he was just shaking hands with and clapping on the back when I got there. I glanced down at the receiving line, in front of a lattice that had the loveliest shower of white wisteria on it I've ever seen. The day itself was as lovely, one of those perfect things Washington comes up with in May to seduce you into forgetting what stinkers it's going to hand out in June, July and August. It was cool, clear and brilliant as blue crystal. The Brents were shaking hands with one of the Cabinet and his wife and daughter, and if they were aware of Hamilton Vair they weren't showing it from where I stood.

They could hardly not have been, however for Ham Vair was obviously just waiting for the proper moment to do something or other in the most spectacular manner he could achieve. He made no move to go down to them, but stayed where he was at the top of the garden, nobody except his unfortunate host anywhere near him. Nobody could miss him there, in his pearly shining new silk suit, spotting his friends with a fine flourish of his hand and what I believe is called the big hello. His blond Nordic countenance shone, and so nobody could miss the true and real flavor of the situation, he'd give an occasional big wink too. It was a kind of cynically arrogant clowning that was clearly embarrassing to everybody but Hamilton Vair. He reminded me of a cocky too-big boy in short pants about to write a bad word on the frosting of his sister's birthday cake.

As I stood there, I heard a man's voice behind me. It wasn't the first man's voice I'd ever heard, nor was the name, as he spoke it at the gate there, a name that had any meaning to me, so I'd automatically turn, as if for example a man's voice had said "Marshall Tito," or "Mr. Lucky Luciano." And it wasn't the voice itself, pleasant as it was, casual, a little too cultivated possibly but not offensively so. I suppose I'd like now to be able to say that what did make me turn, as Ham Vair did too, so that both of us looked around at the same moment, was a profound and far-seeing intuition. But whatever intuitions I have I'd left home that day.

"Mr. Forbes Allerdyce. I'm a friend of Mrs. Brent's. She arranged for me to come."

I thought, if I thought at all, that Vair had turned because of that. It was reasonable he'd take a dim view of any friend of the Rufus Brents. Mr. Forbes Allerdyce was tall, with crisp sun-bleached brown hair, cut like my sons' and Archie Seaton's, good-looking but not sleekly handsome, and his spectacles gave him a kind of air that if not scholarly was thoughtful anyway. He was certainly at home in the world around him.

"I don't believe I've met my host," he said. "Which is he?"

"Right over there, sir." The attendant whose job was obviously to look out for the unknown and uninvited had reacted with instant decorum.

I was glad there was another friend of the Brents', besides me, to help absorb the shock of Ham Vair. My hostess would be glad too, I thought, as I saw her look around, and saw the signal of distress she was hoisting with her arched brows. She wanted to break up the line before Vair got to it, but it was far too pointed a thing to do. She was stuck and she knew it, and I didn't doubt she was wishing she'd settled for the lion and left the jackal at home.

"Lovely day, isn't it?" Mr. Forbes Allerdyce was there at my side. I hadn't realized it till he spoke. He smiled at me. "I'm a stranger here " he said. "Who is the lily of the field in white silk? Or is there a gents' fashion show in conjunction?"

He was glancing toward the wide open space on the upper lawn.

"That's Hamilton Vair," I said.

The smile went off his face. "Oh," he said, a little stiffly. He caught himself then and smiled again. "That's not to be construed as a criticism of my host at all." He laughed apologetically, but there was nothing he could have said that would have made me feel more warmly toward him.

"I think I'll go on down," I said. I'd intended to wait and follow Vair, but there was an emptying in front of the receiving line just then. Mr. Allerdyce still stood there, looking over at Vair as if a gleaming mother-of-pearl silk suit was something he didn't often see. It was certainly in contrast with the grey flannels he had on, admirably cut and admirably worn, that with his suntan and whole casual easiness suggested a winter on a yacht in the Bahamas rather than in Washington, D.C. But I was down the garden then.

"—Darling, you know Mr. Brent, don't you? This is Mrs. Latham, Mr. Brent."

As I looked up at Rufus Brent and felt his warm cordial handclasp, I had the feeling that I had known him, for a long time. It's the sort of thing that makes a woman describe a man as ravishing, I expect. Actually, he was ugly as sin. His nose certainly had a mole on it, if not a wart as advertised by Hamilton Vair. So did his chin, which also looked as if it had been chopped off square before it got altogether out of hand. His nose had been formed with no pattern to go by and stuck between two deep furrows slanting down to the corners of his wide mouth, and his dark hazel eyes were shrewd and alive and wonderfully twinkling and kind under a pair of shaggy black-and-grey brows. He was a big man, a little stoop-shouldered, with a slight but comfortable embonpoint and a watch chain across it.

I am glad I did not call Colonel Primrose and tell him. . . . That flashed into my mind, and with it an extraordinary sense of relief. To try to mind this man's business for him would have been an impertinence as brazen as Hamilton Vair's. And I don't mean that he didn't look perfectly capable of killing somebody. You didn't have to look twice to see that under all the charm and wisdom of that Gothic ugly face there was something as hard as a keg of old nails. It made me wonder if Ham Vair had any realization of how foolhardy his arrogance ·was, against the experience and reserved power of the man he was getting ready to insult, if he could. And it seemed to me that Mr. Rufus Brent had an air of cool and watchful waiting. He looked altogether to me like nobody it was wise to push too far.

"—Lena tells me you're an old friend of hers, Mrs. Latham."

I caught the quick appeal she flashed at me.

"Yes, indeed," I said. "It's so nice to see her again."

She had on another print dress, a sort of teal-blue like Sergeant Buck's Sunday suit, but beautifully cut so she didn't look as lumpy as she did in the purple blotches she wore to my house. Her hat, trimmed with French lilacs, was a pretty hat, but it had slipped like the pink one, so she looked a little dizzy, with her carrot-red hair. She held my hand almost as if she needed actual physical support, the tension that must have been mounting all the time she'd stood there, waiting for Hamilton Vair to approach her husband, a really quite desperate kind of thing. I felt again the strange quality she had, that made her so different from the assured and lacquered women around her. It was a kind of spiritual thing, almost mystical, as she turned that extraordinary sweetness on and off like a far-away light in some lonely sea deep within herself. I could see why she believed in miracles.

I was aware then of a sudden silence, sharp and almost breathless, for an instant, over the garden, and I didn't have to look to know that it was Hamilton Vair's moment. Mrs. Brent's hand dropped mine.

"Hamilton, how nice of you to come!"

My friend was a lady born and a hostess bred.

"You know Mr. Rufus Brent, I believe? Mr. Vair, Mr. Brent."

Hamilton Vair moved a step toward Rufus Brent, evil glee shining in his face. Mr. Brent seemed to grow bigger. Without seeming to change at all, his face suddenly reminded me, in a very different way, of the granite quality of Sergeant Buck's. He bowed slightly.

"Mr. Vair and I have met," he said. "How do you do sir? This is my wife Mrs. Brent, Mr. Vair."

"How do you do, Mr. Vair?"

Her voice carried a long way in the silence. I was proud of her. I'd wondered if she'd been able to speak at all. Neither of them had put out a hand, but it didn't seem as if they hadn't. It only seemed that it was a gaucherie of astonishing proportions that Hamilton Vair had put out his. It looked enormous there, and very empty. I don't know what particularly made it look that way, but it did, and as if suddenly aware of how it looked, he dropped it abruptly. The grin broadened on his face then, lighted with a sudden malice it hadn't had before, and he started to speak.

"Your daughter——"

But whatever Ham Vair was going to say about Molly Brent is lost to the history of these crowded times. People wouldn't put out a hand to touch him, but the gods would, and did. At just that moment, a bird flew over. It was a big bird, not the great auk but no sparrow. A sudden howl of mirth, loud, long and completely spontaneous, broke the silence, and the Hot Rod of the Marsh Marigold State instead of joining it made another and far more incredible blunder. A poor misguided waiter, about five feet high and with occupational bunions on both feet, hobbled up to him with an open napkin, and Hamilton Vair knocked his hand down with a furious gesture that sent his tray of Tom Collins winding left and right, all over the astonished little man and half a dozen guests male and female within winding distance. The waiter stumbled and nearly fell. A large "Boo!" rose from somewhere in the crowd, a clear voice called out "For shame!" and boos and laughter mingled until Hamilton Vair jerked abruptly around and left the place.

The laughter swelled as the little waiter mopped himself off, wet and grinning, a hero for the moment. The Brents had been magnificent. Her face hadn't changed, her husband's belly was the absorber that prevented any emotion from more than rippling across his wide mouth and glinting momentarily bright in his eyes.

V

I don't suppose this is what the poet meant by one touch of nature, but it made a whole part of the Washington world spontaneously and delightedly kin. With the exception of Mrs. Brent, I must have been the only person there who wished it hadn't happened, and not because of the white silk suit Ham Vair could never wear again no matter what the cleaners were able to do. It was his face as he checked his exit, half-way to the garden gate, and looked back. There was blue murder in it. If he'd hated Rufus Brent before, the laughter that echoed in his ears as he left that place must have been utterly intolerable to him.

For a moment at least, the Brents were in. Mr. Brent was the center of a more than enthusiastic crowd, mostly senators. Nor was Mrs. Brent alone on the sidelines. Her suntanned young friend in the grey flannel suit and steel-rimmed spectacles had got to her at last. That was a break too—it's surprising how high and dry the middle-aged wife of the man of the moment can be stranded at times. Mrs. Brent was as transformed as everybody else, smiling happily, eager as a girl, and nobody that I heard was making any cracks about her preferring very young and very handsome men. It would have been the moment, because she was genuinely radiant, talking to him.

"Who is that?"

I looked around. Marjorie Seaton had moved in beside me. She was cool and lovely, bareheaded in a brown linen dress the shade of her own country tan. "Talking to Mrs. Brent," she added.

"His name is Forbes Allerdyce," I said. "He's a friend of theirs."

"Really? I didn't know they had any friends here."

"He called Vair a lily of the field," I said. "He can't be an enemy."

She laughed. "Okay. Are you going home after this?"

She'd stopped laughing abruptly and her brown eyes kindled. "I've got something I want you to see."

There wasn't much doubt what it was. "Okay," I said. I looked at my watch. Whatever my duties to Sergeant Buck's high-class little lady would be, I ought at least to be home at some point during her early arrival. It took me about fifteen minutes, however to work my way back to Mrs. Brent. Her young friend had gone, but the trailing clouds were still there. Her eyes were shining and her cheeks flushed. She'd pulled her hat into place and for a moment she looked as young and lovely as it did.

"Oh, Mrs. Latham, I want you to meet Forbes Allerdyce. He's a friend of my son's. A friend of Rufie's. I'm so happy. You must meet him."

She looked around eagerly. I saw him then, but two or three of the girls Archie Seaton had avoided by not coming had managed to surround him on his progress to the gate. And he had some of Archie's finesse, I thought, because he was gone when I looked next. And I think I must unconsciously have seen there was some kind of discrepancy between Forbes Allerdyce's saying Mrs. Brent had arranged for him to come and the quality of her delight at seeing him. If you arrange for someone to come to a party, you're not as starry-eyed as all that when they arrive. If I hadn't, I wouldn't have inquired about him when my hostess dropped the hand of a diplomat from this side of the iron curtain and held hers out to me.

"Who is Forbes Allerdyce? The young man in the grey flannels?"

She looked very blank. "But darling, I was going to ask you. You brought him, I distinctly saw you, at the gate . . . oh, Mr. Secretary, so nice of you to come. . . ."

So I just assumed the unfortunate contretemps of the lily of the field and the bird of the air had broken things up before Mrs. Brent had a chance to present him, and let it go at that. All that mattered was that Mr. Forbes Allerdyce had made the afternoon a lovely thing for her, and it was very smart of her to have had him there. I saw him again as I drove down Foxhall Road. He was at the wheel of a large maroon convertible, bareheaded, waiting for a break in the traffic. But I had other things on my mind, Georgetown traffic being one of them and Sergeant Buck's Miss Virginia Dolan the other, or I might possibly have examined what Mrs. Brent had said a little more closely.

I put my car away in its alley corrugated-iron garage and walked down P Street toward home. It was the moment in Georgetown when the dusk, still more rose than amethyst, sifts through the trees softening the outlines of the old painted brick houses, making the place what it used to be, a simple unemotional village on the Potomac, with no fanfare and no political connotations, left, right, or center. The day's-end traffic across the bridges from Washington was abruptly over. The street was empty except for a man waiting for a spotted dog to resume his walk and a sedate cat crossing to the other side, her mind on her own affairs. At least that's all I saw till I

got past the next tree and saw the taxi unloading at the curb
in front of my house . . . and got my first glimpse of Sergeant Buck's yellow chick.

She was pure enchantment. I slowed practically to a stand-
still looking at her. The driver was lugging her bags up the
steps, and the yellow chick was still at the curb, leaning in at
the cab window, talking to someone inside. She was slender
and graceful as a flower, and had one foot back like a dancer's, lightly tiptoe on the bricks, poised for a last laughing
word. The driver came back, she stepped away, waving her
hand, and skimmed feather-light across the sidewalk up the
steps. The taxi came by me at that moment, and a head
grinning at me from ear to ear poked itself out the window. It
had been a surprising afternoon and still was. We have group
riding in taxicabs in Washington still, especially to and from
the Union Station, and the one person who'd never get stuck
with any of the characters most of us draw was right there,
his hand up, thumb and forefinger describing the quick circle
as eloquent as his grinning face. If there was a yellow chick
within a mile of the Station, Archie Seaton would always be
the guy to draw her.

And she was okay. I got that, from the happy circle he
pushed through the window at me. I didn't get any more, but
I was as delighted as I had been relieved, by the one look I'd
got of her myself.

She heard me coming and turned.

"Hello," I said, smiling at her. "I'm Grace Latham."

"Oh!" Her eyes bloomed into a smile blue and fresh as
a new morning glory opening into the sunshine. "Hello!"
she said. "I'm Ginny Dolan."

"Hello, Ginny." I smiled again. "It's nice you're here."

I could see a dozen reasons, just offhand, why Archie Seaton
had put so much feeling into that signal of his. She was a
darling, cute as a kitten and very, very pretty. Her hair was
like spun sugar under her little off-the-face blue straw hat with
a white rose nestled at the back of her right ear. Her skin was
petal fresh, she had a moist, not too brilliant mouth and just a
suspicion of a dimple at either end, perfect teeth, a voice that
was nicely modulated and rather diffidently shy, with only a
touch of an accent that wasn't Washington but wasn't any
place else in particular. At least it wasn't Southern. And what
Buck had said was entirely true. She was a very high-class
little lady indeed, as charming and simple as the neatly fitting
navy faille summer suit she wore, dainty and young and as
fresh as her lawn blouse with its tiny turned-down collar and
fetching blue velvet bow.

I pushed the door open and picked up one of her bags.

"Come in," I said. I thought she hesitated for a moment, picking up the other two, but I could have been wrong.

"Would you like to go up to your room now?"

"Maybe we'd better talk things over first," she said, a little primly. I said "All right," a little surprised but more amused, and led the way into my living room. I switched on the light. The dusk was deepening in the garden, painting the old brick wall a soft lovely purple. I pushed Sheila, my Irish setter, off the sofa. She knows better than to be there but she's getting too deaf to hear the front door open any more. I gave the cushions a perfunctory brush.

"Mother never allows dogs on the furniture," Ginny Dolan said. "She says they get hair all over people."

Perhaps that was why she didn't at once sit down. She stood just inside the door looking around her, not rudely but with a kind of objective interest that certainly included the works. Then she took a chair, not the sofa, and sat down, her feet in tailored blue leather pumps crossed in front of her.

"You're a friend of Mr. Buck's, aren't you?" she asked.

I hated to start lying to the girl right off the bat, but then I remembered things had changed. She was being so polite and so very nice about it that I'd have had to pervert the truth in any case. I nodded.

"He said you had a very nice house," she said.

"Home, surely." I corrected her I thought with considerable urbanity. I know Sergeant Buck's semantics too well to believe he'd ever confuse those two terms.

She looked a little surprised, but not much. "That's right, he did say that," she said. "I guess you read his letter. Anyway, I'm new in Washington, of course, but Mother said it was important for me to live in the right place and not to take it for more than one night if I didn't like it."

I saw it was too bad I hadn't read Mr. Buck's letter. I might even have been a little annoyed, if Miss Ginny Dolan hadn't been so patently in earnest and so totally without malice of any kind.

"And it seems very nice." She looked around the room again. "Of course, we have all modern furniture, in Taber City."

It was my plain stupidity that made my jaw drop at that point. I like to think I've become pretty inured to minor shocks. That one wasn't minor. How I'd missed the connection between the yellow chick's home town and the Brent-Vair locus of contention seems hard to understand. Buck had certainly made it clear. She'd never been out of Taber City more than once or twice. I could hear him saying it. Looking at her, beautifully poised and as perfectly dressed as a teen-model for a first-rate Fifth Avenue specialty shop, it was hard to believe—unless I'd underestimated Taber City. I hadn't made the connection in any way.

But, of course, it didn't necessarily mean she knew Taber City's Hot Rod representative on Capitol Hill. It must be a fairly good-sized place—it had a newspaper anyway. I could see "—TY GAZ—" on the center fold of the paper she had under the bag in her lap. At least, I *hoped* she didn't know Hamilton Vair. I'd had plenty of him that day to last me indefinitely.

She'd seen my jaw drop. She could hardly have helped it. "I don't mean this isn't all right," she said gently. "Only, Mother says you only live once and you might as well have a little comfort while you're at it.—But a boy in the taxi said this was a good neighborhod," she added then, with a small tinge of complacency. "I met him on the train. He's very nice, *Eastern*, sort of, but very friendly. I told him a friend of Daddy's had got me a room here."

She turned her blue eyes from the picture of my sons on the table. She'd been examining them with enough interest to make me glad—even at this point—that they were safely out of Washington.

"He said it was a very nice place. He said he used to know a boy who lived here once and he got along all right. He thought I'd get along okay if I didn't stay out too late. You're very strict, he said."

I could see now why Archie Seaton had thought it was all so funny.

"Now, about how much I'm supposed to pay," she said, really getting down to some small but solid brass tacks. "Mother said I wasn't to let myself be gypp—be over-charged. She said Mr. Buck oughtn't to get anything—you know, any commission because he's supposed to be a friend of Daddy's. Daddy'll take care of him. Now, how much do you think it ought to be, Mrs. Latham? Of course, I've got a job, and I'd like to live on it.—But I don't really have to. Money doesn't make any difference to Daddy. He's the sheriff of Taber County."

She brightened again and went on without giving me the chance to answer her.

"You didn't know I got my job in a contest, did you? a talent show? You had to know how to type, of course. That was one of the entrance requirements. But you had to have talent. I danced."

She gave me an incredibly lovely flower-like smile. "Of course"—she didn't exactly shrug but the effect was the same—"I'd have gotten it anyway. We all knew that. It was all set when I graduated from High School in February.

Daddy didn't like it very much, but you know Mother. She thought I'd have a better chance of meeting people in Washington than I would in Taber. She doesn't go for my boy friend. He's all right, but . . . you know." She smiled again. "His father's a big oil man in Taber. He's very rich. But Mother says a girl has to look around. Daddy says he'd rather be a big frog in a little pond, but that's not the way Mother looks at it."

She took one glove off and was starting on the other when she caught herself and became seriously business-like a second time. "Oh," she said. "Mother told me I wasn't to take the room unless it had kitchen and laundry privileges with it. She says if I paid a quarter to use the washing machine. . . ."

"I'll see what we can manage, Ginny," I said hastily.

She took the other glove off. "But you haven't told me how much."

I got up. "Sergeant Buck has taken care of that," I said. I was about to add I didn't think she'd really be there for very long, but she interrupted me with a peal of laughter, as merry and tinkling as the prisms on the mantel lustres when they're moved by the evening breeze.

"Won't Daddy and Mother simply die!" she said. "They haven't seen Mr. Buck for ever so long, and Daddy was sure the kind of lady he'd know is the kind of lady I shouldn't. But you know Mother, she made him write the letter just the same. She said Mr. Buck would probably own half a dozen boarding houses himself now, and we'd get ever so much better rates. And she didn't like what Daddy said, because Mr. Buck was a boyfriend of hers once. She'd have married him if she hadn't met Daddy."

I'd heard Colonel Primrose say Sergeant Buck has led a charmed life.

Ginny stopped laughing, her face suddenly full of apology and real compassion. "Oh, I'm sorry!" she said quickly. "Mother told me to be terribly careful. But you're not the jealous type, are you? Mother said if *she* was a widow——"

The telephone rang then, fortunately. All I hoped was that Sergeant Buck would never, never have to hear what I'd just heard. Ginny Dolan's mother was rapidly becoming Number One on my list. In fact, at the moment she'd quite taken the place recently vacated by Sergeant Buck. As I picked up the phone and answered it, I wasn't sure that third place wasn't held by the young man whose cheerful voice was there in my ear.

"Hi, Mrs. Latham." It was Archie Seaton. "Got a room for rent, Mrs. L.? Oh boy, oh boy, is she a honey! Oh, man! What's she doing here? How long's she staying?"

"Not long," I said firmly. "But she's here now. Would you like to talk to her?"

"No, no," he said. "I'm coming over. I'm taking her to a movie in half an hour. Okay?"

"It's okay with me," I said.

His voice was abruptly serious then, which is unusual for Archie. "Have you seen Marge any place, Mrs. Latham?"

"She's coming here this evening. Why?"

"She left me a note asking if I know anybody named Forbes Allerdyce. Who is he, do you know?"

"He's a friend of the Brents," I said.

"Oh. I wish she'd quit stewing about those people. Tell your dreamboat I'll be right over."

Whoever had taught Ginny Dolan her manners had said you pretended not to hear what anybody said on the telephone. She turned to me with innocent wide-open eyes.

"Where's your television set?"

"I don't have one."

"Oh," she said. "Everybody in Taber City has one. We have three."

"Well," I said, "in Washington, we have Archie Seaton. He's coming over. You'd probably like to go to your room now. You can leave the big bag. I'll have that carried up for you later."

She went blithely ahead of me toward the stairs. "Oh, I'll just leave this down here." She went back and put the Taber City *Gazette* on the coffee table, smiling at me with a sort of demure but happy pride. "It's got my picture in it. I thought you'd like to look at it maybe."

"I'd love to," I said. "Thanks."

She went along into the hall. "How many other roomers do you have right now?"

"None," I said.

"Well, I can probably find somebody for you. There'll probably be some other girls in Hamilton Vair's office."

She stopped on the second step and turned back to me, smiling that shy, delighted smile. "You didn't know it was Hamilton Vair I was coming to work for, did you? It's his staff I'm on."

For the second time she misinterpreted the I dare say stunned look on my unfortunate face.

"You know who he is, don't you?"

"Oh yes." I said it quickly.

She laughed then. "I don't wonder you're surprised," she said kindly. "But Ham Vair isn't as terribly important out in Taber as he is in Washington. Anyway, he has to do anything Daddy says. Daddy's the best friend he's got out there. He wouldn't have got to first base without Daddy. That's why I didn't have to worry about getting the job in Washington. I'm going to be his receptionist. I thought I'd meet more people, that way."

Of course, I should have guessed. Who else would have a talent contest to pick his best friend's daughter for a job in Washington?

She started on up the stairs. "Mother says Daddy and Ham Vair are hand in glove." The musical rippling laughter came down toward me. "Daddy's the hand, Ham's the glove. I guess people in Washington would be surprised if they knew that. So I just laughed when that boy asked me if I wasn't scared coming to the Capital."

The idea was so deliciously preposterous to Ginny Dolan that she laughed all the rest of the way up stairs. It was such complacent laughter, so full of confident assurance, so empty of any possible idea of moral compunction or just plain ordinary everyday ethics, that I was really shocked.

She stopped at the top of the stairs. "You didn't know—" she began, and I stopped involuntarily, waiting to hear what I didn't know this time.

"You didn't know I went to a charm school, did you? They teach you poise, and things like that. It was a wonderful place. I was only there two months, but the lady said I didn't have to stay any longer. I was ready for anything, she said. I could hold my own anywhere. That's when I first decided to come to Washington."

By golly, the lady was right, I thought. Or at least I hoped she was . . . for as I turned on the light in my front guest room and opened the bathroom door, I had a curious little catch in my throat suddenly. Her confident figure in the mirror on the back of the door seemed to me infinitely pathetic. Her slender body was as fragile as if her bones were made of spun glass. I remembered that look on Ham Vair's face as he turned back on his way out at the garden party.

VI

Ginny Dolan plopped down on one of the beds, testing it. "*This* is for me! In Taber, my room's pink. But I like blue. I've got a hot-plate with me. I can put it right over there. Mother says——"

The doorbell rang, so there was one crumb of Mrs. Dolan's practical wisdom I didn't have to sweep up. The Shaw lowboy that Ginny was already mentally converting into her kitchen privileges was only in the guest room to save it from wear and tear. The occupational hazards of running a rooming house were becoming clearer by the minute.

Archie Seaton came in. "Look, Mrs. L.," he said. "Can't you get Marge to lay off the———"

I shook my head quickly, and just in time. Not only did the bizarre situation of having an employee of Hamilton Vair's there in the house occur to me, as he started to say the Brents' name, but the equally bizarre nature of the employee herself. Because as I glanced up the stairs I saw not Ginny but Ginny's shadow. She was hanging practically head over heels over the second floor stair rail. The abrupt silence in the hall as Archie stopped must have struck her as curious too. She rustled her little feet on the floor, unaware of her revealing shadow on the opposite wall.

"Oh, Mrs. Latham!" she called down. "Is that my date?"

"Yes, it is, Ginny," I said.

"Tell him I'll be right down. Just one second."

She ran back to her room.

"——She's here to work for Hamilton Vair," I said quickly. I said it as a warning on the subject of Marjorie's worrying about the Brents, and I didn't realize what a cruel thing it was —to Ginny—until I saw what it did to Archie Seaton. He deflated like a toy balloon hitting a torrid light bulb. I hadn't thought how intense his loyalty to his brother and his brother's chief client would be until it was too late to get back what I'd said.

The next minute Ginny was dancing down the stairs, completely unconscious of what I'd done to her.

"Hi, there, Archie! Do I look all right, do you think?"

"You look swell." He'd rallied, but not very much. "It's just a movie. Let's get going, shall we?"

I went back into the living room with a pretty lousy feeling I'd nipped a beautiful friendship before the bud was even formed. But if Daddy really was the hand in the snakeskin glove that was Congressman Hamilton Vair, there was justice in it. I felt that more sharply when Lilac brought me a late supper tray and I picked up the copy of the Taber City *Gazette* that Ginny Dolan had left for me to see. Her picture was there, all right, and on the front page, and it was Ginny at her best, may I say. I'd half expected a drum majorette's costume, but not at all. It was the exceedingly pretty, wide-eyed, demure little girl who'd sat down to discuss my house-keeping arrangements with me less than an hour before.

SHERIFF DOLAN'S DAUGHTER GOES TO WASHINGTON

it said above it. Below, it said

WINNER OF THE TALENT CONTEST GETS COVETED POSITION IN THE NATION'S CAPITAL.

It didn't say the coveted position had anything to do with Taber City's representative in Congress, but presumably they already knew that out there. The rest of the front page, however, was devoted almost entirely to Congressman Vair. If he rated half a column on the front page of our papers, he rated the works in Taber City.

VAIR ASSAILS RUMORED THREAT TO CLOSE BRENTOOL PLANT

I read.

"Two thousand citizens of Taber County packed the Court House Square last night to hear Congressman Hamilton Vair demand that Rufus Brent, owner and operator of Taber City's largest industry, withdraw his alleged threat to close down the machine tool plant where most of Vair's hearers are employed.

"In a stirring appeal, Vair declared he would abide by his hearers' decision. If fear of their jobs, their homes and their savings, he said, made his investigation of Rufus Brent unwelcome to them, his sense of duty and personal responsibility was such that he would resign the Congressional seat they had three times elected him to. He could not, he said, in honor hold it.

"If a rubber stamp in the hands of the colossus of greed with a wart on his nose was what the people of Taber County wanted in the Congress, then Ham Vair would step aside and let them have a rubber stamp. He did not, he said, believe that Rufus Brent would dare close down the Taber plant, as he had not dared come out openly to make the threat to close it in the first place, but had done it through slimy innuendo in the marble palaces of the rich in Washington, D.C. It was up to the people of Taber to make their choice.

"There was no doubt of the meaning of the ovation Congressman Vair received, when he offered to step down from the platform or go on speaking, whichever his hearers chose. 'It is the will of the people that rules in Taber County,' Vair said, amid thunderous applause."

It was the paragraph heading following that that made me put my coffee cup down quickly.

DEMANDS INVESTIGATION OF BRENT GIRL'S
ACCIDENT LAST FALL.

"Taber's hard-hitting, two-fisted young member of Congress lashed out against what he called the curtain-pullers and closet door-shutters of special privilege. Where but in a man's private life can the people see what any man is, he demanded? Are we to take the gilded utterances of bootlickers, stooges and self-seekers, the paid press and suborned police?

"If my father died in a state institution, would not you have the right to know it? If your daughter or mine had her picture taken escaping from some place in the rain in the middle of the night, would your newspaper kindly not publish it? Would a girl reporter have lost her job the next morning, as the girl unfortunately sent to cover the story I'm talking about lost hers? Would your feelings or mine be considered for one moment?

"If your daughter or mine had an accident on the public road, would reporters be driven from the scene? Would guards at the state's expense be put at the sick room of your daughter? Would you take your daughter, or would I have taken mine, to a sanitarium that specializes in only one kind of case? Was it because it was the nearest place to find medical aid, as a few privileged reporters who didn't lose their jobs were told over the whiskey bottles the next day? Do any of you here believe that story? Would any of you here who has a daughter you love deliberately allow her to be placed in *a geriatric institution* when a hospital was available? Is that why no investigation was ever made? Is that why the police, and the other reporters, were told to lay off . . . or else? Or did special rules prevail because this was a daughter of giant greed and special privilege?"

I skipped over the account of the thundering ovation the speaker was given on that one. The geriatric institution especially must have sounded horrible indeed. Molly Brent's little face, as I'd seen it in the Mother's Day picture between her older brothers kept swimming across the page, among the boos and catcalls that Vair's speech apparently was studded with every time the child was indicated. At the bottom of the page was a banner line: "The United States Senate Needs Ham Vair." On the back page, as I dropped the paper down on the sofa, I saw a small item tucked in above the want ads too late to classify. "Vandalism at Brentool Plant." Tramping down flower beds and breaking windows was laid by Sheriff

Dolan to the high spirits of visiting athletic teams. A warning had been issued to teen-agers.

I'd just put the paper down again when Marjorie Seaton came.

"Your brother-in-law was here," I said. "I've got a house guest. He took her to a movie." I'd decided not to tell another Seaton what my house guest's occupation was. "He said to tell you to lay off the Brents and quit worrying about them."

"I know," she said. "I suppose——" She stopped, stiffening as her eye fell on the Taber City *Gazette* lying there on the sofa. "Where did you get this thing?" She snatched it up, her eyes angry bright. "Where did you get it, Grace?"

"My guest——" I began.

"Because look——" She flung the paper down and tore her bag open. "You look at this. This is the picture they're talking about. I didn't have to go out and look for it. They sent it to her. They sent it to Molly Brent . . . with the clipping of that whole speech of Vair's. They put it in an envelope with the name of her best school friend on the outside. That's why her mother forwarded it to her, and that's why I let her——"

She broke off, still clutching the photograph she had in her hand.

"—Well, I've told you now," she said passionately. "I might as well go on.—Molly's staying with us at the farm. She's been there since January . . . that's why we went so early this year, just to give her a place to be where nobody's trying to drive her clear out of her poor little mind. She was barely able to walk then, Grace. She's wonderful, now, except she's still terrified of everybody she doesn't know.—And this thing had to come."

She thrust it out at me. It was a picture, a sort of printed broadside on cheap paper, of a girl, her head down, her forearm covering her face, running through the rain, clutching at her skirts. She was running toward a car. You could see the license number on it. There were other cars, their license plates spattered with what looked like mud, and illegible. Under the girl's picture was a photostat of a registration card with the same number on it and the name Mary Margaret Brent. The home address was in a town called Madisonburg. Sex female, weight 115, age 18, hair auburn, eyes light-dark brown. You couldn't see the color of the hair or the light-dark brown eyes, as the girl's face was hidden, but she looked the weight and the approximate age. And she looked more than that. Her whole figure was vividly that of a girl in the depths of utmost despair.

In the photograph, you saw why. On the ground, to the other side of the flagpole, were the huddled bodies of two men, and a tavern, garishly lighted, with the doors bulging with struggling men and women trying to break through the cordon of police with drawn guns. Only Molly Brent had managed to get past them, and one great greasy creature in a boiled dinner shirt, his eyes bulging, mouth sagging open, was pointing her out with a fat ring-covered hand, a policeman was evidently starting to run after her. The police slickers and cap protectors pulled down like cowls were shiny with rain. At the foot of the steps lay another body, a woman, her long blonde hair stuck in the black pitchy ooze dribbling from the corner of her lavish mouth, one hand forward on the ground still gripping a small savage-looking automatic, her nails, dark and long, like claws. The rain was washing the black ooze down from her mouth onto the glistening white flesh of her neck and breast.

Molly Brent was running, her face covered. She must have had to swerve wildly to avoid the dark stained gravel around the dead man who lay directly in the path behind her. She may have been with a group of people when her brothers were away, as her mother had said, but as I searched the faces of the people the police were holding back in the tavern doors, none that I could see looked much like a friend I'd want one of my own kids to have. The whole thing was sickening. I hated to look up at Marjorie Seaton. I could feel her standing rigidly there, waiting for me to say something, and I didn't know what to say.

At the bottom of the picture, balancing the cut of Molly Brent's registration card, there was a printed line. "The 2 A.M. Killing of . . ." I've forgotten now what the names were, but they were high-up public enemies, and the woman was the moll of one of them.

"—What was she doing there, Marjorie?" I said at last.

She drew a deep breath. "Oh, my God, Grace," she said, very quietly, ". . . she wasn't there. Look at it, Grace. It doesn't even say she was there. It's just two pictures . . . one of Molly, and one of a police killing in a gangster raid. That thing that looks like a flagpole separates them, they're two perfectly distinct pictures. The fine print says it's the memorial flagpole in the town square some place in Nevada. That's the filthy part of it. Nobody reads the fine print. You look carefully and you'll see . . . but nobody looks carefully. That's what they sent Molly. And here's the companion piece."

She flashed a second picture out at me.

"These are the police holding off the spectators, and the reporters. This is what happened right after the other one . . . when somebody called up and tipped off a woman reporter. Molly was at dinner at her aunt's house. Her parents hadn't gotten the news. The woman took a photographer and went out to the aunt's, and asked for Molly—and asked her for a story. And that's why Molly ran . . . and that's the way she heard about both her brothers. . . ."

I looked blankly at her. Her voice was shaken, passionately angry, and passionately moved at the same time.

"Heard what about them, Marjorie?" I asked.,

She stared at me silently for an instant, her lips white.

"Oh, Grace . . . didn't you know? Didn't she . . . didn't Mrs. Brent tell you? The two boys are dead, Grace. They were both killed . . . in Korea, both the same day. They were Marines. They were both killed, last November. Didn't . . . didn't Mrs. Brent tell you?"

Oh, no . . . she hadn't told me. Whether she thought I must have known, or the picture of my own two sons, one in his ensign's uniform and the other just old enough to start his military stint, made her keep silent, not to disturb me, I had no idea. She hadn't told me.

I took the other picture. It showed the car with Molly's same license plates, smashed and shattered against a tree. Molly was lying on the side of the road, covered with a man's raincoat. A state trooper was holding his arms out to keep people from coming in close to her.

"That's what happened. She was frantic, trying to get home and tell her father and mother before someone got to them the way the woman reporter had got to her. She skidded. That's all that happened. The old people's sanatorium was half a mile down the road, the hospital was ten miles. That's why they took her there. And that's why the woman reporter lost her job—it was rotten journalism in any language—and that's why Molly Brent's so terrified of strangers and frantic at any sudden light. She's never got over that shock, Grace. And she's sweet. You'd love her. She's just a lonely frightened kid they never thought was going to walk again. She adored her brothers. She's just lost without them. And this. . . ."

She picked up the Taber City *Gazette* and flung it across the room into the wastebasket. "It just makes me sick. That's why you've got to get Colonel Primrose, to stop this kind of stuff. There *must* be something. Tom says there's no law. Colonel Primrose can do *something*. I know he can, Grace."

She sat down and took a cigarette out of the box on the table, her hands trembling as she lighted it. "And something else," she said abruptly. "Who is Forbes Allerdyce . . . isn't that what you said his name was? Who is he, and where does he come from? I just don't trust anybody any more."

"I don't know," I said. "He looked attractive, to me. He's a friend of Rufie Brent's, Mrs. Brent told me. She was delighted to see him."

"Oh, really, Grace?" She put her cigarette down, her face lighted up almost as radiantly for a moment as Mrs. Brent's had been. "Oh, how wonderful," she said softly. "That's all Molly needs, Grace. Some man to give her back her confidence in herself, and . . . just in life, really. And the three of them were so close they hardly had any intimate friends. I've thought about Archie. But you know Archie . . . he wouldn't waste his time on a poor scared little rat like Molly. He doesn't even know she's down there on the farm. But she wouldn't be scared of a friend of Rufie's. I'm so glad. And he *was* attractive . . . not like Archie. Sort of . . . civilized-looking, I thought, didn't you?"

She was on her way back to the farm when I got my first startled intimation that Mr. Forbes Allerdyce was a friend of somebody else's too.

VII

I looked again at the composite picture of Molly Brent that Marjorie had left for me to show Colonel Primrose when he came. The flagpole that separated the two halves of the two different pictures actually tied them together, and made them look one and the same scene of rain-drenched horror for the unhappy child running for the car that moments later was a tangled wreck, with her a broken heap under the raincoat beside the road. I put my hand over the tavern side of it. The change was appalling. The tragedy implicit in the tortured little figure fleeing wildly through the rain, having just been cruelly told that both her brothers had been killed, running wildly out to get to her parents before the same cruelty was inflicted on them, was sickening. It was a wicked thing, the use of human tragedy for one man's ambition, if it was ambition and not sheer vindictive malice. But it wasn't illegal. The fine print explained the whole thing, if anybody bothered to read it.

I put it and the Taber City *Gazette* in the drawer under the desk flap, and closed it sharply, startled by the sound of someone fumbling at the knocker at the front door. I looked at the clock. It was a little early for Ginny and Archie. The knocker dropped then and the bell rang, and I suppose it was the dead gangsters strewn about in the composite photograph that disturbed me enough to make me put the chain up on the door before I opened it, after the bell rang, curiously demanding, a second time. I pulled the door open the four inches the chain allows and craned my head around to peek through. For a brief instant, I didn't recognize the man standing there, and when I did, it was the grey flannel suit and blue shirt and silk tie that I recognized first. It was Mrs. Rufus Brent's young friend Mr. Forbes Allerdyce. He had a hat on, which changed him. But I saw then, while he was first speaking, that it wasn't that. He wasn't wearing his spectacles, and even though I knew who he was he was almost unrecognizable.

I stood there for an instant, surprised at seeing him, and I think even a little embarrassed at the suspicious timidity the chain implied. But I felt a surprised pleasure, chiefly, and put my hand up quickly to release the chain.

Whatever went through my mind, it didn't take more than a fraction of a moment. But it was a fraction, and it was long enough.

"Miss Dolan . . . Virginia Dolan," Mr. Forbes Allerdyce said. "Tell her someone's here to see her."

His voice was abrupt, and so rude, actually, that if he'd thrown a glass of icewater at me I could hardly have been more astonished. It also took me a second to translate Miss Dolan, Virginia Dolan, into Ginny, she'd become so entirely Ginny and not Virginia in the brief time I'd known her so vividly in the bright flesh.

"She's the new girl." He raised his voice as if I were hard of hearing as well as stupid. "She got here this afternoon."

"Miss Dolan isn't in," I said. "She's gone out."

"What's her phone number?"

I gave it to him. He said "Thank you," but it managed to be more offensive than if he hadn't.

I closed the door even more abruptly than I'd intended to, and stood there till I'd heard him go down the steps—so surprised by his manners, and so incensed by them for a moment, that I took the fact that a friend of Mrs. Rufus Brent's should be there asking for Ginny Dolan entirely in my stride. Probably Ginny's turning up that afternoon with one of the most eligible bachelors in Washington happily in tow had conditioned me to any other friends she might have, and I was rather pleased, even, when I did think about it.

And she was going to need a friend, however bad his manners to invisible inferiors, because it was quite evident that Archie was through. When I heard them on the porch and opened the door, Archie's car was double-parked at the curb, the engine running, the lights on and the door open. It was the briefest good night in Seaton history as I knew it, and in Ginny's, I gathered from the look on her face, an almost comical mixture of bewilderment and dismay, as he said good night to me and thanks to her and was gone, half-way to his car before I got the door shut. I was as surprised as Ginny, and I felt like a dog. It was my fault for telling a Seaton a date of his was a friend of Hamilton Vair's. I felt a distinct twinge of something like remorse as I saw her standing there looking at herself in the mirror, her bright aura of confidence very dim as she turned those blue wide-open eyes to me.

"I guess boys are different, in the East, aren't they?" she asked. Her voice was as uncertain as the rest of her. "At home they'd at least take you to the drugstore, for a coke or something."

"He probably thought you were tired after your trip," I said. It was cold comfort even if she'd believed it. She shook her head unhappily.

"There was another young man here to see you," I said.

That was a magic formula. The dimmed aura was instantly shining bright again, her blue eyes danced like stars out of a sudden rift in wind-chased clouds.

"Oh, really?" Never has Archie Seaton been wiped off any girl's slate with such speed of light before. "Oh, *I* know!" she said. "I knew he'd come! I bet he was mad as hops, wasn't he? Because I didn't tell you. He was supposed to meet me at the Station, but I ducked him because I had Archie."

She broke into a peal of cascading laughter, sparkling as sunshine.

"I bet *you* were surprised, weren't you? But I keep telling you, Ham Vair isn't as important at home as he is here. He comes to our house all the time, front door and back. But you didn't tell him about Archie, did you? Because he'd tell Daddy, and Daddy's old-fashioned. That's why he told Ham to meet me, because I've never been in a big town before." She laughed again. "Did you get a chance to talk to him? Did he come in? But I don't suppose so."

She'd been hopeful, for an instant there, that a ray of light might have shown, a moment, in the barren cave of my poor existence, but it was all so clearly improbable she'd had to give it up. And I hesitated myself, because I didn't want to have to give her shining *amour-propre* another jolt, or disturb her airy confidence in Daddy's Word as Ham Vair's Law. But still. . . .

"It wasn't Mr. Vair, Ginny," I said. "It was Forbes Allerdyce."

She reacted in two distinct parts. First, she looked slightly dashed, then completely blank. "I don't know anybody named that. At least I don't remember if I do. How . . . how old was he?"

"About thirty, I imagine."

I started to go on and describe him, but she shook her head.

"I don't know many older men," she said. "He must be somebody Daddy knows. Daddy knows a lot of people. He knows more people than anybody else in the whole county. The whole state, some people say. But anyway, could I have a glass of milk? I'll pay ex——"

"That's all right, Ginny," I said. "I'll get it for you."

"I wonder who he was."

"He said he'd call you. I gave him the phone number——"

I stopped as the phone rang then, and turned back, but if it had been an obstacle race I cared to enter I'd have lost by a table and two chairs.

"—This is Miss Dolan." Ginny's face was radiant and she nodded delightedly to me. He might be senile but he was still a man. "Who?"

I'd bent down to pick up a magazine she'd knocked off the coffee table in her burst across the room. There was such a curious note in that "Who?" that I looked at her as I straightened up. I saw the tail-end of the radiant smile just as it disappeared entirely. "O—Oh. It was *you* that came. Oh well . . . just a minute."

She held her hand over the phone.

"That creep," she said to me.

She was shaking her head, frowning. "—What you said, that's not his name. What's he coming to see me for, I'd like to know? He's got a nerve, hasn't he?"

I could hardly have been more surprised, and she was waiting for an answer.

"I don't know, Ginny," I said. "Perhaps if you ask him . . ."

"Okay, but I just don't want you to get the idea I'm friends with an old creep like he is. Why! He wouldn't dare call me up at home. Daddy'd kill him if he did."

Her cheeks were warm and her eyes bright with indignation.

"Well, I'll get you some milk," I said. It all seemed very odd to me. "I'll put it in your room." I went out and closed the door, thinking that perhaps what she was going to say to that creep wasn't for any ears of mine. And her belligerence was certainly genuine. When I passed the door again on my way up from the kitchen I heard her distinctly.

"I will not. What would Daddy say? It's too late and I'm going to bed."

But she didn't. I didn't hear her go out, but I knew she was gone. The air pressure funnelling up the stair well was like an invisible hand pushing my bedroom door in as she opened the front door, pulling it silently to when she closed it, with a pause in between as she pressed the catch to leave it unlocked for her return . . . and I got a book, seriously beginning to wonder, now, about the hazards of rooming house keepers, and started downstairs to wait up for her a second time. I didn't think Sergeant Buck, or Daddy either, would approve of the yellow chick's safari into the night. Because Daddy, even if he was a friend of Ham Vair's, was beginning to sound all right to me. Something shone out of his blue-eyed child each time she mentioned him that made me feel that in his perhaps odd way Daddy was a pretty solid citizen. At least Ginny had real respect for him, and that's a tribute to any parent these days. She was really proud of Daddy.

I stopped as I came into the hall, relieved for an instant, thinking I'd heard her come back. I went quietly to the stair rail and looked over. It was Lilac, swaddled in the strange garments she wears at night, creeping along the hall not to disturb me. I saw her old hand reach out and put the chain across the door, and she sat down then in the Chippendale chair beside the card table. I faded quietly back to my room. If Lilac was willing to conspire against me, it was all to the good, and the unshirted hell she'd give Ginny Dolan when she came in would be the best thing in the world for her. And after all, and in spite of his advanced age, Mr. Forbes Allerdyce couldn't be such a creep if she was willing to go out with him at that hour.

So I turned my light out with confidence, and that's why it seemed so perverse that I can never remember such a hagridden night. The dream I kept waking from to find myself trembling with empty terror dogged me the minute I closed my eyes again. A girl was running wildly through the rain. Sometimes she had no face, sometimes Molly's, the way I'd seen it in the Mother's Day photograph, and then she'd have Ginny's face, the belligerent little face at the telephone, only now static with terror as she called "Daddy! Daddy!" The rain pelted down on a dark screen that hid the featureless terror behind her, whether it was Ginny's face or Molly Brent's. I was worn out when I finally waked, and it was eight o'clock and Lilac there with my breakfast tray, her moon face as bland as whipped owl's grease, no evidence at all of her night watch.

"It's a lovely day, Miss Grace," she said. "A day in *ten thousand.*"

It was a pretty good day, even for Washington in May. It was china-blue again. The Silver Moon rose on the old brick wall glistened like a sunlit snowdrift sprinkled with the dust of yellow gold. I looked back at a Lilac too amiable by far not to be up to her eyebrows in duplicity even if I hadn't known all about it.

"That's one consolation," she added.

It was that too, I thought. Neither of us mentioned Ginny, and that was another. I picked up the morning paper. Happily there was no mention of Hamilton Vair on the front page. I glanced at the society column. There was a brief account of the garden party. Vair's name was listed and Forbes Aller-dyce's was not, and there was no mention of wild life. In fact a curious peace had settled on the Brent-Vair front, for one day at least, so I turned to various other scandals and threats of scandal, and poured a cup of coffee. The phone rang then, and it was Colonel Primrose.

"Oh," I said. "I'm *so* glad you called."

There was a brief instant of silence. "What's the matter, Grace?" he asked quietly, and I knew I hadn't sounded my usual early morning self. He doesn't call me "Grace" unless he's being serious, or worried, or irritated at me beyond the lengths of his very long endurance. He calls me "Mrs. Latham." It was a custom originally designed to appease Sergeant Buck, no doubt. "—is it that girl?" he asked abruptly, and I knew then he'd been keeping his fingers crossed, knowing more of his sergeant's friends than I do. "What's her name . . . Virginia?"

"Ginny," I said. I stressed it, which was a mistake.

"—Yes, Mrs. Latham?"

Her bright little face popped in at my door, fresh and lovely as one of the Silver Moons on the garden wall. "It's for me, isn't it?"

In Taber City they dive for telephones. In Washington, they're going to have a lady wrestler named Latham, if I go on developing the strength and agility I managed to exert to hang on to mine. It spluttered and crackled, with Colonel Primrose trying to find out what had happened to me or to his connection.

"Call me later, will you," I said. "Tonight, if you can." I put it down without waiting for an answer.

"Oh, you didn't have to do that, Mrs. Latham," Ginny said quickly. "I'm not in any hurry. I thought you called me. I could have waited."

She was so genuinely sorry I hadn't realized her business wasn't so urgent that I couldn't take a little time out for my own that I was quite touched. Miss Ginny Dolan's small spun-gold universe was a web with every strand leading directly to the bright little creature perched exactly in the center of it. It seemed cruel—and futile—to try to disabuse her of any such notion. And she looked completely enchanting. All the formless featureless terror of my dream was palpably ridiculous. There wasn't a shadow of a line to indicate Lilac had read any riot act to her or that she'd been on safari with an old creep in the midnight world along the Potomac. She had on a simple navy blue crepe dress that fitted her like an angel's skin, crisp white organdie collar and cuffs, a strand of small ladylike pearls around her throat, a small blue beanie on the back of her head behind the soft sunny halo of angel's curls around her face. Her blue eyes were clear as dew-drops on a yellow rose. I'd forgotten how really lovely Miss Ginny Dolan was.

"I just came to tell you I was going out so you wouldn't have to worry about me," she said. "And I wondered . . . do you . . . don't you have keys your guests can have?"

—Not with me responsible to Sergeant Buck, young lady, I said to myself. "Sorry," I said to her. "There's always some-one here to answer the door."

"Okay," she said. I saw her covert glance. She wasn't sure Lilac had played the game.

I thought it might as well be time we quit playing games of any kind. "Look, Ginny," I said kindly. "You *are* a guest——"

I didn't get one word or one syllable farther. Her face lighted up merrily. "You don't have to tell me that, Mrs. Latham." Her laughter was like a mischievous summer breeze ringing all the silver bells in a flower garden where little sum-mer breezes aren't supposed to go. "We're not as backward in Taber City as everybody seems to think. Daddy's sister had to take guests. She didn't like anybody to call them roomers either. Of course, she had to quit, because when Daddy got prominent all kinds of crummy characters kept coming around. Daddy said there were just too many jerks trying to use his connections without his sister helping out."

She put out her hand and touched my arm. "I know how it is. Lots of older women aren't trained to do anything to make a living. My aunt wasn't. I don't think people should be ashamed of taking people in. They have to live somewhere."

She gave me such a sweet and really understanding smile that I felt momentarily like a dog for still having three empty rooms on the third floor. I could also have wept from sheer downright frustration, and I dare say I looked it. She broke into another laugh that was more like an amused giggle. "You looked exactly like my mother, then," she said, and for an instant I had an impulse of genuine sympathy for the woman. "Only you're prettier," she added. "Mother's let herself get awful fat. It makes her look ever so old. You don't really look old at all."

I've never heard of sugar-coated cobra venom, but no doubt it exists. My sympathy for Mrs. Dolan died a-borning.

And as for trying again to explain to Ginny that she was not a roomer, the hell with it, I thought, until I could get a slate and a pencil or until Sergeant Phineas T. Buck got back home. I mopped up my saucer, where I'd spilled my coffee at some point in all this, and poured another cup. Ginny had moved to the door. It was an illusory respite.

"Oh, Mrs. Latham. . . ." She just that instant remembered what it was perfectly apparent had been the whole reason for her coming. "I almost forgot," she said brightly. "It's the *funniest thing.* You know when you said 'Forbes Allerdyce,' last night? You 'member?"

I wouldn't have bothered to answer if she hadn't waited, wide-eyed and so falsely bright that she glittered like a tinsel doll.

"Well!" She laughed, really surprised that she could have been so stupid. "I didn't know you meant *that* Forbes Allerdyce. We used his . . . his nickname. He's an old friend of . . . of Daddy's, out in Taber City. He's so much older, I just didn't think it was him you meant."

As my eyes met hers—those awful adult eyes that all of us have faced in our time—she wavered. But she went stoutly on. "And I'm having lunch with him today."

"I thought you said he was a creep," I commented mildly.

"Oh, well, *you* know. That was at home. He's different here. He's ever so nice." She caught herself quickly. "I mean, he sounded very nice on the telephone.

"Well, that's fine," I said. I took a sip of my stone-cold coffee to indicate, I hoped, that the landlady would like to be left alone. But the yellow chick wasn't through.

"And there's . . . there's something else, Mrs. Latham," she said.

The going was harder this time, the brightness more labored. As I looked at her, I had a sudden twinge that was almost a heartache . . . or one in miniature, anyway. She was trying so hard to keep her shining ingenuous little façade intact that it was pathetic, in a way, and rather valiant, if misguided.

"I . . . told you a dreadful story," she said. "I told you I . . . I was going to be Mr. Vair's receptionist. You 'member I told you that?"

"Aren't you?"

"No, I . . . I'm not," she said quickly. "I . . . I was just pretending. I'm not going to work for him at all, really. I don't know exactly . . . exactly what I'm going to do. Maybe I'll . . . I'll just stay here a few days, and buy Daddy a present and go back home again. I think that's where a girl belongs anyway, don't you?"

"I wouldn't be surprised," I said.

"Well, anyway, I just wanted to tell you so you won't tell everybody you see you have one of Mr. Vair's staff at your house.—You'll promise, won't you, Mrs. Latham?"

There was a kind of small but terribly earnest desperation about her that seemed very out of proportion to the matter in hand. I think that's when I truly began to be disturbed about the yellow chick.

"Because . . . I don't really know Mr. Vair as well as I pretended."

She tried to keep her blue eyes glued to mine. "You see, I . . . I don't know him at all, ackshually, Mrs. Latham. Why, if he . . . if he came in this door I . . . I wouldn't know him from Adams," she said emphatically.

"Well, that's good, Ginny," I said. "There are a lot of people who think he's very bad to know."

Her little jaw dropped and she stood there looking at me wide-eyed.

"Oh, that's not right," she said then, earnestly . . . and this set the keynote for all the lectures she was to give me, like a child mimicking a grown-up, half-scolding, half-severely didactic, setting me straight for my own good. "That's just his *enemies* say that. That's that old Brent's crowd. They're out to get Ham because he's telling the truth about them. You don't know, but I do. I listen. My bedroom in Taber's right over the back porch and I hear everything. I've heard lots of things would surprise you, Mrs. Latham, if you knew anything about politics. Anyway, we're on Ham's side because Daddy's getting pretty tired of old Mr. Brent. He's cost Daddy more money than you've ever seen, and Ham's going to take old Mr. Brent to the cleaners. Why, Mr. Brent won't let a slot machine be any place in the plant, or any place where he owns the land. He's driven Daddy's biggest contributors right out of the county. That's cut Daddy's take these last two years like nobody's business. You just don't know."

VIII

"Of course, Daddy's different," Ginny said. "He doesn't hate Mr. Brent, personal-wise, like Ham Vair does. There's a lot of things Daddy has to do, political-wise, but he wouldn't do anything mean. Daddy says what's the use of doing things that keep you awake at nights and don't pay off in the daytime to make up for it? That's Daddy. Things have to pay off or he won't touch them."

It seemed . . . practical, I suppose. I didn't know, but I was getting surer Daddy would always know what he was talking about.

"But . . . I don't know," his daughter said. "Money comes where money is, that's what Daddy always says, and this job somebody's offered me pays a lots of money."

I looked at her. "What job, Ginny? Who's offered it to you?"

"Oh, it's just a silly old job. Some friends of mine thought I'd be wonderful at it. Because a teacher of mine said I was a born actress. Would you think so, Mrs. Latham?"

I didn't know. I was worn to a frazzle with the mental gymnastics of jumping from hoop to hoop that she juggled brightly in front of me. Or maybe it was just hunger, and relief that it was a television job or something, and not whatever vague and awful thing I'd first got it into my mind she meant. It was then that Ginny Dolan first became aware of me, myself.

"Oh, you poor dear!" She made a dive toward me and patted my arm again, all sweetness and kindly light, the sort you use to comfort the aged and really pooped. "You must try to eat your breakfast. And don't you worry about me, Mrs. Latham. I can take care of myself. Let me pour you some coffee?"

"No," I said. "No thanks." I wasn't sure I could manage, but by golly I was going to try.

She tiptoed out, closing the door softly, and in an instant I heard her swooping happily down the stairs. The front door slammed, shattering, and music to my ears. And before I could try to sort all the shocking bits and pieces and fit them into some kind of a picture I could look at and try to understand, Lilac was in the room.

"You ain' eat your breakfas'," she said.

"I haven't had a chance," I said back.

"I'll get you some hot coffee. An' here this. The shofer in the kitchen, wait for an answer."

She handed me a small informal envelope and the engagement book from my desk downstairs. I opened the envelope. "Mrs. Rufus Robert Brent" was engraved on the parchment flap of the double card.

"Dear Mrs. Latham," I read. "If you're free this evening will you dine with me at half-past seven? My husband has been called out to the Taber City Plant, and I've asked Forbes Allerdyce to come in for dinner. I told you that I had seen miracles in other people's lives. I truly believe we now have one in ours. You were so kind the other day I want you to share it with me. Cordially and gratefully, Lena Brent."

I read it again. I don't know whether it was a sort of nagging uneasiness, or actually the wide-eyed way she'd spoken of miracles that noon at my house, that worried me. Miracles tend to disturb me, especially if they're in human form. Or perhaps it's the people who seek miracles.

I scribbled a note of acceptance. "I won't be here for dinner, Lilac," I said, when she came back. "And I'm going down to the country, to the Seatons', for lunch. I don't suppose Ginny'll be here for either, but you stay, won't you?"

"Yes, ma'am," she said . . . with so much emphasis that it even struck her as too much. "I mean, I ain' bother goin' any place tonight," she added blandly.

The dogwood that sprinkles the protecting fringe of beech and chestnut oak on either side of the white rail gate into the Seatons' farm, four miles along a country lane from the main highway, was almost gone. Inside, the oyster-shell road makes a wide bend through the woods and comes out between the bois d'arc hedges, sweet with clipped-back honeysuckle and multiflora roses, that divide the fields. Across the pastures I saw the rambling old red brick farmhouse that the Seatons have never tried to "restore" to a spurious grandeur it never had. It lies comfortably on a knoll, the grass sloping pleasantly down a couple of hundred yards to the river, one of the broad estuaries of the Chesapeake actually, blue now along the golden-green marshes and hazy white in the water, an ungainly old tub that I knew belonged to Archie Seaton waddling up and down beside it. A couple of dogs were on the pier, running back and forth, barking at a lone blue heron flapping in leisurely unconcern off down shore to broader marshes. I made the white-ribbon turn around the boxwood garden to the end of the house. And that's when I first saw Molly Brent.

I saw her a suspended fraction of a moment before she saw me, and before even the dogs there and the three little Seatons saw me—they were all so entranced—at the end of the gallery that runs along the river front of the old house. For a brief instant the small group held, Molly Brent the center of it, her head like a fireball of burnished copper bent over the net she was weaving. If it had been five centuries ago on the Adriatic, and a Botticelli there, it would have been a perfect Madonna of the Crab Net, with the smallest tow-headed Seaton at her knee, a little colored boy about ten kneeling solemnly beside her holding the ball of twine. The two other Seatons, four and five, were squatted soberly in front of them beside a pair of colored twins not much older, and the dogs were squatted around, watching too. They were all so absorbed that none of them heard me come, or if they heard they couldn't for an instant break the circle of enchantment around the copper-haired girl who was weaving, the long black bobbin flying skilfully in and out as she knotted the white string. I don't know whether it was the dogs or the little Seatons who broke first, but it was the girl I saw. She was like a sudden flame springing from a small stick of lightwood, on her feet, a slender vivid splinter of light held motionless for an instant, her face white as her cotton shirt, before she turned and was gone in a flash as the young Seatons and their dogs raced toward me.

"It's on'y Grace, Molly!" Tommy, aged five, stopped and ran back shouting to her. Then he came running on to me. "That's on'y Molly," he said soberly. "She had a accident. She's scared of people she doesn't know."

He said it with a definitive sobriety that marked him as senior officer present.

"Let her alone, then," I said. "There's some stuff for you kids in the back seat."

Then his mother was in the front door. "Hi, darling."

"Molly ran," her son said.

"Okay. You run too. Dogs and children scatter. You're eating lunch in the orchard. Scoot, all of you."

She held the screen door open for me. "This place is a madhouse. I don't know how Molly stands it. How are you?"

Inside there was peace and quiet, and only eight dogs, a Llewellyn setter in a basket with seven silky pups, all busy with the problem of nutrition and reasonably silent. I bent down to look at them as Marjorie went back into the hall.

"Molly! Come along. It's Mrs. Latham, I've told you about her."

She shook her head at me from the doorway. ". . . I don't know," that said. But I heard a hesitant step on the stairs, and in a moment Molly Brent came in, her face pale and unsure, only a shadow of the face I'd seen for an instant bent over the crab net. It was still very lovely. Her eyes still dominated it, with its high delicate cheekbones, and the curious description of them on her driver's license, light-dark brown, was true. They were dark brown, as dark as old sherry, with amber flecks like sunlight in them, and warm and lovely as her hair, burnished copper in the sunlight, sleeked back in a donkey-tail that emphasized the lovely pure lines of her face.

"This is Molly Brent, Grace. Mrs. Latham, Molly. What about making a cocktail for us, will you?"

She put her hand out shyly.

"Hello, Molly," I said.

Her smile was a frail light in contrast to the glowing warmth that had made her such a radiantly vivid picture waeaving the net, but it was a light.

"How do you do, Mrs. Latham?" Her voice, low and not too sure, was still curiously like her mother's, and she had another quality of Mrs. Brent's, that strangely lost intangible sweetness that was a light of its own.

She went quickly down the pine-panelled room to the bar on the old dough mixer. "A martini, Marjorie?"

"Please, darling. And not all gin. How about you, Grace?"

As she turned to me the Llewellyn raised her head and growled. The pups went very silent. Marjorie looked quickly out of the window. A lump of ice dropped to the floor as Molly Brent stiffened, frozen motionless there.

"Oh, it's Archie Seaton," Marjorie said. She managed to make her voice casual, for Molly, but her dark eyes on me were accusing. I shook my head quickly to say "Not me."

"It's just Archie, Molly," she said. "Tom's youngest brother. We've told you about him."

Somehow I didn't think that was going to be too reassuring, knowing the Seatons' ribald estimate of Archie's private and public life. I saw Molly Brent put the pitcher of martinis down, her face magnolia-white as she tried to control that fear of hers that was like shock itself.

"You don't have to stay if you'd rather not."

But it was already too late.

"Hi, Marge. Who doesn't have to stay where?"

Archie was right there in the hall, and before Molly could take more than a few steps he was in the doorway. She froze stiff again, her face so white that it made her shirt look yellow and her hair like a shiny copper cap totally apart from her. Her eyes were fixed on Archie, but I think she was too blind to see him. And I wasn't sure I was seeing him myself. Maybe it was Ginny Dolan's influence, but it seemed to me he'd aged, or something. He wasn't grinning, and there was nothing comical about the set of his simian mug as he caught the scene in front of him.

"Molly, this is Archie," Marjorie said. "Now run along, darling. The kids are in the orchard."

But Molly Brent was too paralyzed to run.

"Hello, Molly," Archie said. He turned to me. "Hi, Mrs. L. 'Scuse me, Marge, I left some stuff in the car." He turned and went out, and Molly flashed across the room and out like a streak from a fireglass. And Archie stepped back in.

"Molly who?" he asked quietly. "Is that——"

"Molly Brent." Marjorie's cheeks were flushed. "I suppose

you've heard all about her, like everybody else in Washington."

He stood looking at her for an instant, and went over to the window. We could see the glint of her hair in the sun. The children were already running toward her to drag her back to the picnic.

"Why the hell didn't you tell me she was here? I wouldn't have come barging in and scared the daylights out of her. That kid's no dipso."

"Of course she's not!" Marjorie said sharply. "She's just a frightened——"

"Okay, you don't have to get sore at me." He went over to the bar, picked up the martini pitcher and held it up to the light. "I'll have to teach her how to make a cocktail. Who else knows she's down here?"

"The Brents and ourselves."

"Is this connected with your asking me about this guy Allerdyce?"

"That was a mistake." She was flushed and angry. "It never occurred to me you'd come barging in, you never come here unless we drag you. I needn't have bothered about Allerdyce. He's a friend of Molly's brothers, and he . . . he's an answer to a prayer. It was the shock of her brothers' death, and the way they hounded her out and told her about it, that wrecked her. She adored them. And she's never mentioned their names the five months she's been here."

He was listening intently. "And you're counting on this guy——"

"I'm more than counting on him. Mrs. Brent says he's charming. She may bring him down tomorrow. She wanted me to come up tonight to dinner, to meet him. But Tom's had to fly out to Taber with Mr. Brent, because Vair's kicked up another row there. But that's nothing to you. You don't give a damn about any——"

"Just keep your shirt on, will you, Marge? Let me ask you something. You've got Molly Brent here. Do you think Vair's crowd is trying to find out where——"

Her eyes were blazing now. "My God, they've tried everything. They call the house. They call Mr. Brent's secretary, and Tom's secretary. They've sent registered letters with return receipt demanded. You can see why. If they could get a picture of her the way you just saw her. . . . But I don't know what they want, except that it's to hurt Mr. Brent. I just know if she had some friend of her brothers . . . they were such wonderful people, she adored them so!"

Archie Seaton lifted the martini pitcher to the light, poured still more gin in and looked at it critically. "If you and the Brents are so sold on that idea," he said, "don't you think it might have occurred to the Vair outfit too? If you wanted to find Molly, wouldn't that be the smart way to do it? Dig up a friend of her brothers'? They're dead. Who's going to know the difference?"

Her face was a sharp blank. "Mrs. Brent would now. She'd know."

"Maybe. What if the friend really was a friend, and a louse? And Vair dug him up?—You see, you asked me who this Allerdyce is. And I happened to find out. I think he's a phoney, and I damn well know it's Ham Vair he's working for."

Marjorie's face was grey. "I . . . don't believe it." Her voice was like old straw with the wind rustling through it.

"Okay, you two." He brought us each a cocktail and took his to the couch by the window. "That's why I came down here. I thought you both ought to know quick what's going on.—When Ginny and I got to your house last night, Mrs. L., there was a guy across the street, and when he spotted Ginny, he cut out down towards Wisconsin. That's why I dumped her so fast." He gave me a fleeting grin. "He went to Nick's place. The phone booth there's open, and when I got in he was browbeating the hell out of some girl. 'Look, sister, it's not my idea, it's the boss's. You damn well get off your tail and come on, I'll be there in three minutes.' I decided to stick around just in case. You told me Ginny was here to work for Vair, but if he was talking to her, why didn't he just come over when she got home, instead of this cloak-and-dagger stuff? I trailed along, and it was Ginny all right. She came out of your house, sore as hell. He had a maroon convertible parked up the street, and they went out Massachusetts to a big white brick house on Woodley Road."

He glanced at Marjorie.

"You may know the glamorous Sybil Thorn who's bank-rolling Ham Vair's campaign. It was her house, and she had the door open before they got on the porch. And that was okay. So Ginny's working for Vair, so she goes to his unofficial headquarters. So that's her business. But this guy had to practically drag her there. I stuck around, in case she had to walk home or something. She comes out at half-past two, dancing a jig all the way to the car.

"It looked like dirty work to me, for a green kid anyway. I stuck along with the guy after he got Ginny home. He went over to the Penn View. That's a fleabag out by the Station, behind the Senate Office Building. That's when I found out he was this Forbes Allerdyce you were talking about . . .

except that the night clerk's an old joker that never forgets a face and he says the guy was there last year and Forbes Allerdyce wasn't his name then. While he and I were shooting the breeze, Allerdyce puts in a call to the House Office Building. The old fellow listened in. A man answered and Allerdyce said, 'She's okay, I'll see you,' and hung up. So there you are. You figure it."

I'd been figuring it, in a series of pictures with sound, each sharply focussed and very disturbing.

"Look," I said. I told them about Allerdyce's introduction of himself at the garden party, and Ginny's "that creep," and about Mrs. Brent's note.

"—I think you'd better call her, and damned quick," Archie said quietly. "Before the miracle man gets working on her."

I looked at the clock. "He's taking Ginny to lunch."

Marjorie's face was white. "You call her, Grace." She sounded like a bloodless automaton. "Just tell her he was at Sybil Thorn's. She'll understand the rest."

She gave me the number and I dialled it. A maid answered. "Mrs. Brent's down at the swimming pool," she said. "Hold on, Mrs. Seaton. I'll try to get her."

I thought she sounded relieved, as she identified me by the humming over the rural line.

"She's down at the pool," I said.

Then, surprisingly quick, because I know the pool's down a series of terraces and Mrs. Brent moves heavily, I heard the click of the phone being picked up. And I heard a voice I recognized. It wasn't Mrs. Brent's.

"Are you calling for Mr. Brent?" Mr. Forbes Allerdyce asked.

"No," I said. "But I'd like to speak to Mrs. Brent, please."

"Mrs. Brent's rather busy, I'm afraid." There was a subtle, not quite impertinent note in his voice. "I'll give her a message . . . or you can leave your number. She can call you later."

"Don't bother," I said. I put the phone down, my adrenalin rising. The maid must not have told him it was Mrs. Seaton, but I didn't think of the possible significance of that, merely the subtle offensiveness he'd managed to convey.

I told them about it.

"—The miracle man's moved in already," Archie Seaton said. "What more do you want? Both Ginny and the night clerk wouldn't be wrong about his name, would they? Maybe there was a friend of Rufie Brent by that name. You wouldn't think this is just a fluke? A guy at a party not knowing the hostess, knowing Vair's new hired girl, turning up johnny on the spot the day Mr. Brent's called out of town on a mess of Vair's making and his lawyer's out of town with him?"

He took his pipe off the table and went over to the door. "You two better get together. Figure out what we do. Maybe Forbes Allerdyce was a friend of Rufie's. Rufie's dead. He can't say."

He pushed the screen door open. "But Seaton's not dead."

Marjorie got up quickly. "Archie . . . where are you going?"

He grinned at her, more like himself, or the self I knew.

"I'm going out to speak to my nephews and nieces, Mrs. Seaton," he said. "I think I'll adopt the scared one with the dark red hair. Her brother's friends can clear through me."

IX

"—He'll scare her to pieces," Marjorie said desperately, and she waited to see Molly Brent come flashing back to the house. But it was after lunch when she came, and she wasn't flashing. She was trudging five yards or so behind the rest of them, like a small bit of driftwood in their wash, or a young squaw respectfully to the rear of the big chief and his happy band of braves. It had plainly become a man's world.

"Now, where's this crab net?" Archie said, very business-like. It was about ten feet from him in plain sight, where Molly had dropped it when she fled from me. One of the twins ran to get it.

"She made it all herself," Tommy said proudly. "Come on, Molly."

She did come on then, when Archie didn't even look around, her eyes wide, with the air of a fawn approaching a mound of hay that might or might not conceal a dog or a gun, and settled herself on the step, her head turned just enough to see them.

"It's good, Uncle Archie, isn't it? *Isn't* it?"

He examined it critically, without a word, for minutes. It would have been absurd if it hadn't been so important to his breathless audience. And to Molly Brent. I saw her swallow as she waited.

"Not bad," Archie said. "Not bad at all." He was detached but generous, and Molly breathed again, a shy glow of pleasure in her face. "—For a girl," he added. "Where's the bobbin? We'll finish it."

He'd struck fire there. Molly's chin went up and she leaned forward to watch him. The color flushed back into her cheeks and the spark in her eyes faded as she saw she was watching a master. He drew the bottom square together. "There we are. You kids get the pole and bring me the pliers, we'll see how she works. I'll be back in a second." At the top of the stairs he turned. "Hey, Molly, see if you can find some tape, will you? There's a roll in that chest of mine in the cellar. It's black."

He came on without waiting to see if she was going, went into the house and waited for us. I glanced back as I went in. Molly was lighting out around the corner, whether to get the tape as directed or to escape I had no idea.

"Did you try to get Mrs. Brent again?"

We had, several times. "The line was busy," I said.

He nodded. "I'm staying here tonight, Marge. I'll sleep on my boat if you'd rather."

"She . . . she wouldn't tell him Molly's here. And he's going to be with her for dinner. . . ."

She sounded like somebody whistling in a desperate wood, trying to ignore the creeping steps behind.

"If he knows it's Ginny's landlady he's meeting, ten to one he won't be at dinner. Maybe I'm all wet but I'd like to stick around, if you don't mind—till Tom gets home. When are you going, Grace?"

"Now," I said. I got my bag.

"I mean to the Brents'? Could you get there early and talk to her?"

Marjorie followed me out. "Wait," she said. "I've got some apple blossoms for you." She went back and brought them out to the car, and glanced around. Archie was back with the crab net detail again.

"Listen, Grace. I don't want Archie to stay . . . I don't want Molly to know I'm frightened. But I am. Some way, this is just the sort of thing I've been waiting for. There's been a man around all the time . . . somebody stole those pictures from the Madisonburg paper who could pass for a newspaper man, and there was somebody attractive enough to make a nurse of Molly's go overboard for him. He walked out on her the day I went to get Molly. And Sybil Thorn's been mixed up with some strange characters. Her last divorce was practically blackmail, with a very smooth operator. We know her husband's lawyer."

Her hand tightened on the window ledge. "But if I get jittery, Molly'll sense it. You see Mrs. Brent. She's fey, but she's good, Grace. And call me, will you? But of course Archie's right. If he recognized you last night, or this girl told him and Sybil, he won't be there. And you *talk* to Ginny . . . will you?"

But I couldn't talk to Ginny, when I got there, because she wasn't home. I gave Lilac the apple blossoms, instead of tossing them out on the Benning Road, which would have been the smartest thing to do, and went upstairs. And I saw that if Ginny hadn't had lunch with Forbes Allerdyce, she'd been to his hotel. There were three books of Penn View matches on her dressing table, and the rest of her day was writ large in a pile of unopened bundles on her bed. Also on her dressing table was one item she'd opened and used. It was a large jar of expensive skin food that Ginny Dolan needed about as much as she did a medicated chin strap. In the box on the sales slip that said "How Sold" was written "Chg." The price, with a question mark after "Tax," had been written in in the girlish hand of my starry-eyed roomer, and all the slips there carefully filed . . . at least they were anchored down by the powder jar on the dresser.

And I didn't go to the Brents' early, because with Ginny Dolan an open-work chatterbox and Mrs. Brent part of the day at least with Allerdyce, her eager heart in control of her tongue, there seemed very little chance of his not knowing who was coming to dinner to meet him. I think I was more relieved than I'd care to admit when I got to the Brent house in Nunnery Lane off Foxhall Road and saw he wasn't there. The maroon convertible was distinctly absent and no cars in the cobbled courtyard at all, except one with a new University of Maryland sticker on the window, a battered old black sedan that I vaguely took to be one of the servants'. There was certainly nothing Ivy League, which meant I had a clear field to warn her to beware of miracles.

The house they'd taken is a magnificent Palladian job. I'd known it a long time, and never thought of it as being particularly remote until I drove in then, past the concrete pillars, a sign on one of them saying "Dead End." There are only three houses in the Lane, one on either side and one at the dead end, each of them with extensive grounds planted and walled to make them as private as possible. The Elliotts who live in the end house were abroad and the house on the right was boarded up, being gradually eaten away with the joint erosive of weather and lawyers' fees, having been tied up in an estate quarrel and empty for years. The Brents' is on the left. And the maid who let me in and took my jacket was as reassuring, I thought, as the absence of Mr. Allerdyce, for she was just as sultry and just as sullen as the sprig of precious springtime I'd left behind in my own house on P Street. I gathered we were known to each other, but I couldn't place her. She was what Lilac calls a settled woman, but as Lilac is what Sergeant Buck calls a pillow of her church, and I've lived in Georgetown all my life, there are a lot of familiar faces I can't put names to. She went ahead of me along the black-and-white tessellated marble hall.

The library and the so-called morning room beyond it, that opens onto the terrace and the lawn sweeping down to the rim of dense planting at the far end of the slope, are the only rooms downstairs in that house that don't need at least twenty people to take the formal chill off the luxurious gold velvet period furniture and brocaded walls. The library in particular was never designed, even then, for the woman standing there. Mrs. Brent was by the long table in the center with a silver bowl of lilies of the valley in her hands, getting ready to throw them out, I supposed. They were old and ratty, and undernourished in comparison with the hand-painted flowers all over the nebulous floating chiffon of the hostess gown she had on. It was astonishing, a garden club version of the Woods of Dunsinane in head-on collision with a rainbow. And the contrast between that costume and Molly Brent's rolled-up jeans wasn't any more startling than that between Mrs. Brent's flamboyant carrot hair and the sleek shining copper of her daughter's.

As she came forward, that lovely smile of hers was the only thing that kept her from being really bizarre. "I'm so glad you could come." Her face was shining with happiness. "Forbes is making us a cocktail. I'm so glad he could stay."

I was so taken aback that it took me an instant to absorb the shock.

"But I told you, Mrs. Latham," she said. "I wrote you. I met him yesterday . . . it was such a pleasure. Rufie used to talk about him so much, but we'd never met him. And he's been here all day, it's been such a joy. He didn't want to stay until I told him you had sons of your own, you wouldn't mind if he wasn't properly dressed. And look what he brought me."

She was still holding the silver bowl, in both hands, like a fantastic priestess radiantly holding an exalted chalice.

"They're my favorite flowers. The boys always sent them to me, and Rufie told Forbes how I love them."

It was the flowers he'd brought her, not the bowl. They were wizened yellow things, around for at least a week.

"—I'm afraid they're pretty far gone, but they were all I could find."

"They're lovely, Forbes."

I'd heard a faint tinkle of ice against crystal, but I hadn't heard any footsteps before he spoke. My back was to him now, and in an instant I was going to have to meet him face to face. My heart missed a beat, I imagine, as I turned.

"I want you to meet Forbes, Mrs. Latham," Mrs. Brent said happily.

It was clear that Forbes Allerdyce hadn't been in the least interested in Mrs. Brent's dinner guest . . . until she turned and he saw her face. I think shock is the only word that describes his reaction then. Even the ice in the cocktail pitchers on the tray responded to the sharp inertia that pulled him up. He was frozen, motionless, for a bare instant. Mrs. Brent was entranced by the heady stale perfume of the lilies and didn't see him. And I don't know quite how to describe what happened next, because nothing overt happened, but it was something so sharply dangerous, and so malevolent, developed with such psychic speed and intensity, that I can still move unconsciously backwards remembering it.

But at that point I still had some advantage. I'd got ready for him, and I haven't lived in Washington all my life without developing a respectable lacquer, as standard equipment to meet the changing scene that turns up some pretty odd characters in the standard order of Capital procedure. So I could say "How do you do, Mr. Allerdyce?" without any effort at all.

"How do you do, Mrs. Latham?"

As he went on and put the tray down on the table, I saw that in spite of his pleasant voice it wasn't just a jolt Mr. Forbes Allerdyce had got; it was an instant trauma, and it was followed by an almost uncontrollable seizure of rage that took everything he had to suppress. It seethed around him in an aura as visible as the heat waves flowing from a stove. His whole body was cataleptic in that rigid fury, and there was a split second there when everything inside me was a silent but screaming panic. I thought, *nothing but physical violence is going to absorb this. It's the instant in which the killer is unleashed.* . . .

I didn't breathe there, for an instant, and then I saw him move, the rigid catalepsy slowly dissolving. It probably wasn't more than a second or so in duration, but it seemed a kind of hideous eternity to me. And Mrs. Brent came back from some nebulous shining cloud where terrestrial atmosphere is not likely to reach.

"I told Forbes you had two sons," she said.

"But you didn't tell me I'd already met Mrs. Latham," Allerdyce said. "I really didn't expect my sins would find me out so quickly." He was stirring the cocktails. "Which will you have, Mrs. Latham? A Manhattan, or a martini?"

"A martini, please." I sat down and pulled up a small table. My hands and knees were neither steady . . . and I didn't yet know which of his sins that I was connected with he meant. "Put it there, please, will you?" I motioned to the table, when he brought the cocktail. I smiled up at him. "Which of your sins are you talking about, Mr. Allerdyce?"

His grey eyes tensed as they met mine. He smiled pleasantly and went back to the table.

"I don't have to ask what you'd like, Mrs. Brent."

Her pale blue eyes widened enquiringly as she looked at the Manhattan pitcher he'd picked up. If he'd been a magician, and the Manhattan he poured then a chinchilla rabbit, and she a child of five, her eyes couldn't have shone with greater or more enchanted wonder.

"Oh, Forbes," she said softly. "How did you know? Did . . . did Rufie tell you?"

The tremulous joy in her face was appalling to me. As the ratty lilies of the valley could have been sprays of fresh-plucked butterfly orchids, the cocktail might have been Olympian nectar, from the joy with which she took it.

And there was something wrong with the scene. I sensed that in a sudden shaft of antagonism that came my way. I was spoiling, somehow, what had been planned as a much more touching play. It wasn't coming off with the full flavor of sentiment it had been designed to have. I saw the faint ridges in the side of his face, though he was smiling.

"Rufie told you!" Mrs. Brent said. Her eyes were moist. "They always made a Manhattan for me, in that little shaker. Rufie brought it home from college especially for me. Did he tell you that, Forbes?"

He nodded, smiling. I was conscious that there should have been a speech at this point, and I'd soured that too. But his smile was easier, and the atmosphere was clearing. I was aware of that because, conscious of him as I was from the instant I'd seen him, caught in that paralysis of seeing and recognizing me, this was the first time I was aware of really seeing him himself. His worn sports jacket and flannel trousers were pleasantly out of a well-tailored past that like his steel-rimmed glasses gave him the cultivated look of the Ivy Leaguer, and the sun that had given him a healthy tan had bleached his cap-cut hair so that outwardly he was a combination of Old Nassau and Nassau B. W. I. that was really very attractive. Somehow it also matched the old sedan nosed into the service wall better than it would have matched the maroon convertible . . . except that it didn't match the University of Maryland sticker on the sedan window. That was a false touch that you'd have to live in these parts to know.

"You should have told me more about Mrs. Latham," he said, smiling. He came to the chair next to Mrs. Brent's and perched on its arm, putting his glass down on the table and taking out a pack of cigarettes.

"Here, Forbes." She raised a flushed and happy face to him and pushed the leather box on the table toward him. "Save yours, dear."

She thinks he's poor, I thought . . . and suddenly the sedan, the old clothes and the ratty bunch of lilies of the valley fell into place and it was a good thing I hadn't drunk that full three-ounce almost undiluted martini he'd given me.

"You didn't tell me I met her yesterday," he said easily. "But you've got to promise not to throw me out before dinner, Mrs. Brent. Because it smells wonderful."

She laughed. "Don't be silly, Forbes." It obviously didn't matter to her what sins he'd committed. She was in a kind of enchanted fog, looking at her cocktail, happy that Rufie had remembered, and touchingly grateful to Allerdyce for bringing the knowledge to her. And I'd be the same, I thought, except that neither of my kids would ever tell any of their friends that it's yellow roses Ma likes and she hates martinis and takes her poison straight when she can get it. . . .

And a sudden light flashed into my mind and I felt a chill creep down my spine. *That's what's wrong,* I thought. *It's all false. The Brent boys wouldn't be such saps. That's why this is going sour and why he's so furious. Because I don't believe it, I'm spoiling his show. The garden party doesn't matter. He can use that to make himself look frank and candid. But the rest of it I'm ruining. He didn't expect anybody so unlike Mrs. Brent to be the friend she was having in to meet him . . . who'd know that's not the way normal boys act. . . .*

X

Normal boys don't *bleat about their mothers* . . . The Brent boys in the Mother's Day photograph with little Molly between them, twinkling deviltry in their eyes, had been intensely normal. They weren't saps, dripping that kind of stuff about their mother's favorite flowers and favorite cocktail. Molly wouldn't have adored a couple of brothers who were capable of doing that. *This man is a phony.* He was smiling at me, Ivy League and State Department from tip to toe . . . the smiler with the knife under the cloak, I thought. I smiled back at him. Two smilers; but the knife I was trying to conceal, a stage prop in futile hands, was no match for his.

He smiled at Mrs. Brent then, and with what a difference . . . contrite and most engaging.

"I crashed the party, yesterday," he said. He made an amiable pretense of rising. "I'll go quietly." He laughed then, and waited an instant for her to speak. "I wanted to meet you," he said.

"But Forbes!" She wasn't as shocked as one could have been. "But . . . why? My dear boy, why didn't you just come and *see* us? You knew a friend of Rufie's, and particularly Forbes Allerdyce. . . ."

"I know," he said gently, and almost sadly, and I supposed, if I'd had the whole day's continuity instead of ten minutes in the middle of the third reel, I wouldn't have been as skeptical as I was. "I couldn't. Because . . . well, I had to see *you*, first. I had a picture of you, in my heart. I know it sounds crazy, to Mrs. Latham. But it's the first party I've ever crashed." He smiled at me. "That's why I latched on to the first attractive woman I could see."

Mrs. Brent was way out beyond mere techniques. "You might have got into a lot of trouble, Forbes," she said reprovingly. And then dinner was announced. "Come along, both of you." She was laughing at him then. "—I hope you don't mind, but we always dine in the morning room when there's only ourselves. It's so much cosier."

Again I saw the brief suspended pause. It wasn't till dinner was nearly over that I saw the reason. He hadn't expected to dine in the morning room, and it startled him. I wouldn't have known why if his napkin hadn't slipped off his lap or if I hadn't been telephone-conscious; for as he bent over to pick it up I saw the line had been busy because the phone was out of use. It was on a table at the far side of the room, and the mouth and ear bulbs of the telephone bar were each resting on a pile of magazines.

I got almost at once a curious instance of Mrs. Brent's perceptive telepathic nature then. "You know, it's the first day the phone hasn't rung almost constantly," she said. "It's been such a relief."

"Your husband called," Allerdyce said.

"That's his private line. I mean the regular phone. Nobody's called, since that woman. People are so rude in Washington."

"She may have thought I was rude." He looked at me, smiling. "The connection was so bad. There was such a hum——"

Mrs. Brent looked startled, and anxious. "Oh, but you should have told me, Forbes. That's—you must always let me know when that line calls. I'll just call her." She pushed her chair back. "Excuse me, will you? I'll just go in the library. You pour the coffee, please, Mrs. Latham. It isn't too cool on the terrace, is it?"

It was. It was very chilly. I felt the prickles of it down my spine, and especially when Forbes Allerdyce, who'd opened the library door for Mrs. Brent, came up behind me, not speaking. He came on around to where the coffee service was on the low table in front of me.

"You know," he said affably, "I don't know why I should, but I thought somehow it was you who called." His brows lifted with a sort of self-deprecatory amusement. "I thought perhaps with the gate-crashing that was the reason you dislike me. Because you do, don't you?"

"Do I?" I smiled at him. "What do you take?"

"One sugar, black, please."

As I handed him the after-dinner cup and saucer my hand wasn't nearly as steady as his.

"It's too bad, you know," he said. "Because Mrs. Brent's terribly lonely. We've had a good time, re-living Rufie today. He was a nice kid. I got to know him best when I tutored him, at M. I. T. He was a whizz in math but a wash-out in English. I had a job squeezing him through on a D minus. But I'm leaving in a minute. You can tell Mrs. Brent all about it."

He smiled at me with apparently quite genuine amusement. "It's interesting, though. What's all the defensive armor for, Mrs. Latham? Or is it protective? You women with sons. . . . Are you planning for one of yours to marry the Brents' daughter?"

It was too dark for him to see the start that gave me. It was so extraordinarily revealing of what was uppermost, I thought, in his own mind that it was frightening. But it was chiefly interesting because it was the clearest indication I'd yet had that he didn't know my status in re. either the Brents or the little lady my roomer. Either Ginny hadn't told him and Mrs. Thorn her landlady's name or she'd so thoroughly communicated her own opinion of me that they hadn't conceivably connected me with the garden party and Nunnery Lane.

"And I hadn't realized Molly was so close to Washington," he said. It was an invitation I resisted with no effort. He stood up and put his cup in the tray. "Well, I'll clear out now. Good luck, Mrs. Latham."

The sardonic amusement in his voice lingered behind him. In a moment I heard Mrs. Brent.

"Forbes, you're not . . . but of course, I know you have other things to do. Here. I brought you some of Rufus's cigars. No, take them. It's been such a joy. . . ."

The phone hadn't been inadvertently disconnected either, because it was connected again when I went inside and looked. Mrs. Brent wouldn't have believed it anyway, even if I'd been unwise enough to try to make her believe it. If I hadn't already been aware of that, I would have been when she came back and saw me in the library.

"You don't know what today has meant to me," she said. She settled in a chair and drew her chiffon painted draperies around her, folding her hands with a gesture of resignation and peace, lightened with a wistful and tremulous hope that was poignantly moving . . . and acutely disturbing. "I've missed my boys so terribly. I never met Forbes. But the boys talked about him a great deal. They were always planning to bring him home. But you know how these things happen. Once he had a skiing accident. And the boys were always so full of life, and so busy. But it's Molly, not Rufus and myself, that I'm really happiest for. She worshipped her brothers, and she's been so lost. Now——"

"Mrs. Brent," I said. I knew there was nothing I could say that would pierce this hypnotic cloudland of lilies of the valley and star-drenched memory, but I had to try. "You don't think you're being——"

"Hasty?" That serene and lovely voice interrupted me. "No, Mrs. Latham. I didn't tell him Molly was . . . very near us here. I must wait till Rufus comes. But you know. . . ." She smiled with sudden pleasure. "I need young people, and so does Molly. I've missed them so. And Forbes knows a girl here that's just my daughter's age."

I caught my breath. No pause Forbes Allerdyce had made to absorb and readjust to sudden shock was more cataleptic than the one that held me suspended there as she went blissfully on.

"She's young and attractive, and she needs a position. She's just come to Washington. He's bringing her to see me tomorrow. She could be a sort of secretary-companion, and someone young, for Molly. They're starting in right away, to clean out the swimming pool and get it ready."

I got up. I hadn't intended to. It was quite involuntary.

Mrs. Brent smiled. "You're holding the gate-crashing against him? He was afraid you would, poor boy. But if you'd been here today, you'd understand. I do. My boys did shocking things. If I'd known it yesterday. . . . But I'm just so glad I didn't. Today has been delightful to me." That perfectly lovely smile came to her lips again. "You live here where everybody's suspicious of everybody. That's one reason I haven't liked it here, and that's why Forbes, knowing all the intimate and homely things that only the closest friend could know, is such relief and such joy to me. Even Mr. Vair doesn't frighten me now, Mrs. Latham."

She laughed then. "That's a miracle in itself. I was so nervous and overwrought the other day. I want you to forget it. But I know you will."

She came to the door with me. "There's just one thing, Mrs. Latham." She looked disturbed again. "You know Marjorie Seaton much better than I do. You don't . . . you don't think she'd . . . that she's a mercenary person, at all, do you?"

"Not in the least," I said.

"No. Of course she isn't. It's just that . . . well, it was she I talked to a minute ago. Her husband's my husband's Washington attorney. It's a . . . a very valuable account. But I don't think that would influence her judgment on . . . personal matters. Do you?"

"It wouldn't," I said. I couldn't tell her I knew Molly was at Marjorie's, and well.

She was pleating and unpleating her chiffon drapes. "Of course, it was so terribly foolish of Tom Seaton to say my husband had threatened to close down the Taber City Plant to make those poor people starve."

"He didn't say that, Mrs. Brent." I didn't care how sharp I made this. "That's quoting Edson Field, and he's been Hamilton Vair's chief lackey ever since Vair first started attacking your husband. I know Tom said nothing of the sort. I was at the dinner party and heard him myself. Edson Field deliberately misquoted him."

She stood there in a bewildered fog, struggling with a genuine wish to believe the best. "Oh, well, I'm so glad you told me." She smiled happily then. "I'll tell Forbes tomorrow. He was really distressed. He didn't believe it . . . about my husband, I mean."

She shook my hand and said good night. "I've depended so much on Marjorie. I don't believe she'd . . . tell me Molly was happy, just to——"

—Just to keep her, and keep us obligated to her on her husband's account . . . was clearly what was struggling in her mind, but it was too awful a thing for her even to admit to herself.

"I'm sure she wouldn't, Mrs. Brent," I said. *But wait a few days*, I thought. *Wait till Allerdyce starts undermining Marjorie too as well as Tom Seaton. And wait till little Miss Ginny comes and sweetly and shyly raises those morning-glory blue eyes.*

I got into the car and switched on the engine. She stood uncertainly in the doorway for a moment, and I saw her close the door then and take back into that palatial emptiness the doubts and apprehensions that had sprouted in so brief a time, since her call to Marjorie, and would no doubt burgeon monstrously now she was alone with them.

I went on home to call Marjorie myself. She might as well be prepared . . . and prepare Molly, if there was any way to do it.

The P Street curb was lined with cars. I have a garage of sorts, up a narrow crooked lane that used to be an alley and isn't much else now. I don't like to go there at night any more. In the old days—or they seem a long time ago—it used to be a friendly noisy place with every rickety stoop crowded with colored people laughing and calling to each other, radios blaring from inside the lighted doors behind them. Now the stoops are empty and doors closed, and the only light that lazarus light from the television panels seeping through the windows. I don't mind driving up it, but it's a long walk back.

That's where I ended, however, because I couldn't find another space nearer home. It was all right, in front of me with my headlights on, but as I looked in the mirror and saw the lazarus-tainted darkness closing in behind me, and knew I had to close the garage doors and walk back alone through the silent shadows, a sudden panic took hold of me. As I made the jog in the lane and my headlights reached the big old cotton poplar crowding the rusty corner of my garage, and saw a man standing there, I think it was as close to sheer unmitigated cowardice as I've ever been in my whole life. He stepped out, then, as I came up, into my headlights, and I saw it was Colonel Primrose.

I've been glad to see him before, but never so glad I stalled my car in the middle of a back alley. And it was fortunate he was there. I'd have gone through the alley full of its empty shadowy terrors with no trouble, but I'd have walked down P Street and into my own house and run smack into Mr. Forbes Allerdyce there. That I didn't was about the only break we'd had. What with the curiously basic, if at times dubious and certainly unpredictable, moral instincts of Miss Ginny Dolan, it put off, for a few more precious hours, Allerdyce's finding out I was her landlady . . . and that gave Molly Brent the only ghost of a chance she ever had.

I suppose that for everybody in the world there's one dependable and enheartening presence whose appearance restores courage and sanity to one's universe. Colonel Primrose is that for me. Seeing him there, slightly rotund, those black X-ray eyes of his amused at first, at my genuine delight, and then contracting like some old parrot's as he saw it wasn't for himself alone, I could feel all my panicky tension relax. It didn't seem in the least odd to me to have him turn up in a dark alley, beceause he always turns up when I really need him.

"What's going on?" he asked, when he'd padlocked the rusty doors for me.

"I thought you were on the West Coast."

"Chicago, this morning."

We were out in the alley and he'd given me that tip to toe business to see if I'd visibly deteriorated since he'd seen me. I gathered I'd held up. He said "It's good to see you again, Grace," and smiled at me. "I thought I'd better get here. I don't trust you when you're as glad to hear my voice as you were this morning. There's no use deluding myself. What's the trouble? Is it all this girl of Buck's? What's Archie Seaton hanging around your house for?"

I stopped in the middle of the alley. The shadows were just shadows, and the light from the screens not the least eerie, except that it made his grey hair look as if he'd got a blue rinse and his face unnaturally grave.

"Archie?" I said. "What do you mean?"

"He came out—up the area steps—just after I saw another young fellow go in. I had a short talk with him. He said you were at the Brents' and due back at quarter to eleven. I figured you'd come here when there wasn't any space round the house. Is Archie serious? What's all this about Brent and Vair, and Allerdyce and Molly Brent? Where does Buck's girl come into it? What about going back to your house and meeting the young lady and this Allerdyce?"

"*No,*" I said. I came to a halt. "He doesn't know I'm Ginny's landlady. I don't want him to know it, not if I can help it."

I saw it wasn't the blue light that made him look so grave. Nor did it account for the quality of the searching gaze he fixed on me.

"You haven't lost your mind, have you, Mrs. Latham?" he inquired.

"No," I said. "Or I don't think so. I know it doesn't make much sense."

"My dear woman," he said patiently, "I've never asked you to make sense. I'm fond of you as you are. All I want you to do is begin at the beginning and use words I can try to understand. If you don't want to go to your house, we'll go to mine."

"I don't think Sergeant Buck would approve of that," I said.

"He isn't here."

He must have felt my heart sink then, and I couldn't tell him one of the chief reasons I was so glad to see him was that it meant Buck couldn't be far off, and if he could get his infant albatross off my neck, Allerdyce needn't ever find out about my connection with her, and I might escape the Seaton treatment long enough to be a little use to Molly Brent when they got her away from Marjorie and out there at that place in Nunnery Lane.

"What's happened between you and Buck?" he inquired suspiciously. "He's been telling me for the last week what a high-class lady you are, and you seem disappointed he isn't here."

I'd forgotten Sergeant Buck had looked at my long empty dining-room table and offered to sell his colonel out.

"I'd just . . . hoped he'd be here to get Ginny another place to live," I said. "You wait till you see her. She's completely enchanting, and very hard for me to take."

I had an old-fashioned reluctance to go to his house alone, at that hour of the night, that I can see now was a sort of premonition. It's a beautiful old house, but there's a BOQ air about it and always a slight odor of fresh paint and plaster that comes from Sergeant Buck's military standards. I sat down uneasily. I'd never been there except at a party, more than once or twice in my life, and then with Buck's baleful eye on me.

Colonel Primrose brought each of us a nightcap, if that isn't a Freudian way of referring to a scotch and soda under the circumstances, and his amusement didn't make me any more comfortable.

"Now tell me," he said, and I told him. I began with the hairdressers', and told him about the dinner party with Tom Seaton and Edson Field at it, and about Mrs. Brent's extraordinary visit to me. I was feeling more at home by then, except that every time an old board creaked I expected to see Buck's land mass loom up in the doorway.

"And tonight, she doesn't feel Vair's the menace she thought he was the other day," I said. "I'm to forget what she said then. But it's Molly, really, Colonel Primrose."

I told him about the composite picture and about this afternoon at the farm.

"That was a composite picture in itself. You couldn't believe the girl with the kids as I first saw her was the same one, if you'd seen her when Archie barged in. What Allerdyce'll do to her I don't know. You didn't see him tonight."

I told him about the telephone, and the lilies of the valley and the Manhattan cocktail, and that last passage with me on the terrace.

"It looked like association of ideas, for him to jump at the conclusion that I'm a scheming mother with two marriageable sons," I said. And I told him about Ginny and the creep under another name. "But he did know about the lilies, and about the Manhattan, and Mrs. Brent hasn't a doubt in the world that he was an intimate friend of her boy Rufie. She's hypnotized. She suspects both the Seatons already. If I'd told her about Archie Seaton's following Allerdyce and Ginny out to Sybil Thorn's and that I thought he was one of Vair's men, I'm sure she'd have asked me to leave the house at once."

"I don't doubt it at all. You were very wise not to."

"And he's really diabolically clever. I've no doubt she's made up her mind by now that the Seatons can't be trusted, and little Molly's as good as back there."

"You're probably right there too." He thought for a minute. "Tell me about Buck's girl, now."

"I wish you'd quit calling her Buck's girl," I said. "Her name's Ginny, and she's perfectly angelic to look at and sweet as sugar pie."

"She sounds like sugar-coated rat poison."

"That's my fault. Maybe because, in this instance, I do have two marriageable sons."

He smiled. "I'm glad you haven't lost all your subjectivity."

"I'm going to lose everything, if you don't get Ginny out of my house," I said. "I'm not longing for a dependent child, the way poor Mrs. Brent is. And you've got to understand about Ginny. Daddy's the hero in her life, and she's on Vair's side because Vair belongs to Daddy. He may be a big shot in Washington, but in Taber City, Daddy's the big shot. That's why Sergeant Buck ought to be able to do something, if he and Daddy are such old friends. But chiefly, I want to get her a respectable place to live in."

"She's out tomorrow, if you want her out," he said.

"Good," I said.

"—But I suppose you realize you won't have any contact at all with Mrs. Brent and Molly, if she does go?"

Pleasant humor masks both vigor and a kind of impersonal ruthlessness in Colonel Primrose, as I've known for a long time now. He was looking at me with what I ought to have seen was a half-rueful, half-sardonic gleam in his eyes. And I ought to have known—just after I'd been talking about Allerdyce jettisoning the Seatons—how easy it was going to be for

him to jettison me . . . like dropping a bomb on a sitting
duck in a front-yard lily pond. He was kind enough not to
print it in block letters, unless it wasn't kindness but the basest
sort of practicality. Anyway, it was too late even then to do
anything about it.

XI

"You're forgetting Mr. Brent," I said. "He's no fool."

He smiled and shook his head at the same time. "You
aren't forgetting something, are you? It's perfectly possible
Allerdyce did know the Brent boys, and Vair got hold of him
for just that reason? I take it there was an Allerdyce in their
lives. This could be his name. He could have been going
under a false name when Ginny and the night clerk knew
him. He seems to be sure of himself, and he did know those
details—about the cocktail and the flowers. You say he tutored the Brent boys?"

"He said he tutored Rufie, at M. I. T. Rufie was a whizz in
math but a wash-out in English. He helped him squeeze
through with a D minus."

"He said that?"

I nodded. As the Latham boys settled for D minuses in
English more than once, as I remembered, the point seemed
academic.

He thought again for a moment. "Your realization of one
thing, tonight, made it possible for us to go on," he said, very
gravely. "It was absolutely first-rate. You mustn't forget it for
a minute. Don't try to tell Mrs. Brent that Allerdyce is a
phoney. It just can't be done, Grace. It sounds heartless to say
this, but in the confidence racket, when there's a willing vic-
tim, like Mrs. Brent, reason and evidence and facts are use-
less. Any policeman can tell you heartbreaking stories. People
think the police are callous. They aren't. They're just helpless."

He was silent again for a moment. "Archie's probably right
about one thing too. Brent and Tom Seaton being out at
Taber City just at this time isn't a coincidence. And you might
as well count on something else too. Mr. Brent'll go along on
this. If Mrs. Brent is convinced, she'll convince him.—And
don't look at me like that, my dear. I'm just telling you facts
that are basic training for any police officer. There's nothing
harder to stop than somebody who wants to believe a miracle.
Most of the time, all you can do is pick up the pieces after-

wards. You told Mrs. Brent I don't do miracles. You mustn't ask me for one yourself."

"I'm just asking you to help Molly Brent," I said. "If you'd see her, you'd understand."

I got up and took my jacket off the back of the chair. I knew now how Marjorie Seaton must have felt when I brushed off her plea to get Colonel Primrose in the first place, that night after dinner, in the powder room after Edson Field and the rest of them had been ripping the Brents to pieces and roasting them with such pleasurable malice.

"I do understand," he said quietly. "And I'll do my best for her . . . and you. I just don't want you to expect too much, too quickly. I've seen too many people with hungry hearts open to this sort of disaster. But I'll do my best." He came over to me. "I missed you, Grace, on this trip. Look around you. When we're through this business, will you entertain a proposition to come here and be here permanently? It's going to be very empty when you go tonight. . . ."

There were a couple of places at the curb that were empty too, when we got up the street to my house, and a light in front of the second floor. When I saw the light in the kitchen was out, I knew Lilac's vigil was ended. Our guests were gone.

"Ginny's still up," I said. "Will you come in and meet her?"

"It's a little late. I'll meet her tomorrow. I also want to meet Molly Brent. Will you drive me down?"

I don't know why it took that to bring Marjorie Seaton sharply to my mind when I'd been sitting right beside a telephone in his house. I said so.

"Call her now," he said. "Tell her exactly what I've told you. Anything she says to Mrs. Brent about Allerdyce will play right into his hands."

If he expected me to do it immediately, he didn't know Ginny Dolan.

I went in and back to the living room. The pleasant aroma of a good cigar—Mr. Brent's—was there. The ashtrays had been neatly emptied and the windows opened to air the room. I noticed that the green glass battery jar full of apple blossoms that hid the pictures of my two sons was neatly in place. And I don't know whether it was because Colonel Primrose was back or I really was suspicious of everybody, as Mrs. Brent had said, but when I went to put my car keys in the small drawer in my desk where I keep them I saw it had been opened. There was a large smudge of a thumb print on the polished mahogany and my extra front door key was gone. I locked the back windows, put the chain across the front door and went upstairs. Ginny was waiting for me at the head of the stairs.

"Mrs. Latham . . . you didn't have to stay out on my account," she said. She said it almost severely, like a grownup scolding, and it's been a long time since I was scolded, by anyone except Colonel Primrose. "I could have had my company in the dining room."

"That's all right, dear," I said. I turned the hall light off. Her packages were all opened on her bed, and my heart sank when I saw a brand-new white bathing suit lying on the back of the chair. "Good night," I said. But that was too easy. In three minutes she was tapping on my door.

"Mrs. Latham." She put her spun-sugar head inside. "Could I talk to you?" She came on in. "About my room. Can . . . can I keep it, Mrs. Latham? Because this . . . this friend of mine, he said this wasn't a . . . a regular house. He said this"—she waved her hand generally around—"this stuff you've got isn't old. It's *antique*. He says anybody that lives here doesn't have to take . . . roomers. But I . . . I don't want to move."

"Then you don't have to," I said. "Is he the one who took the front door key out of my desk?"

She looked at me wide-eyed for a moment. "I . . . I don't know," she said. "They . . . they're all funny people." She stood there silently for a minute. Then she said, "Do you . . . I mean, you've heard of a man named Edson Field?"

I nodded.

"Well!" she said. "That's why I came home early tonight. This friend of mine who was here was supposed to meet me out at this other lady's house, but Mr. Field was there. I don't like him. He thinks this other lady's going to marry him, but she isn't. She lets him think so, but tonight I heard her talking to . . . to somebody else on the phone, I guess Mr. Field sort of . . . of found out, because he started drinking too much, and I came home. I'm not narrow-minded, but some things I don't like. That's not politics. Daddy says politics is dirty business but he says keep sex out of it. He says there's a lots of things that don't mix and sex and politics is one of them. He says it makes trouble sure as you're born. So I . . . I came home."

I was silent. A lot of people had wondered why Edson Field had beaten his pen into a ploughshare for Ham Vair.

"She oughtn't to act like she's going to marry Mr. Field and let him get a divorce when this friend of mine that came here says it's Mr. Vair she's going to marry when he's senator. Do you think? Anyway, I came home, and Archie came. But then this . . . this friend came, and Archie went. We were down in the kitchen, and I told him it was . . . it was business, and he went out the downstairs door. Lilac's very nice, isn't she? I mean, kind."

I nodded.

"Well, anyway." She stood there undecided for a minute. Then she said, "I guess I'd better give you . . . I mean, I've got some money, to get back home on, and maybe you'd better keep it for me. Would you?"

She sidled out the door without waiting for an answer, and in a moment she was back. She had a blue moiré silk envelope, the kind you carry a toothbrush and toothpaste in when you're travelling, and she put it on my dressing table.

"It's two hundred dollars," she said. "You keep it for me, will you?"

I looked at her. It was a little too close on the heels of the missing door key.

"You don't think your friend Forbes Allerdyce would steal your money, do you, Ginny?"

"—I don't know what he'd do," she said, with devastating candor. "And neither do you. But I guess I'm nervous, because I'm not used to that much cash money."

When she'd gone I waited an instant, and I called Marjorie Seaton. I needn't have bothered, because Archie'd called her, and Mrs. Brent had called her again, after I'd left Nunnery Lane.

I told her what Colonel Primrose had said.

"I expect he's right," she said. "But it's too late. And she's asked me to come and see her tomorrow, and I've got to go. I'm sorry I've messed it. I'm expecting you and Colonel Primrose down to supper tomorrow night."

I called Colonel Primrose then. I'd had an idea Marjorie'd be up, but I didn't mind waking him.

"I've got a thumb print for you," I said. I told him about the front door key.

"Mrs. Latham," he said patiently, "—will you go to bed and go to sleep? Archie's already got Allerdyce's prints, through his friend the night clerk. See that your chain's on the door.—Buck's coming tomorrow."

That seemed a slight non sequitur, but perhaps not. It may have been merely a premonition on his part that Buck's return would be far more troublesome than one missing front door key. If so, he was very right.

I'll long remember the meeting of the Sergeant and my little roomer, in my living room the next morning. Buck had come up from the kitchen, in his teal-blue suit, freshly pressed, and that tie pristinely awful, and I called up to let Ginny know he was there, and heard sunbeam steps dancing down the stairs and down the hall. And for an instant, the charm school failed Ginny completely. She took one look, her blue eyes popping open like a child's who'd heard about a dinosaur but had never actually seen one. She didn't say "Oooh, gee!" but that's what she looked like. It was only an instant, and then she swallowed and came on, her demure enchanting little self. In the blue cotton dress that matched her eyes and the white beanie made of petals on the back of her bright curls, she was about the prettiest thing I've ever seen. And Sergeant Buck was a gone goose.

"Oh . . . Mr. Buck! I'm so glad to meet you!"

She put her hand in his. It was like a butterfly on a hand of bananas. "Daddy's always talked about you ever since I can remember. And Mrs. Latham's said such nice things about you. . . ."

Whether she was leaving her mother out in deference to me or to Mr. Buck, I'd no idea. But poor Buck. All he could do was hold his breath, as if he'd shatter this airy bubble of dream stuff. And just at that moment, there was a honk-honk from the street. Ginny's bright head bobbed around, her face sobered for an instant, it brightened instantly, and if I'd thought for an instant that the yellow chick was dumb I thought so no longer.

"That's for me," she said. "That's a friend of mine." She looked demurely at Buck. "Would you come and meet him? Daddy always meets all my friends. . . ."

Sergeant Buck cleared his throat then, and amid the jingling of all the mantel lustres said, "Sure, Miss." He mumbled something about getting his hat, and he really looked punch-drunk as he barged across to the basement door.

Ginny turned to me, her eyes wide. "Gee!" she said. "Jiminy!" The car honked again. She flashed around, ran along to the front door and flung it open. "Just a minute!" she said sharply. It was more of an order than an apology. "This is Sunday!" she added.

Buck was back on the double. I didn't like to dash to the front window till they'd got out, but I did then. I saw him giving Mr. Forbes Allerdyce at the wheel of his old sedan a semi-salute as Ginny ran around to the other side. There was a dismaying note to the scene. Ginny had a beach bag in her hand that she'd not brought into the living room, and I saw the swimming pool deal was still on. But I felt a relief that was far greater than I'd have been willing to admit, for I was really worried about Ginny since my dinner with Mr. Forbes Allerdyce, and the sight of that monolithic mass on her side must have given anybody some pause.

If, however, it took the pressure off Ginny Dolan even for a moment, it was only to compress it to blast both her and me, when that moment passed and another came. And if we'd been back in enchanted days when natural laws weren't so rigid as they are now, and fairies were respectable, and one had offered me the privilege of changing one single event in that week in Washington, I know without hesitation which I'd have chosen. I'd have made it the Rufus Brents who went down to West River to the Seaton farm for dinner that night and not me and Colonel Primrose, and I'd have done it for their sake as well as Molly Brent's.

It was dusk when we got there. The dogs were awake but not the children. I saw there was only one boat down at the pier. The waddling old hulk that belonged to Archie was gone.

"He and Molly are out in her," Marjorie said. "I hope she doesn't sink, but I guess they can both swim."

It wasn't till we got in the library that I saw how tense she was.

"Will you make yourself a drink?"

Colonel Primrose watched her with that pleasant sort of detachment he has about people, women especially, and mixed her an old-fashioned first.

She took it almost mechanically. "Well, I've really messed everything." Her voice was bitter. "I've convinced the Brents I'm hysterical. Too hysterical for Molly to be around. Mr. Brent's back. He left Tom out at Taber."

Colonel Primrose nodded. "Tom called me this morning.— Are they taking Molly?"

She shrugged. "They didn't say so in those words. But . . . Mr. Brent's sold on Allerdyce. I . . . I never could have believed it. She called him last night and he got a plane at once and came home. He talked to Allerdyce. Of course, he'd already talked to Mrs. Brent for a couple of hours. And of course too, Grace's little friend Ginny was there. The two of them were working like beavers cleaning out the swimming pool. Mrs. Brent was down there with them while I talked to him. Then she came up."

She shook her head slowly.

"She sent for Allerdyce. I had to tell him I knew he'd gone out to Sybil Thorn's, and he was wonderful. He's terribly, terribly good . . . I'll give him that.—Of course he'd been to Sybil Thorn's. He'd been there because he used to know her, and he knew she was a friend of Vair's and was supposed to be putting up the money for Vair's campaign. He went there to see if he couldn't get her to hand over the negatives of some stolen pictures. . . . That's what *I* did."

"I told Grace to tell you it was no use."

"I know. She did tell me. But it was too late, I was stuck.— It makes me so furious." She was close to tears, of anger and frustration. "I've lied, and everything else, to keep the Brents from knowing about those pictures. I knew Allerdyce was just waiting for a chance to tell about them . . . and I gave it to him. He was just torturing them under the pretext he was a friend, and deeply shocked, and everything. And he offered to clear out, a noble gesture . . . and it worked. Mrs. Brent started to cry and Mr. Brent said 'Sit down, son.' So I came home. And all I care about is Molly. He knows she's with us, of course. He couldn't help it, the way Mrs. Brent talked to me. It's just a . . . a wicked shame. . . . And the big bunch of apple blossoms I took up to her just lay on the hearth and withered."

When she turned to me, I saw she was close to tears of compassion too.

"You saw Archie and that crab net yesterday," she said. "I could have choked him about that. What he did after that was a lot worse. He took the kids down to try it and left Molly. She just sat on the porch and watched them. Then he came back and said 'So long, everybody,' and left. This morning he came back."

She blew her nose, half laughing and half crying.

"He came in, said 'Hello, everybody,' and went down in the cellar and started hauling up all his old gear for that tub of his. He must have made forty trips, busy deal, not even speaking to any of us except Tommy. He let him help. He got it all piled up out on the front steps, Molly watching him. He didn't even see her. Then he said he guessed he'd go to work on his boat. Her poor little face fell so even Tommy saw it. So he said, 'Uncle Archie, can't Molly go too? She can help.' I know Archie hadn't prompted him, and it was perfect. Molly said, 'I can scrape paint, Archie.' It looked as if he didn't think so and didn't want her to even if she could—exactly the way I've seen all the Seatons treat their kid sister. He just didn't want any part of her. Then he said, 'Okay, Ragweed. I guess you could help lug the stuff down anyway. And don't drop it.' "

She was more than half laughing now.

"Poor kid, he'd put all the stuff you couldn't possibly lug without dropping in one pile, the crab net and a batch of line I knew he'd uncoiled so she couldn't help but get tangled up in it, and everything. So she tripped and stumbled along after him, and he'd stop and say 'Come on, Ragweed,' and then put his stuff down and help straighten hers out, as if he'd known all the time she'd be a hell of a lot of trouble. And then, when they got clear down there, he sent her back for *his* sweatshirt. She ran all the way up and back. It almost broke my heart. She was so happy she was shining. Just a whole chunk of her life fell out. She was right back where her brothers were bossing her around. Archie was wonderful. I never knew what a sweet wonderful guy he was before."

She batted the tears out of her eyes and smiled at Colonel Primrose.

"It's silly," she said. "But it was really sweet. Archie was just the brother she's needed to make her snap back. That's why I can't bear to think I've messed it up so."

"They're still out?"

She nodded. "He took enough stuff to last a week. I was afraid he had some crazy idea of taking her out and breaking down in the middle of the Chesapeake. I wish to God he would, now. I guess they're having supper out, and there's a moon tonight. She hasn't been out with anybody for so long, or out after dark at all. She's still been afraid of the dark, and sudden lights terrify her, even when she's inside. Oh, if I'd only got Archie down here months ago! But I guess I never really knew him till today."

The butler announced supper then, and not even Colonel Primrose was aware of the hideous prophecy concealed in the shadows of the words she'd spoken. It was about quarter to eleven. We were back in the library and he'd looked at the grandfather clock in the corner a couple of times.

"I'd like to see her, and I'd like to see Archie," he said. "I don't suppose they've sunk."

He smiled, and so did Marjorie. "That thing of Archie's couldn't sink or it would have done it years ago. Maybe we can see them. Would you like to go down on the pier?"

Colonel Primrose got up.

"Will you come, Grace?" Marjorie asked.

I shook my head. I suspected he'd like a chance to talk to her, and I knew it would do her a lot of good to talk to him. I didn't expect all the dogs to go with them. The only one left was the Llewellyn setter, who'd deserted her pups, out in the kitchen now, for the library fire. We'd been there about ten minutes, though it seemed longer to me, not used to the noisy silence of a country place. But even though I was acutely conscious of all kinds of unfamiliar sounds, it was the setter who heard the familiar one first, and I didn't hear it at all, even when she raised her head and growled the first time. She growled again and then got up from the hearth, the hair on her shoulders rising, her muzzle pointed towards the open window behind the dough mixer at the end of the room.

XII

I felt the cold prickles up and down my spine, and it took me a second just to manage to turn and look that way too. I couldn't see anything, and there was something there. I heard it then, the faint far-off scrunch on the oyster-shell road and the soft velvet throb that was a motor of some kind. I'm not a complete coward in town, but there in the country I certainly was, and I don't think I've ever been so near screaming as I was at that moment, until I thought of the children upstairs. And I still couldn't see anything, because of the light in the room that drew a sharp curtain in front of the frosty milky glow of the moonlight outside.

That's when I slipped across in front of the growling dog and switched off the library lights. I could see then, and I saw the car, moving slowly, without any lights, along the lane up to the house. The moonlight on the oyster shells made a solid white ribbon to guide it. The moonlight was on the car too, and I could see that it was dark but not black. It was the maroon convertible. The top was down, and in it were three men, two in front and one back. I was already frightened, but to see the car coming steadily on, with no lights, and with three men in it where I'd expected one only, was paralyzing. They must have seen the lights go off, but they came on. And that had a kind of nauseating effrontery that I can't describe —as if the three men in the car knew that Majorie and Molly were alone on this isolated farm, and it gave them a gangster's liberty and a gangster's courage.

The scrunch of the white-walled tires and the velvet purr of the engine, the growling dog behind me, were the only sounds except the heavy tick-tock of the old clock, like some evil metronome punctuating the silence of the gradually lightening room. Then I moved. I ran across the hall and through the living room onto the front gallery. I didn't want to call to Colonel Primrose and frighten the children, but I thought I'd be able to duck down past the apple tree there and see him and Marjorie at the pier, and be able to call them. But I didn't call. They weren't down on the pier.

The two people coming up from it weren't Marjorie and the Colonel. They were Molly Brent and Archie. I saw them in the moonlight. It was too late for me to call, they were too close to the house . . . and I knew then that was why Marjorie and Colonel Primrose, seeing the boat already docked and the two coming up, had gone the other way, out toward the orchard, to let them take that moonlit walk together up the grass from the River. And it was too late . . . because in that instant there was a sudden flash of bright light from the boxwood circle, a beam swooping down the hill, wavering an instant and focussing, and another flash then, and Molly Brent and Archie caught in it, her copper head buried suddenly in Archie's sweatshirt, his arms around her and his face extraordinary with shock and rage.

Then as the dogs started barking over in the orchard, the headlights of the car burst on, the motor roared and the car shot around the boxwood circle, and I saw the dogs come streaking and crying across the field and Colonel Primrose and Marjorie running after them towards the house. The blinding after-vision of the floodlit scene was so vividly on my retina that I didn't see anything else for a moment, just the image as it had been. Molly in a bulky sweatshirt and dungarees clinging to Archie, and out the other way billowing masses of apple blossoms lighted up like great banks of snow through which the dark forms of the dogs were bounding, and behind them Colonel Primrose and Marjorie, and the sound of the car disappearing down the road toward the gate.

Then it dissolved and I saw Archie again, running up to the house with Molly in his arms. I held the screen open and hurried on ahead of him to turn the lights on in the library again, as fast as I could so a new light coming on wouldn't terrify her. I didn't know whether she'd fainted out there, but her eyes were wide open now when Archie laid her down on the sofa.

"It's okay, Ragweed. Buck up, old girl."

His voice was miraculously offhand. She had hold of one of his hands and he was brushing her hair back from her forehead with the other.

"Everything's okay, Ragweed."

Her eyes were raised blankly to his, the golden flecks in them lost in brown depths, her face white and terrified. She tried to sit up.

"Better stay there a minute. What about a tot of rum, Mrs. Latham.—You remember Mrs. Latham, Molly."

Her eyes moved to me and she nodded. "I don't want anything," she said faintly. "I don't like the taste of it."

I think Archie started to say what the hell difference did that make, but he grinned instead.

"I guess you're all right. I'll let you sit up now."

He moved her feet around with his free hand. Her hand tightened its grip on his and her breath stopped an instant as she saw Colonel Primrose come in with Marjorie. If anything had disturbed them recently you'd never have guessed it, but Marjorie's eyes were blazing underneath, and I know Colonel Primrose well enough to know when he's in such a boiling rage he can hardly speak. Outwardly they were doing as good a job as Archie was, not to alarm the girl any more.

"This is Molly Brent, Colonel Primrose," Archie said. He ignored her death grip of his hand. "She doesn't look this bad, usually. It's my clothes she's got on. She fell overboard and got herself all wet."

"You look awfully dry," Marjorie said.

"It wasn't me fell in," Archie said amiably.

"You mean you didn't go in after her?"

"She can swim. I did toss her a line, though. Didn't I, Ragweed?"

Molly nodded, a little smile flickering in her eyes. She let go his hands and looked down at her paint-spotted outsize dungarees, and pulled one bulky knee down further over her leg as she looked shyly at Colonel Primrose. He came over and held his hand out to her.

"How do you do, Molly," he said, and she hesitated a moment and raised her hand to him.

"He did say he'd come in and get me if I wanted him to," she said, with a quick smile. "But my brothers always said if a girl's clumsy enough to fall in she ought to drown. So I'm not used to being fished out. We had a sailboat at the lake and one of us was always getting dumped."

Her face went slowly blank then, and she put her hand down and took hold of Archie's again. "Who . . . who were those people up there?" Her voice was small and strained, but somehow fundamentally steady. "Were they the same ones who . . . who did that when . . . I mean the other time it happened to me? When my brothers . . . ?"

"Look, Ragweed." Archie picked up her hand and rubbed it with both his. I don't think his voice was as fundamentally steady as hers. "That's what we're going to find out. That's what Colonel Primrose is here for. We don't have to worry about that stuff. They've gone now."

"You're not going?" She asked it quickly and breathlessly.

"Well, not till the boat's finished." He grinned at her. "So up with you, my good girl." He stood up and pulled her to her feet. "Bed for you. Here, I'll give you a ride up. I don't want you to fall and break your arm, you've still got barnacules to scrape." He picked her up as if she were Tommy or one of the twins.

"He's teasing you, Molly," Marjorie said. "He's had the bottom scraped."

Molly Brent smiled again. "I know it. I kicked the bottom when I was overboard, just to see. But we do have the galley and cabin to do."

"Say good night to the people, Ragweed. And you better come up, Marge. She'll be asleep before she gets her shoes off."

"Good night, Molly," Colonel Primrose said. The smile on his lips faded as Archie carried her out, and I saw his black eyes snapping. He went over to the bar and poured himself a drink. He was angrier than I'd ever seen him, so definitely so that I thought it was best for me not to speak till I was spoken to.

"I wish to God I'd stayed here." He shot a glance at the gun rack over the pine dresser. But when Archie Seaton strode back into the room, his face ridged and white, and went directly to the rack, he shook his head. "If we'd been here, Archie . . . but we weren't. He won't come back. He got what he was after."

"I guess so," Archie said. His eyes were hard steely grey and dangerous.

"*They*," I said. "There were three of them."

They wheeled on me then.

"Two in front, one back. They had hats on; I couldn't see their faces. I couldn't see them at all till I turned the lights off. But I recognized the car. It was the maroon convertible."

"The———," Archie Seaton said. He didn't stop there. With that pigmentation he's not the deliberative silent type. It made the casual job he'd done to keep Molly on an even keel more admirable than I'd thought while he was doing it.

"That won't help," Colonel Primrose said patiently. "Get yourself a drink and relax."

"I don't want one." He sat down on the sofa, leaned forward and put his head in his hands, kneading the pink stubble on his sunburned skull. "Oh, brother, this is it," he said softly. "The poor little devil. I've worked her like a horse today. I was scared sick when she went overboard. I don't know how I kept from going in after her. I don't mind telling you, this big brother stuff is all right, but I don't know how long Seaton can keep it up. Oh boy, this is really it."

He looked at the cushions where Molly Brent had been as if part of her was still there, and it probably was, a dream part . . . and his never handsome face had a kind of light in it and a selfless tenderness that it would be ridiculous to call beauty but that was something like it. A feather from love's bright wing had brushed Archie Seaton, and the wonder and loveliness of it had left him a little dazed and overawed.

Then Marjorie came back. "This is one bad dream she won't have to struggle through. She's dead tired. She was asleep before I got the light off."

"Well," Colonel Primrose said curtly, "let's take stock of things. Three men came here, Marjorie. Allerdyce of course. I'd guess a professional photographer. And somebody who knows this place. Who's that?"

She shook her head, looking silently at him.

And suddenly I knew. "Edson Field," I said.

"Is that a guess, Mrs. Latham?"

"It could be," Marjorie said slowly. "He knows the place. He's been here. I guess we'll know tomorrow . . . or the next day."

Archie's face hardened. "If that swine. . . ."

"Take it easy, Archie."

Colonel Primrose's voice was as close to the machine-gun

crackle that Army officers are apt to carry into civil life like a bad hangover as I've ever heard it.

"Let's get some things straight here. Time's running short. We can't stop Field from writing anything he wants to, any more than we can stop Vair from calling Mr. Brent a thief, a liar, or any kind of blackguard he wants to call him. And so far there's not one damned thing we can do about Allerdyce, and anything we try to do until we get something on him is going to blow up. Believe me, we can't afford any more mistakes . . . if we want to help Molly Brent."

He looked from one of us to another, his eyes hard. "Let's get this clear. We're up against what many people in Washington are up against . . . the maddening frustration of decent men and women in the face of debased political and moral values. We're particularly up against the frustration of trying to make the Brents face a reality they don't want to face, and a heartless, cynical, corrupt crowd like Vair and Allerdyce and the rest can move right in and destroy everything that matters to such people, because they're blind and deaf and begging to be hoodwinked."

He stopped abruptly. "Sorry. I didn't mean to make a speech. But this is the whole Capital scene today. Men's reputations and lives are attacked every hour of the day for political reasons and their health and sanity ruined and their families destroyed. Molly Brent's an incident. Ginny Dolan's just as typical. She's unconscious, I'm sure, that she's a shill, a come-on girl, for a pair of ruthless gamblers like Allerdyce and Sybil Thorn. Even Ham Vair's a product of the corrupt politics of our time. Allerdyce is using him, as he's using Ginny Dolan, and Vair's too crass and stupid to know what's happening to him. But this is beside the present point.

"Let's not make any more mistakes. If we want to save this girl, let's face some facts ourselves. The Brents will take Molly home right away. That's plainly what Allerdyce is working for, this business tonight will clinch it. And there's no use hoping Mr. Brent won't be deceived. We'd be insane not to figure Allerdyce as a very good, very careful, *professional* operator. Mr. Brent might not be deceived for long. It might be long enough.

"You can do something right now, Marjorie. You're on the spot already . . . go phone Mr. Brent and tell him what happened here. Go wherever you've got a phone Molly won't hear if she wakes. You might as well stick to your guns, now."

She went out without a word. He turned to us.

"Until we can dig up something about Allerdyce or he makes a mistake, we're helpless. If I went to Mr. Brent, what would I say to him? We believe the fellow's a phoney, we have no evidence at all. He's given them a strong impression he's not. The FBI have no record of him. Neither has the Pentagon. He's never been in jail, he wasn't in the Armed Forces. Tom Seaton may have some influence on Mr. Brent. The chances are both the Seatons are discredited. Above all, we're in the position of trying to prevent a crime from happening . . . a hundred times as hard to do as solve it after it's happened. We can trace this man Allerdyce eventually, yes. It takes time, and time's what we haven't got."

"What have we got?" I asked, a little bitterly, I'm afraid. "You're the frustrating thing around here. There's one person you can question about Allerdyce. Ginny Dolan knows the man. Her father knows him."

Colonel Primrose smiled patiently. "This is what I particularly want you two to get clearly in mind. Ginny Dolan is not to be questioned at all. She's . . . almost the one person we've got to depend on when Molly Brent goes back into that house with her parents and Allerdyce. You tell me you think Ginny's okay, really, Archie. And you, Mrs. Latham, think her father's a sound guy and there are things he doesn't stoop to. That's why we've got to keep her at the Brents' house if we can, and as long as we can. She sounds to me like a weak reed. I may be wrong. One thing's sure: she's about all we've got."

He looked at Archie. "If she could meet Molly. . . ."

"I've asked her to come down here."

"Make it tomorrow, then. At that, it may be too late."

He got to his feet and put his glass down on the table. "I said Ginny's about all we've got," he said quietly. "We have one other chance. It's our best chance, I think. It's not pleasant to think about it, and it may be dangerous.—We think Allerdyce isn't what he claims to be. Mrs. Brent is completely sure he is. There's one person who's going to know, for sure."

I looked at him a little bewildered. He seemed to have accepted the idea that Allerdyce was an impostor, now. He hadn't accepted it the night before.

"That absolute knowledge could be pretty dangerous. We don't know what Allerdyce is really up to. It could be . . . several things. I'm assuming he's looking out for Allerdyce and going way beyond helping Ham Vair. I'm assuming also he's gambling for great stakes, and gambling all he's got. He won't stop at any risk."

Archie looked up slowly, his face tense. "Who are you talking about, Colonel?" he asked. "Who's the person who's sure to know?"

"Molly Brent," Colonel Primrose said.

XIII

It was a grim drive back to P Street in Georgetown, Washington D.C., . . . for Colonel Primrose chiefly.

"What are you doing, trying to incite Archie to murder?" I demanded, as soon as he'd closed the Seatons' gate. "What possible chance has Molly got? You didn't see her yesterday when she was frozen absolutely rigid with fear when Archie barged in. You'll have her in St. Elizabeth's in a week. And you haven't any right to use Ginny this way . . . especially now Archie's in love with Molly. It just isn't fair. . . ."

It was an embittered monologue that continued on as monologues, female, are likely to, long after I'd said it all and gone back over it all, in the same and different words, until I suppose it was a diatribe, not a monologue. I know we were almost to the District line before his silence became so oppressive I decided I might as well hush.

"If you're through," he said, very urbanely, when I hadn't said anything for three or four unhappy miles, "let me tell you I'm not inciting Archie to murder, I'm not driving Molly to St. Elizabeth's, and I'm not selling Ginny down any river she isn't already embarked on. I have an idea that Allerdyce started this thing legitimately—from Vair's point of view—and saw a chance for a side deal. That's the river he's embarked on. And everything's very shipshape, all sailing directions thoroughly worked out . . . but he's a phony just the same. He's made at least one minor but interesting little slip, which you picked up——"

"Me?" I said.

"You. And I believe he's making another that's not a slip but a crucial blunder."

He stopped for a moment. When he spoke again I was startled at the anxiety in his voice, and ashamed of myself.

"I can only pray I'm right, Grace. I've thought of everything I can, not to have to put it to the test. I've even thought of trying to get Archie to persuade Molly to marry him tomorrow morning. But it's a brother, not a lover, she needs right now—or thinks she needs—and until she's ready to meet Archie on the other terms, I think the shock of having them even implied, when she's just begun to find a little security for her heart, would spoil her chances for a growing and really beautiful relationship.—I suppose that sounds odd for me to be saying."

We'd stopped for a light on the Benning Road. I looked cautiously at him. It sounded so odd that I wondered what had happened to him.

"If she has her brother snatched away from her now she's barely found him, it would be a bad shock," he said quietly. "She's got to find out for herself that he's more than a brother. That's what I'm putting my entire faith in. You see, I do really believe that love is strength . . . and I believe Molly Brent has found a strength that none of you think she has. It may sound cruel, but I believe putting it to the test is going to be the best thing that could happen to her. I'm not upset at her going back to Nunnery Lane. People have to grow up, Grace. That's the trouble with her mother. She's still a child. You remember that when Molly's car accident happened, she was dashing home to help her parents? That seems important to me."

"It's . . . rather rough doctrine, isn't it?" I asked.

"All good doctrine's rough." He smiled faintly. We were silent going through the empty streets toward Dupont Circle to get to the P Street Bridge and home.

"I'm counting on Allerdyce not to know rough doctrine when he sees it," he said then. "He doesn't know Molly has found life's worth living again. He's judging her on the basis of all the rumors he's heard—even though he may have started them himself. He's judging her by that picture of her running through the rain, without knowing why she ran . . . and he's judging her by tonight, I imagine, not realizing that when she has a man's heart to bury her little head in she won't run again. That's a major error I think Allerdyce is making. I believe youngsters have a lot more guts than people give them credit for, Mrs. Latham."

"I hope you're right," I said.

"People take for granted the incredible valor of Iwo and Kaesong, but they're afraid to trust the same kids to meet the hardships of Main Street."

"I'm glad my sons have grown up, if you're turning into an expert on youth."

"You could easily have eaten their hearts out if you'd put your mind to it. I suspect Molly Brent was a factor in keeping her mother from completely absorbing those two boys. That's another thing I'm counting on. You must see by now the basic error Allerdyce's operating on. In fact, you pointed that out last night too."

We'd put the car in my alley garage and were walking back down P Street.

"I seem to have been a lot more acute than I was aware of," I remarked, not having the faintest idea of what the hell, if I may be permitted to say so, he was talking about, or what were these fine flashes of insight he was so kindly attributing to me. Or I thought kindly, until he chuckled then and I caught the slightly wry aroma that was mixed in with his apparent amusement.

"My dear Mrs. Latham," he said, "you have the highly developed faculty of all reasonably intelligent illiterates. Old Lafayette can't read or write, but he never forgets anything he's told or anything he sees."

Lafayette's his ancient cook . . . chef-cook, Lilac calls him, which is her highest form of praise for a colleague.

"Your trouble comes when you try to think. If you'd stick to reporting facts, you'd be a big help. It's when you decide you know what a fact means that you foul things up. I only hope you've told me everything you've seen now . . . and I'd be a fool to count on it."

If he'd been gifted with tongues, he couldn't have uttered a clearer truth. I might conceivably have searched my own heart just then, for its sins of omission, and come up with a dilly. But we were at my house. There was a chink of light over poor old Lilac's kitchen shutters and the cause of her continued vigil was clearly shining out through the slats of the inside shutters in Miss Ginny's windows on the second floor.

"The yellow chick's still up. Will you come in?" I asked.

"Not now. It's too late."

I looked at him cautiously again. He's not normally so sensitive about time. It had begun to look to me as if he were deliberately avoiding Ginny Dolan.

"Look, you're not being fair," I said. "She's really very sweet."

"You were calling her an infant albatross last night."

"Okay, suit yourself." I put my key in the lock. "One thing," I said. "Ginny's got to start going to bed or I've got to get in earlier. I'm going to lose a cook if I don't."

"There's always Lafayette . . . when you move down to our house."

I opened the door, and almost flattened my nose against it as I started in automatically and it came to a grinding halt.

"That damned chain," I said.

"But two nights ago Ginny left the latch off, didn't you tell me?" He was suddenly interested.

"That was before Allerdyce took my key." I started to add, and before she'd entrusted her two-hundred-dollar nest egg to my keeping, but I heard the soft patter of her feet on the stairs.

"She's coming down. You've got to meet her."

I looked at the narrow opening in the doorway, realizing I was about to see Ginny as Allerdyce had seen me. But I couldn't see her at all. I just heard her.

"Is that you, Mrs. Latham?"

There was an anxious quality in her voice, and even scared.

"Yes, Ginny," I said.

"Just a minute." She pushed the door shut to release the chain, opened it then and vanished around behind it.

"Come in, Colonel Primrose," I said. "Ginny, I want you to——"

"Oh, but I've got my hair up, Mrs. Latham——"

"That's all right. I'm sure the Colonel won't mind." I looked back at him. "You don't mind pin curls, I hope?"

"I'd better get used to them, I hope," he remarked.

Ginny was backed up against the wall. "I'm ever so sorry I'm . . . I'm such a mess, Mrs. Latham.",

She looked really scared, and very embarrassed. She hadn't looked at my escort.

"This is Colonel Primrose, Ginny," I said. I expected to see the charm school rally to her defense, but it didn't.

"How do you do, sir?" she said.

"Hello, Ginny."

He put his hand out, and Ginny gave hers a quick wipe on the seat of her bathrobe and put it out to him. Illiterate as I may be, I couldn't have rated high as a reporter in his mind then, and he must have thought I'd made up the charm school. As revealed in the hall light, the yellow chick, her hair in bobby pins tied with a blue silk net, a slight shine of skin food on her lovely, earnest and scared little face, those blue eyes round as a pair of lesser moons, didn't look like anything I'd described. She had on pajamas and a flowered silk dressing gown, hastily tied around her middle, she was bare-footed, and she looked very like a ten-year-old who'd waited up to see a dissolute parent safely to bed. She also had an odd air of responsibility that was rather moving, in a curious way.

"Why don't we go and sit down?" I said. "Would you like a little bourbon, Colonel? What about a glass of milk, Ginny?"

"I'd love some, thank you," Ginny said.

She sat down diffidently, straightening her dressing gown, aware of her bare feet without knowing what to do with them.

"Why don't you sit on the sofa and put this over you?" I asked. "It's chilly." I tossed her the afghan on the back of it and got a quick flash of gratitude. But it was Colonel Primrose her eyes were fixed on, as he stood at the cellaret in the dining room making a drink for himself. He came back as I came in with a glass of milk for Ginny.

"Did you have any supper?" I asked.

"Oh yes, Mrs. Latham. Uncle Phinney took me downtown. He had devilled crabs but he wouldn't let me eat one."

I was a little startled, as I hadn't realized she had any

relatives in town. Colonel Primrose's face can only be called a most extraordinary study. I thought at first it was because her having a relative here might make a great deal of difference in his plans . . . and quickly realized it was little less than a dawning horror inadequately suppressed. He put his glass down hurriedly.

"Uncle Phinney says a lots of people break out if they eat sea food," Ginny said.

"I didn't know you had an uncle here," I said, and she popped into full bloom then, herself again, and smiled at me, her eyes brightening.

"Oh, he's not my really uncle. But he's such an old friend of Daddy's he said I could call him that."

She turned that full morning-glory gaze on Colonel Primrose then.

"He thinks you're just wonderful, Colonel Primrose," she said, and the terrible truth really hit me so squarely amidships that I sat down quickly, and didn't really dare even look at Colonel Primrose.

Uncle Phinney . . . short, or something, for Phineas. For Phineas T. Buck.

Colonel Primrose cleared his throat and picked up his glass.

"Yes. Of course," he said . . . with great poise, but the shock had told. "Buck and I are old friends."

"That's what he said," Ginny answered brightly, and straightened up, back in her stride now she and the Colonel had found a common ground on which to communicate. "He said you'd cohabited together in the same house ever since you both retired."

Colonel Primrose put his glass down again, not spilling much. It was only by a superhuman effort, or maybe pure chance, he hadn't choked, and a mild stroke wouldn't have surprised me. He's never been so amused at Uncle Phinney's semantic disabilities as I have. Ginny went happily on.

"Of course, Daddy's told me all about you. He was in France with Uncle Phinney."

You could see who'd impressed Daddy, in the regiment, and it wasn't its colonel either. I looked sweetly at him, and Ginny, aware that somehow the atmosphere was disturbed, pushed the afghan off her feet and sat up.

"Well, I think I'd better go to bed if you'll excuse me, please, Mrs. Latham," she said. "Good night. Good night, Colonel Primrose."

"Good night, Ginny."

He got up and Ginny pattered out and off up the stairs.

"—Uncle Phinney, for the love of God," Colonel Primrose said, helplessly.

He'd ignored the more serious allegation, and I raised my brows, and I swear he blushed. Then he laughed a little, picked up his glass, finished his drink and was serious again.

"That girl's scared," he said quietly. "Does she know what Allerdyce is up to?"

"I don't know," I said. "It's Vair she's working for . . . or she thinks it is."

He nodded. "I imagine we'd better pull her out of there. She could be in a worse spot than Molly Brent."

I was relieved, because, somehow, Ginny Dolan had become pretty important in my book too.

I'd gladly have sacrificed myself, however, on the altar of sleep, when I let the Colonel out and went upstairs. But she was still up.

"You look half dead, sweetie," I said. "Don't you ever go to bed?"

She was waiting in the hall and she really looked tired. There were circles under her eyes, enviably blue, not liver-brown like the circles I get and no doubt had at the time, as it was almost two o'clock once more. She followed me into my room.

"Mrs. Latham," she said. "That's Colonel Primrose, isn't it?"

"Why, yes," I said. I looked at her blankly. "Why do you . . . ?"

"Is . . . is he as famous as Uncle Phinney says he is? I mean, about . . . catching people . . . doing things?"

Probably not, I thought, Buck's veneration for his chief being not short of idolatry. But I nodded. "Why?"

"I . . . just wondered." She looked up then. "He's . . . he's a friend of yours, isn't he?"

I nodded again.

"That's what Uncle Phinney said. He said that's . . . that's how he got me this . . . room here."

She was blinking her eyes, and I thought she was going to start to cry.

"He said . . . we weren't paying anything at all, for it." She blinked still more and swallowed. "So . . . so maybe I . . . I'd better move. He said I was only here till he got back and found some place. So I . . . I guess. . . ."

The tears were very close to the surface. And my heart sank. I didn't want Colonel Primrose to sacrifice Molly Brent for her, but I didn't want her sacrificed to Allerdyce and Ham Vair either.

"And if you . . . if you'd just told me I was *company*," she said. "I wouldn't have . . . I mean, I didn't know, Mrs. Latham."

By golly, it was me that was almost in tears then.

"Look, Ginny dear," I said. "If you'd like to stay here, I'd love to have you. You don't have to move if you don't want to."

"Oh?" She ran over and put her arms around my neck and buried her face in my shoulder. "Oh, I'm sorry! I was awful, Mrs. Latham! I was just awful!"

"No, you weren't. You're very sweet."

I patted her back, and I was startled at how frail her little body was. "Don't cry. Please don't cry, Ginny. You weren't awful, and it was Archie who started it. It was his fault, and mine. Not yours."

She raised her head and fished in her pocket for a handkerchief. "He must have thought I was awful dumb." She batted her lashes then to get rid of the tears. "Can I really truly stay here, if I'm . . . if I *act* all right? If I'm not in anybody's way?"

"You're not in anybody's way, Ginny," I said. "But there's one thing you've got to do, and that's go to bed."

She nodded obediently. "I was just afraid to go before you came in, because I . . . I was worried. I didn't want anything to . . . to happen to you, on my account."

"What do you think's likely to happen to me, on your account?"

She shook her head. "I don't know. It's just that I . . . I'm. . . ." She didn't seem to have a clear track on that one, because she gave it up. "Daddy says if people are nice to you, you're a skunk if you aren't nice to them in return. And you've been ever so nice to me." She put her bare foot out and ran her toe along the crack between the wide floor boards. "I guess it's this big house I'm sort of scared to go to bed in when I'm alone. In our house, we've only got two rooms upstairs and Daddy's little den and they aren't as big as this room. And you've got all upstairs. What's up there?"

I supposed just the idea of rooms she didn't know made the house seem bigger and emptier. I'd had the stairs leading up to the third floor walled in during the oil rationing and a door put there on the second floor landing.

"There's nothing up there, Ginny, except three more rooms and a couple of baths and a hall like this one," I said. "They're my sons' rooms and a guest room they use. You can go up and look at them some time. It isn't really a big house."

"But I like it. It's not like that place I . . . I go to. That's big. It's not like a house. It's like a movie set, with all that stuff in it too. Except the swimming pool's nice, I 'spose. But it sort of gives me the creeps. I don't wonder that woman's bats, and she sure is. But *he's* sort of nice. It's a funny thing. I always thought he was sort of a . . . a stinker. But he's not, really."

I was holding my breath then, for fear she'd . . . do what? I didn't know. I was only conscious that I was torn between wanting her to be at the Brents' and wanting her to give them up at once . . . not to be a sacrifice for anybody, and still to be there, if she could be, if Molly Brent came home.

XIV

"But you said I had to go to bed." Her eyes were sparkling suddenly. "And I'm going right away. Uncle Phinney brought me back at ten o'clock. He must think I'm five years old. And I sort of thought Archie'd call me up, maybe. But he didn't."

She'd got to the door by then. "You know, I thought Archie was . . . well, he just didn't have a job yet, was why he wasn't working. But I bet he's got a lots of money, hasn't he? Because that old car of his . . . and last night, he wasnt embarrassed, not taking me to a restaurant, like a fella'd be if he didn't have the money to pay for it. You know what I mean?"

"I think so," I said.

Her eyes sparkled again. "I think he sort of likes me even if I am dumb. And I'm crazy about him.—He's going to take me to see his family tomorrow. He wouldn't do that if he didn't . . . didn't like me, would he?"

Oh, dear, I thought dismally. "He takes a lot of girls to the farm, Ginny," I said.

"Oh, I'm not *jealous.* I can tell he's known a 'lots of girls before he met me." She took a quick dancing step around the door. "Well, good night, Mrs. Latham And . . . thanks a lots . . . you know what I mean."

I said "Good night, Ginny," but I was beginning to suspect she was incubated in a chain process of some kind, to start and stop and go back and come again. She was back in half an instant.

"Oh, by the way, Mrs. Latham . . . did you put my money some place?"

Her eyes slipped sideways to my dresser drawer where I'd put it and left it.

"No, but I will," I said. "I'm sure it's safe. Why?"

"Well, I thought I might give it to . . . to Uncle Phinney to keep. But I'd rather you would . . . if you'll put it some place."

I should have given it to her then, to give to Uncle Phinney. But I didn't, and next morning, when Colonel Primrose was downstairs, and Lilac had the washing machine going and there wasn't pressure enough to give me a dribble to get the toothpaste out of my mouth, was the first time I remembered again. I got toothpaste all over it, and then I heard the water go on full force where I hadn't turned it off, and dashed back and put the blue silk traveling case on the top of the john while I finished brushing my teeth. I'm not complaining about the drawbacks of semi-Georgian plumbing, though I've swallowed more milk of magnesia in paste form, waiting for the water pressure to pick up, than they've dispensed at any hospital. I'm only explaining why I forgot Ginny's money another time, because Cononel Primrose was in a hurry, Lilac said, coming up again while I was hurrying to get a dress and some lipstick on.

He was also disturbed, about Ginny.

"She's sold Uncle Phinney a tale. He says she's just 'socializing' with this Allerdyce. I'm afraid he thinks you're trying to keep Ginny from meeting other high-class people."

"Did you tell him the whole deal?"

He shook his head. "I don't want him to half kill this fellow and get sent up for assault and battery. You may remember Uncle Phinney is a violent man. And anyway, I don't think he'd believe a damned word I'd tell him without getting Ginny to confirm it. I certainly don't want that to happen."

I gathered there'd been a slight case of insubordination in their common habitation that morning. It wouldn't have been the first time. I vividly remembered one instance when Buck's offside and subversive intervention on behalf of a woman came very near getting her hanged for murder. She'd lived directly behind me on the other side of the garden wall. Colonel Primrose had moved over to the windows and was looking out, and no doubt it was being recalled to his mind too.

"I needn't say Buck thinks she's white with a blue rim around her.—And after all, she is working for Hamilton Vair."

I suppose it was that that reminded me abruptly of what I'd put in my desk drawer to give him when he came back, and that had slipped my mind both the other times he'd been in the house. That was the picture of Molly and the newspaper with Ginny's picture in it. I took them out now, and took the picture of Molly out of the envelope, putting it on the desk under the Taber City *Gazette*. Colonel Primrose stopped what he'd been saying suddenly.

"What's that?" he asked. He stepped out on the terrace and started across the lawn, and I followed him. I saw what he meant then. A section of my border, in front of the brick wall, was badly trampled. A couple of molded bricks from the coping had been knocked off and were in the middle of a clump of broken peonies. Two deep footprints in the mellow earth marked where a man had landed heels down when he jumped, a tulip plant still crushed under one of them, the other fairly distinct in the soft dirt. The clump of budding peonies was ruined.

"They were perfect, yesterday at five o'clock," I said stupidly. "I was out here looking at them."

I looked back at the wall, stunned really, because an eight foot wall isn't the easiest thing in the world to get over and for years I've regarded it as a sufficiently safe boundary. I don't even bother to close the French windows in the living room at night in the summer when it's hot.

Colonel Primrose looked back at the house. He went toward the terrace then, uncomfortably like a cat stalking an invisible pigeon. The terrace extends clear across the house, so there was no dirt he could find any prints in, even if somebody had trod there—or so I thought until he stopped again and pointed down. There were no entire footprints, but the blue wisteria petals fallen from the old vine were smashed and mangled, distinct evidence of somebody's standing there.

He was looking up at my open bedroom windows.

"You didn't hear anyone here, last night?"

I shook my head. "And of course Sheila's deaf."

"Did you and Ginny sit up and talk?"

"A while."

"Right above here?"

I had to nod again. He was silent a moment. Then he took my arm.

"Come inside," he said. "You'd better tell me what you said. Leave that corner of the border the way it is. I'll have Captain Lamb send a man out."

Captain Lamb is Chief of Homicide of the District Police and an old friend of the Colonel's.

His eyes brightened without warmth. "I think they can do a moulage on that footprint. Maybe we'll have something to question Allerdyce on after all."

"But . . . why?" I said. I was still dazed. I've taken that wall for impregnably granted for so many years, and its failure plus Sheila's deafness seemed to leave me extraordinarily undefended.

"He doesn't trust Miss Ginny any more than I do."

"But he doesn't know I have any connection with——"

"Listen, my dear." He closed the screen door. "This man Allerdyce is a professional operator. Once it occurred to him that Ginny's landlady was a friend of Mrs. Brent's and could know a good deal about him, it would be child's play to make sure. If he didn't want to risk a simple question of Mrs. Brent, he could make a simple deduction.—You said he thought he'd recognized your voice on a country line. You saw the Seatons' orchard when his lights went on last night. He was here that same night." He pointed to the big battery jar of apple blossoms, now sprouting green leaves under the buds where the petals had fallen. "You don't see bunches of apple blossoms in Georgetown every day. Marjorie even pointed it up by taking Mrs. Brent a bunch of them."

When I heard footsteps in the upstairs hall, it took me an instant to remember that Lilac was still up there. She was on her way down the stairs when the door bell rang. Colonel Primrose looked hastily at his watch.

"What were you and Ginny talking about——"

He broke off and looked around, listening. I was still in a semi-daze from the footprints outside and I didn't for a moment realize what had happened. I'd heard a voice but I hadn't for an instant heard what it said.

"—Will you ask her if she'll see Mr. Rufus Brent?"

"Oh no!" I whispered, as Colonel Primrose moved away from the window. "Don't go!"

Lilac was in the doorway. "Mr. Rufus Brent, Miss Grace . . . right in here, sir," she said, and all Colonel Primrose had time to do was shake his head at me. It was prohibitory, I knew, but on what level, universal or particular, I had no way of knowing, and I certainly couldn't keep my mouth entirely shut.

Mr. Brent's step came along the hall. It was slow, I thought, like that of a man with a heavy load on his shoulders. And indeed, he was such a man, even if the load was an invisible one. It was not entirely invisible either, I was aware at once, as he paused in the doorway, dwarfing it the way Sergeant Buck dwarfs it. I'd forgotten how large a man he was.

"How do you do, Mr. Brent?"

The garden party twinkle was gone from his eyes, and it seemed to me the Gothic old face was more heavily lined and the clefts from that extraordinary nose with the mole on it to the corners of his mouth a good deal deeper when they weren't lightened with the broad warm smile he'd worn then. He smiled now, but he was too preoccupied for it to be very cordial, and I was still too preoccupied about my own problem to be cordial myself. He shot a glance across the room.

"Oh, I'm sorry," I said. I'd forgotten the two hadn't met. In Washington you take it for granted everybody knows Colonel Primrose. I introduced them and they shook hands.

"Sit down, won't you?"

Mr. Brent hesitated. It was obvious he had not expected anybody else to be there. He sat down then, in the big cherry-red wing chair by the fireplace, turned in the spring and summer so it faces the room. "This is a pleasant house, Mrs. Latham. Is it Colonial? When was it built? It's an interesting bond. I noticed it as I came in."

It was obvious that Rufus Brent had not come to discuss what bond of brick work my house was built with, and equally obvious that that was all he was going to discuss with a third party present, and of course, I had no way of explaining Colonel Primrose's interest, his profession and his standing in it. But Colonel Primrose got up almost at once. "I must go, Mrs. Latham."

Mr. Brent rose and they shook hands again. "Goodbye, sir." Colonel Primrose bowed to me, all very formal, and went out, and came back immediately. "I'm sorry, but I had a hat, didn't I, Mrs. Latham?"

He had a hat and he knew precisely where it was. For some reason I've never known, he doesn't put it on the table or the chair in the hall, he puts it on the chair just inside the dining-room door. I excused myself and went out to find it for him.

"It's in the dining room, I think," I said. "Unless Lilac moved it."

He had it in his hand. He also had a piece of paper in his hand that he gave me. I glanced at it quickly and saw he'd scribbled out the minor slip that Forbes Allerdyce had made, that I'd reported to him with no idea it had any meaning. And it was minor, but I saw instantly—now it was written out for me—that it did have a point. He'd written after it, "Use if you can."

"Of course . . . thank you," he said, ostensibly about the hat. "I'll call you tonight. Goodbye, Mrs. Latham."

I put the note in my jacket pocket and went back to the living room and to Mr. Rufus Brent . . . and I stood motionless for one instant there in the doorway, staring at Mr. Brent, my breath caught and my heart racing, and I tore back into the hall to the front door.

"Colonel Primrose . . . quick!" I called to him.

He was only a few steps down the street. We ran back into the living room. Mr. Brent was slumped down in his chair, his eyes staring, breathing heavily, his face congested in the most extraordinary mask of pain and acute anxiety. He was conscious, but not of me and Colonel Primrose, as his fingers clutched at the upholstered chair arm. Lilac had come up from the kitchen and we sent her out for Mr. Brent's driver, who'd been standing by his limousine at the curb when I ran out for Colonel Primrose. He and the Colonel lifted Mr. Brent and got him on the sofa while I got my doctor on the telephone. Mr. Brent lay there, his collar and belt loosened, just staring up, conscious but oblivious to his surroundings.

It wasn't till then that I saw what had happened, or why it

had happened. Beside the empty wing chair, on the floor at the side nearest the empty fireplace, was the Taber City *Gazette*. I picked it up quickly. The composite picture of Molly was under it, where it had fallen from his hand. I held it out to Colonel Primrose, terribly distressed and stunned, actually, by my own hideous responsibility for what had happened.

"—I took it out of the desk to give to you, when you were at the window, just when you saw the broken place in the border. When he came I didn't even think about them over there. He must have picked the *Gazette* up, and this. . . ."

He gripped my shoulders and shook me. "Stop it. What's done is done. The doctor's coming?"

"Right away."

"Go outside then and wait, and pull yourself together."

He went over to Mr. Brent, slowly beginning to focus and be aware of us, took his wrist and counted his pulse. He nodded to me. "Go on out." As he drew up a chair by the sofa and sat down, Mr. Brent's eyes moved under their shaggy brows and rested on him, trying to adjust, still bewildered.

"You watch for the doctor, Lilac," Colonel Primrose said quietly. "Go on out in the garden, Grace."

"Shall I call Mrs. Brent?"

"Wait till the doctor comes."

It was one of the longest half hours I've ever spent. I saw Lilac drawing the living-room curtains, and Colonel Primrose and the doctor talking gravely together in the hall, and finally Colonel Primrose came out. It was a warm day with a familiar sultry overtone contradicting the cloudless sky. He motioned toward the iron table and chairs underneath the old locust tree at the end of the garden, and I followed him there, out of earshot of the living room. He didn't speak for a moment, and when he did he didn't make any attempt to conceal the irony that had developed.

"He has to take a long rest, with no emotional or business strain."

There didn't seem much need for comment on my part.

"Nature's warning," he said, and I knew he was quoting. "He seems very much better. He's flatly refused to go to a hospital, but he'll rest here for a while."

"Is he going to be able to get up . . . ?"

He shrugged. "It's dangerous, for a man of his age and weight. There's no law. He knows his own mind."

"Do you suppose," I said after a minute, "that this is what Mrs. Brent really had in the back of her mind? I never could see Mr. Brent killing——"

"You didn't hear him in there just now. If Vair had been there he'd have tried it. But I agree with you. He's not likely to set out and find him to do it."

"Did you tell him it isn't all Vair? That Allerdyce———"

"He's just had a heart attack, Mrs. Latham," he said dryly. "However, the doctor's coming back. Brent's agreed to wait for him."

In spite of the heat, there was an icy pall hanging over the garden. I shivered a little. Mr. Brent seemed curiously secondary, as I looked over at the mangled border and at the bruised wisteria blossoms under the bay window below my room upstairs.

"What's . . . going to happen to Molly?" I asked.

He shook his head. Then he looked at his watch and got up. "I told Tom Seaton to meet me at lunch. I'll see him and get back." He stood there thinking an instant. "Is Ginny likely to come bursting in?"

"I wouldn't predict anything about Ginny," I said. "But presumably she's over in Nunnery Lane, and will be till five or so. Unless Allerdyce. . . ."

"Mr. Brent wouldn't let us call his wife. He doesn't want her to know about this. I don't want Allerdyce to know it. It's important indeed for him not to know it. If Mr. Brent were out of the picture———"

He shook his head. "There's no point in not looking at possibilities. There's a great fortune at stake here. Mrs. Brent's entirely under Allerdyce's influence. If he finds out what happened here, it would be simple for him to make a situation Mr. Brent might not recover from. Ham Vair might be more use to Allerdyce than Allerdyce's ever been to him. Molly Brent wouldn't be much of an obstacle, would she? There'd be a good many ways of getting rid of her, with her presumed history of emotional instability. That's what's frightening about it."

He started on. "Just see he stays quiet. If he tries to get up or leave, call me."

He was gone then, and I sat there, numbly remembering those flashing lights at the Seatons' farm the night before. Her presumed history of emotional instability. . . . It was a ghastly thought, and her white rigid little face as she confronted Archie the first time flashed horribly into my mind. The ways of getting rid of her could be as simple and awful as the way to get rid of Mr. Brent . . . only to a living death that would be worse than death.

XV

I could hear the springs on the sofa strain as Mr. Brent shifted his heavy frame, and I got up quickly and hurried to the window, my knees weak then with the sudden relief of hearing a relaxed snore coming from the darkened room. The frail thin end of a wedge of hope pushed into my mind. At least Molly Brent was still safely at the farm. Mrs. Brent wouldn't bring her home without his consent. He couldn't yet have made up his mind entirely. He wouldn't have come to see me if he had. If Colonel Primrose could talk to him, maybe there was some hope still. I'd forgotten, I expect, that when the hounds of hubris are in full cry, as they seemed to be on the trail of the Rufus Brents, hope's a fool, a firefly light into the quicksands of despair.

It was a strange vigil I kept out there. There were hundreds of people—many thousands, indeed, I imagine—holding their breaths, waiting for the Czar of the Industrial Techniques Commission to open his mouth and speak, their economic lives dependent on what he said . . . and I waited, holding my breath, praying I'd hear just another relaxed, long-drawn snore. Washington is a cockeyed place.

At half-past two the doctor came again, and went shortly after, and as Colonel Primrose signalled me to come in I caught just the end of a brusquely exasperated parting medical advice. "—That's up to you, Mr. Brent. If you won't go to a hospital for immediate rest, there's no use wasting my time or what very little's left to you. Good day, sir."

I thought as I came in that Mr. Brent looked a little startled at that, and I imagine it had been a long time since anybody had spoken that plainly to him—which was no doubt one of the troubles of the whole business of Molly Brent and the picture that was now over on my desk face down under the Taber City *Gazette*. Power makes an iron curtain of its own, and with everybody, from Mrs. Brent and the Seatons to his whole secretarial and administrative staff, diligently protecting him, he probably had no real idea of what was going on at all. He looked incredibly better than he had when I saw him slumped in the fireside chair, and better, actually, than he'd looked when he came in first. He was sitting up, his tie and collar in place again, his hair combed and face washed.

"I'm very sorry, Mrs. Latham. . . ."

"I'm just distressed, Mr. Brent, that you——"

"Where did you get that picture?" he asked. "Where did it come from?"

His voice was quiet and controlled, but I looked at Colonel Primrose. I didn't want the man to have another attack because of what I'd done.

"—Mr. Brent." Colonel Primrose drew up a chair across the coffee table from him. "You're going to resent what looks like interference in your private affairs. Under the circumstances, I'm going to risk that. I strongly urge you to listen to me, and to think seriously what your course ought to be."

Mr. Brent's eyes resting on him were steady. "What circumstances do you have in mind, Colonel?" he asked evenly.

"The circumstances your daughter is in, Mr. Brent. That composite picture that you saw.—A picture that you have not seen yet, but that I believe was taken last night, at the Seatons' farm, that Mrs. Seaton told you had been taken. I believe you will see it . . . distorted and misused as this other has been distorted and misused."

"These are political——"

"Mr. Brent . . . I would not risk exciting you—believe me —if I did not believe it is drastically important, for your daughter's safety, to make you see that your problem here is no longer a political one. I ask you, for the sake of your daughter, to listen to me."

Their eyes held unwaveringly for a long instant.

"I'll listen to you," Mr. Brent said.

"Vair is not working alone. He was not at the Seatons' farm last night. He was dining here, in Georgetown, until eleven o'clock. He has agents, Mr. Brent. There's no doubt in my mind that one of them is in your house, perhaps now living under your roof . . . that he was not a friend of your sons, that if he knew them at all it was very slightly . . . and that there's the strongest prima-facie evidence that he was and is an agent of Vair's and he's there, in your house, with the purpose of injuring your family. I urge you to take serious steps to test the truth of those statements . . . and equally serious steps to test the truth of his. You owe that to your daughter . . . whatever your attitude toward your wife and yourself may be."

Mr. Brent said nothing for a moment.

"You are talking," he said then, "about Forbes Allerdyce."

"I am indeed."

"Very well, Colonel Primrose."

I was so relieved not to see any plethoric flush on his face or any anger or resentment flashing out from under those drawn and shaggy brows, that I relaxed myself, for the first time since Colonel Primrose had started.

"I'm giving you credit for honesty in this matter, Colonel.

Perhaps now you'll listen to me. I didn't see Allerdyce at the garden party. I was pretty much surrounded by top brass, after the Vair episode, which Mrs. Latham will remember, I'm sure." The glint of amusement in his eyes was brief. "The next morning I was called out of town. We were threatened at the Taber City Plant with a work stoppage that I put entirely at Vair's door. When my wife called, late Saturday night, very much upset by what Mrs. Seaton had said, and told me among other things that Allerdyce had crashed that party to meet us, I was very much surprised, and frankly worried."

He stopped to answer the question that Colonel Primrose started to ask.

"—Surprised, and worried, because it wasn't in character. I'll explain that later. I got a plane and came home at once. I talked to my wife, and when Allerdyce came I talked to him, at some length. He explained the gate-crashing affair, and having two sons of my own, I can understand that, Colonel Primrose, better perhaps than you'd think. I was entirely satisfied in my own mind. And now, Colonel—and Mrs. Latham—let's get one thing straight. I have had to become in my life a reasonably good judge of men, and I know how to spot a phony . . . I think. And I assure you that Allerdyce was a friend of my sons . . . of Rufus Jr. in particular. He knows intimate details of their lives. He could not have known those details if he had not had a long and intimate association with them—for there is no other way he could have learned them. I gave him a pretty exacting going over, Colonel. He never faltered and never made a slip of any kind."

My hand went to my jacket pocket, but Colonel Primrose shook his head.

"I've no doubt he has intimate knowledge of your sons' lives, Mr. Brent," he said quietly. "He's playing a very carefully and astutely prepared rôle. He can't afford to make mistakes, and he's not likely to. I suggest, Mr. Brent, that he's a trained professional investigator . . . that he started out investigating you for Hamilton Vair, early last fall . . . and that somewhere, in the course of that, he came across some person, or some material, or both, that gave him the background he's using."

"I'm sorry, Colonel." Mr. Brent spoke with quiet decisiveness. "There is no such person, and no such material. I thought of that. On your premise, it's a reasonable supposition. But Allerdyce knows facts about the boys, about my wife, and about myself, that no other person could have told him, and that there are no records of. There was, at one time, material out of which he could have learned those facts, perhaps . . . my sons' letters home, that my wife and Molly both kept, from the time they started leaving home. Letters to them from the boys on trips, in school and college, Europe, Korea. But those letters are not in existence."

"Are you——"

I caught myself. I'd started to ask if he was sure.

He looked at me composedly for an instant. "I'm sure," he said simply. "I know they are not in existence, because I destroyed them. And I'm a thorough man, Mrs. Latham."

He was also a painfully unhappy man, and not as harsh and adamantly hard as his voice and words tried to show him to be. His face worked almost imperceptibly as he drew a deep painful breath.

"I destroyed them, I mean, with my own hands—all of them. I did it because my wife—and Molly, when she was lying there in the hospital, never going to walk again, the doctors thought—were living in a past that was dead and couldn't ever come back, clinging to it. . . ."

He stopped again for an instant, and went on steadily.

"We were devoted to our sons . . . myself no less than my wife and daughter. But they were dead, Mrs. Latham. We had to realize that, if we were to go on living . . . if Molly and my wife were to live at all. That's why I destroyed the letters. It was hard to do. It may have been wrong. I think now it was. Time would have healed it all, without such drastic surgery on my part, and it was a cruel shock to my wife. There are no letters, Colonel Primrose, and no records. None, of any description."

Colonel Primrose sat there, attentive and imperturbable.

"I needn't say it's been very hard for all of us to bear," Mr. Brent said wearily. "Allerdyce's coming has meant a great deal to my wife. You didn't know her before last November. You can't know what it means to see her happy again. I destroyed the boys' letters. I can't destroy this new happiness, Colonel Primrose . . . not without a great deal more reason than anyone's given me.—Marjorie Seaton's been under a strain with Molly. She was overwrought, yesterday. It's easy to misinterpret people's actions. But I'll also say this. I'm not too bull-headed not to respect intelligent disinterested opinion. If he isn't Forbes Allerdyce, if he's masquerading, then I want to know it, and at once, so my wife won't be hurt worse than she has to be hurt. I am not a pig-headed fool, Colonel Primrose."

As the Colonel started to speak, he raised his hand. "Let me say one thing more, sir." There was a flicker of light in his eyes that grew irrepressibly until they were twinkling much as they'd done as he stood in the receiving line there in front of the bank of white wisteria at the garden party. "I said the gate-crashing seemed out of character. But it's an interesting thing. I think it had greater influence on my acceptance of him than any questions and answers."

He laughed then, for the first time since he'd come to the house.

"He's not as much of a priss as I'd expected him to be. I imagine he learned something from them. I can see what Rufie and Robbie would think of him. If you'd known them you'd understand. They weren't barbarians, by a long shot, but they were full of the Old Nick. Their escapades didn't always seem as amusing at the time as they did when I thought about them later. Rufie's term for him fits. What I'm saying is, it fits Allerdyce, but it also fits Rufie. That's why I don't think I'm deceived, Colonel."

"What is the term, may I ask?"

Mr. Brent laughed again. " 'Exemplary,' " he said. "I think their letters first used it when Allerdyce tutored Rufie, in college."

"They'd known him before that?"

"Some time before. They met him when they were visiting on Cape Cod one summer. At least that's my first memory of him. They talked about him a good deal. My wife reminded me what I'd forgotten. He was coming home with them one vacation but he caught something. Measles or mumps. Then he was in Boston when Rufie was at M. I. T. and had to have a tutor."

"Would you mind, Mr. Brent, if I look into that tutoring?"

"Do you doubt that my son had a tutor named Forbes Allerdyce, Colonel Primrose?"

There was an undertone of steel in Mr. Brent's voice.

"I'd like to be sure the Forbes Allerdyce in your house is *the* Forbes Allerdyce," Colonel Primrose said calmly. "Let me tell you why. You said he'd made no slips. I'll tell you one. It's a very small matter. But it's not a blunder that a person such as he represents himself to be would make."

"Explain that, sir," Mr. Brent said quietly.

"You of course wouldn't remember the marks your son received in the subject Allerdyce tutored him in."

"His marks would mean nothing to me."

"But they would mean something to a tutor. Allerdyce told Mrs. Latham what his mark in English was. He helped Rufie, he said, to squeeze through on a D minus. The A-B-C-D system of marking of course is in use all over the country. But it was not then in use at M. I. T., Mr. Brent. I happen to have done work there, as many Military Academy men do. That marking system was adopted very recently—in this present year. But even if Allerdyce had correctly said he helped Rufie to squeeze through with an 'L' for Low, that would still ring false . . . for any respectable tutor would *guarantee*

what they now call a 'C' mark. I suggest you will find this is
not the man who tutored your son. He does not speak the
language of an exemplary tutor, Mr. Brent."

Mr. Brent was silent for a moment, his brows drawn together. "Check it, then, Colonel. But I don't want him to
know you're doing it. We are in his debt, not he in ours."

As he got up and stood there, not steady, I looked appre-
hensively at Colonel Primrose.

"If you don't go home and rest, Mr. Brent, you'll have an
impressive list of pall-bearers," he said quietly. "That wouldn't
help Molly, or Mrs. Brent—especially if I happen to be right
and you wrong. We sent your car away. If you'd like her to,
I'm sure Mrs. Latham will be glad to drive you home."

Mr. Brent, I'm sure, thought it was pure kindness that
prompted that offer, but I knew better.

"I don't want my wife worried," he said simply. "Perhaps,
if it's not too much trouble, you'd both come? I'd like you to
meet Allerdyce, Colonel. I think you'll change your mind
when you do. And maybe I should rest for a while."

That's how Colonel Primrose and I were present when
Molly Brent came to Nunnery Lane.

Mrs. Brent had snatched her from the farm, indignantly
and without warning of any kind, just in the clothes she had
on, with daubs of paint on her white shirt and faded blue
jeans. It was only the pure accident of Colonel Primrose's
going back upstairs for one more word with Mr. Brent that
kept us there till she came. It was a strange scene from the
beginning even, when Colonel Primrose and Forbes Allerdyce
met, with such polished ease on Allerdyce's part and urbane
courtesy on the Colonel's, with Allerdyce thereafter doing his
subtle best to ease us out. I'm not sure, indeed, that that
wasn't why Colonel Primrose went back upstairs. Standing
there waiting in the black-and-white marble hall, I could feel
the tension Allerdyce couldn't control, though he had no idea,
he'd said, where Mrs. Brent had gone, and I saw the telltale
pause for an instant when he heard her car coming in, and
saw the flicker of rage behind his steel-rimmed glasses as
Colonel Primrose came down the stairs a minute later. And
Allerdyce had to stand there, pretending he didn't know, too
late to readjust . . . unless he was figuring the devastating
readjustment he was shortly to make to demolish both Colonel Primrose and me completely. It was Mrs. Brent's
chauffeur who opened the door.

The three of us stood there, motionless, as Molly Brent
came in, slowly, like a bewildered frightened waif caught up
off the streets and brought into a palace, her eyes, amber-pale,
fixed straight in front of her, her copper hair in a slicked
donkey-tail at the back of her small trembling head. Her

mother, bustling in after her, gave her a little push, not un-
kindly, on into the marble chessboard hall. I was off to one
side, Colonel Primrose at the foot of the stairs. Mrs. Brent
had eyes for nobody except the young man midway between
stairs and door in the center of the hall.

"Molly dearest . . . this is the surprise I told you about.
It's *Forbes Allerdyce*, dear. You remember Rufie's friend,
Forbes Allerdyce? Well, here he is, darling! Forbes, this is
Molly. . . ."

Molly Brent came to a halt. It wasn't an abrupt halt but a
kind of incredulously bewildered stopping, as you'd stop, I
thought, if somebody said "Here's a ghost. I want you to meet
him," . . . or it was even like the ghost of a ghost, the way
she stood there, as if not sure she'd heard. Then she closed
her eyes, and opened them again, her lips parted.

". . . Who?"

It was little more than a breath she drew.

". . . Forbes Allerdyce, darling. You remember, Rufie's
friend. . . ."

Molly had turned her head slowly and was looking at her
mother. Her amber eyes darkened with a haunted and utterly
dumbfounded disbelief.

"Forbes Allerdyce. . . ." It was a question and an excla-
mation of total incredulity whispered all at the same time. Her
eyes widened still more as she stared blankly at her mother.
Mrs. Brent's face was alight and radiant with confident happiness. Molly moistened her lips. The pulse in her throat was
throbbing, but she'd quit trembling, her body motionless and
almost rigidly still. She turned then and looked at Allerdyce,
smiling at her, pleasantly amused at her amazed incredulity
rather than embarrassed at it.

"Hello, Molly," he said.

She closed her mouth and swallowed.

"You . . . you're Rufie's Forbes Allerdyce?"

Her eyes were fixed on him with the most extraordinary
expression in them. I couldn't tell whether it was doubt, or
what, and if it was, if it was doubt of him or of herself. "You
really are?"

"Really am." He smiled engagingly.

"Oh!"

Her eyes were dark, the pupils expanded, her face so pale,
as she whispered that, that it was like milk under the copper
cap of her hair. She turned her head slowly, and her eyes
rested on me. I'd never seen on anyone's face the expression
that was on hers then. She didn't speak, but something in her
face that had been doubt certainly, but doubt so naked it was
really horror of a sort, changed then, the instant she recognized me, to a relief so lightning fast, and so profound, that it

looked really to me then as if the doubt had been not for Allerdyce but in some way for herself, even for her own sanity.

There was a swift flash of light in her eyes. She turned back to Allerdyce.

"Oh!" she breathed again. "—I just couldn't believe it was really you. I . . . I've always wanted to meet you . . . so much. I . . . never knew you were . . . still alive."

XVI

Allerdyce closed the door almost before we were out of it.

"Goodbye. Do come again, won't you both?"

I might have imagined the ironical amusement in his smile but I didn't make it up in the tone of his voice. And there'd been a couple of times there in the hall when I knew by that taut, almost invisible suspension of his that he wasn't amused. One was the brief space of Molly's incredible indecision, before she said "I . . . never knew you were . . . still alive."

He'd laughed then, not pretending it was any particular feat on his part. "Very much so, I'm happy to say. What made you think I wasn't?"

"Oh, just . . . just the plane crash," she said, still breathless, and Allerdyce, smarter by far than I am, because I'd forgotten Colonel Primrose hadn't met Mrs. Brent—or perhaps acutely aware of someone behind him that he couldn't see—brought him promptly forward.

"Mrs. Brent, this is Colonel Primrose."

What happened then was as bewildering to me as Molly's extraordinary reversal . . . for while I didn't understand that look on her face, it seemed a reversal to me.

"This doesn't make sense," I said. "What did she *mean?*" We were headed out the gate into Nunnery Lane, and I stopped the car before we got to the concrete entrance pillars. I wanted to get this thing settled before I got into the Foxhall Road traffic. "She *knows* Forbes Allerdyce is dead. You didn't see the look on her face when she saw me. She looked as if she'd lost her mind, for a second there. Truly she did."

"I noticed." He was scowling, trying to think, I suppose. "But you saw one thing. The whole block against talking about her brothers is gone. I was afraid when she came in. . . ." He didn't finish, but he didn't have to. It hadn't alarmed me. I'd seen her in frozen terror at the farm. Coming in the door at Nunnery Lane, she'd been bewildered and frightened, but not the way she'd compulsively been when she saw my car in the drive at the Seatons', and again when Archie had barged into the library. She was like a log jam in a river . . . one released, all released, and life could begin to flow in normal movement again.

"And he changed the subject very quickly, I thought." It was just then that Allerdyce had brought Colonel Primrose forward to meet Mrs. Brent, and she'd cast her surprised glance at me. She hadn't told me in so many words she no longer needed him, but she'd obviously meant me to understand it and was distressed that I hadn't. And that's when Colonel Primrose had done the other thing that so startled and bewildered me.

"What on earth did *you* mean? I thought you didn't want them to know Mr. Brent had had a heart attack?"

"Allerdyce already knew it. You must have seen that."

I hadn't in the least.

"The way he looked at Mr. Brent when he came in . . . watched him take out a cigar and put it back, watched him when he took that elevator upstairs."

That was a discreet mahogany-panelled job to the left of the library fireplace. I'd forgotten it was there until Mr. Brent had gone to it instead of walking up.

"But how?"

"I'd forgotten you're a stranger here in Washington. Get somebody to tell you about the leaks sometime. Anything that happens to Mr. Brent is news."

"His driver," I said.

"Not necessarily. You've got neighbors with friends on newspapers. Doctors aren't always close-mouthed, especially when annoyed. Your phone was giving out a busy signal for some hours."

In front of us a car swung out of Foxhall Road into the Lane. He reached over and sounded my horn sharply. It was Archie Seaton. He pulled up on the other side. Through the glass his face looked grey-greenish, like some simian character that would be pleasanter to avoid. In the normal light as he came across to us he still looked tough, with a seething angry flush on his face. It was no polaroid glass that had taken the blue out of his eyes and left the sea-grey film over the alarm and bitterness visible in their depths.

"She there?"

Colonel Primrose nodded. "What do you think you're doing?"

"I'm calling on Miss Brent," Archie said evenly. "I also brought her some of her clothes and things. The old bat didn't even give her a chance to get her toothbrush. Ginny was there, she'll tell you. It makes me so goddam sore——"

"You keep out," Colonel Primrose said quietly. "Her father's had a heart attack. That'll keep her and Mrs. Brent busy. Leave her stuff at the door and don't try to see her. And take out the note you wrote her and hid in a pocket. It won't get to her."

Archie grinned a little. "It seemed like a good idea."

Colonel Primrose smiled faintly. "It wasn't. Listen carefully. You can help Molly now or you can wreck everything. You can start giving up the big brother act, but you've got a job to do first. It's up to you to find out what she knows about Allerdyce. She knows the name, she didn't know his face."

He told him quickly what had happened, Archie listening silently.

"Do you know the Elliotts' caretaker?"

They're the people who own the empty house at the dead end.

"If I don't I'm going to."

"Molly's room's at the back over the dining room, or that's where the maid was putting fresh flowers. There's a balcony outside. I don't know if Allerdyce has moved in yet——"

"Today," Archie said. "Ginny told me."

"He's probably in the wing then. They don't keep a dog. You ought to be able to get the general layout, from next door. Use your head and don't do anything foolish. Come to my house as soon as you can. I'm assuming you wouldn't be welcome at the swimming pool."

Archie grinned. "You're so right. The Seatons are out. Socially, this is. The old Toolmaker hasn't fired Tom yet." He looked at us. "Or has he?" he asked, with sudden bitterness.

"Not as of one-fifteen today."

"I'm on the job then. I'll see you."

He took a step toward his car and turned back, his heart so naked in that ugly mug of his that I could have wept, I felt so sick with anxiety and so sorry for him. "How was she, Grace? How did she take it? Has she——"

It was hard to answer, I was so bewildered myself. "Much better than I'd have thought," I said.

"I see her everywhere I look . . . that crazy donkey-tail, and those yellow spots in her eyes when she laughs. No wonder she misses her brothers, they must have had a lot of fun together. And it's no wonder the poor dumb old dame's nearly bats, the stuff they used to pull on her. She told me a lot of it. Gosh, she's sweet. Molly, I mean."

He grinned and shook his head like a Chesapeake coming up with a pintail in his mouth. "I guess I'm bats too. So long."

"Watch yourself Archie."

I started the car. I could see him in the mirror when I

turned into the Road. He had his trunk open, getting something out of a suitcase.

"How did you know he wrote her a note?"

"I didn't," Colonel Primrose said. "But she wouldn't get it, and he'd go through hell thinking she had got it and wasn't answering."

"You sound as if you knew about these things," I said.

He looked at me, and then back at the road. "You underestimate yourself, my dear. Watch it. That's a police car coming."

My sudden spurt was purely reflex and watching the patrol car after it passed, purely conditional response. I saw it turn into Nunnery Lane.

"There's no traffic in there," I said.

"There may be."

I glanced at him, but let it go at that as he went on. "It's too bad too that Archie's upset about his brother. It's damned unfortunate."

"What happened?" I hadn't thought to ask him when he came back from lunch.

"Just more of the same. Vair's knifing Tom Seaton on the War Assets deal on the Brentool Plant at Taber City. Calling for an investigation of Tom's firm. It seems a case of Scotch is involved, and the loan of a tenant's cottage on the farm for a month, to one of the Surplus Property people. He happens to have been a classmate of Tom's at Virginia. Vair calls it bribery."

He took a deep impatient breath. "This whole business stinks. I'm not saying that giving presents is a good thing, but it's a custom of the country. All kinds of luxury trade have been built up on it. Game farms, fancy fruit and food packaging outfits advertising to that effect. The Internal Revenue abetted it, allowing gifts to be deducted from income tax. Nobody ever pretended it was bribery until it was convenient, lately. All I object to is the pot blackening the kettle, the self-righteous plucking of the mote and ignoring the beam . . . and the assumption men's souls are so cheap they can be bought for so little, while the big takers aren't touched."

"Is Tom worried?"

"Of course. Every decent legal firm in Washington's worried. It takes a long time to build up a reputation; one irresponsible investigation in Congress can wreck it. If Tom loses the Brent account it won't be the only one. The decent firm suffers, the shyster firms thrive on it."

He shook his head. "The Brent situation is the complete paradox. Brent knows exactly what Vair's charges amount to

—when they're made about him. When they're made about
Seaton's firm, he's like everybody else. Where there's smoke
there's fire, and they did give a certain man a case of Scotch
and they did have him and his wife and kids at the farm. It
had nothing to do with Mr. Brent's getting the plant. Who's
going to believe that with Vair beating his breast?"

"But nobody's going to stop him beating it," I said. "Tom
doesn't think you . . . ?"

"This business of the Brents back there might just possibly
turn out so we can." His voice was quiet, but it had the same
steely undertone as Mr. Brent's. "By means of two
people . . . Allerdyce, and Ginny Dolan. It could just possibly be that Vair's overreached himself.—Do you know if
Ginny's seen him, at all, since she's been here?"

I shook my head. "I don't know, really.".

"Will you find out?"

There was a parking place in front of my house. I pulled
into it.

"She's probably home, unless she's out with Uncle Phinney," I said.

"Damn it, Grace. . . ." He glared at me for an instant,
and then he laughed. "The less I see of Ginny the better. I
don't want to give her the idea I'm trying to get her to do
anything. Find out about Vair, will you, and let me know?"

I could hear Ginny's radio going, as I went up the steps,
but so reduced in volume that I wondered if she was sick. I
put my key in the door, and hit that blasted chain again. Then
I waited to hear her come down the stairs. But she didn't
come, and I closed the door and went down the area steps to
the kitchen.

Lilac gave me a black sultry stare. "You comin' in this way,
now?"

It was a milder rebuke than I expected.

"They been reporters here, 'bout Mr. Brent. I ain' know
nothin'."

Her eyes followed me suspiciously to the stairs. "The police, they been here too." I stopped abruptly. "They been all
over the back garden. Captain Lamb hisself came with 'em.
They gone, now."

If Captain Lamb, Chief of Homicide, had come himself we
were in high echelons indeed.

"I guess they won't be back," I said, and when she said
"Hm," I went on up to the hall, not really wishing to argue
about it. I expected Ginny to pop over the bannister, but she
didn't. Her radio was still playing softly, but that's all I heard
till I closed the basement door and went on upstairs. She was
standing there in the door of her room, but I had a curious

sharp impression that she hadn't been standing there very long.

"Did you . . . ring the bell?" she asked. "Cause I . . . I didn't hear it, or I'd have come down."

She didn't look at all happy, but I couldn't tell whether she was scared or just very uneasy . . . or a little guilty, even, about whatever she'd been doing in my absence.

"I came in the kitchen door." I looked at her again. "Ginny, what's the matter, dear?" She looked as fragile as thistledown, almost transparent, she was so wan, with no light in her face and her eyes clouded. "Look," I said. "You're losing weight, aren't you?" Heaven knows she didn't have much to lose.

She nodded. Then she said, "Can . . . may I come talk to you, Mrs. Latham?"

I said "Surely," quite automatically, and automatically went on into my room.

"Did . . . you know the police were here, Mrs. Latham?" She asked it tentatively, still holding the door, as if not sure she could come in or not.

"Yes," I said. "Come in and sit down. They came because somebody climbed over my wall, and stood down there on the terrace, listening to you and me talking last night. Or so Colonel Primrose thinks."

She didn't seem surprised. She just stood solemnly, her eyes on the window, thinking.

"Who would it be, Ginny?"

"Oh, him, I guess," she said soberly. "I guess he doesn't trust me any more than I trust him."

"Then why do you have anything to do with him?" I asked. "Don't you think——"

She went over to the chaise and sat down. "I don't have anything to do with him, really. That's the whole problem. He was supposed to be working for . . . for politics. But he's not. He's a dirty double-crosser."

"What is he working for, then?"

"That's just what I said. That's the whole problem. *They* said it was all right, he was just working for some extra money on the side, and these people have got so much they wouldn't miss it. But . . . there's this girl, Mrs. Latham. I don't think that's right."

I started to ask another question, but I remembered Daddy's dictum and waited, watching her small heart-shaped face and wide unhappy eyes fixed on the carved post at the foot of my bed.

"That's the trouble. That's why I just don't know." She looked up at me. "Did you know Archie's brother had a big

farm on a *river?*" she asked, and I nodded. "Well!" she said.
"He took me down there to lunch, today, and it was just the
nicest thing. Marge—that's his sister-in-law—she acted just
like I'd been there before, and I was perfectly welcome, and
that's not the way a lots of people act when a fella brings a
girl they don't know, especially if she's . . . if she's——"

"Pretty?" I supplied it. Her cheeks colored a faint pink.
"You can say it, because you're really very pretty."

"Thank you." She said that with a ghost of a smile that
went about its business of vanishing at once. "Well,
this . . . other girl." She looked at the window and lowered
her voice. "This other girl was there. They told me she was
bats, but she's no more bats than I am. But she's sort of
scared, till she knows you. And she was down painting the
kitchen in an old boat when I and Archie got there. And he
was ever so nice to her."

A smile sparkled in her eyes at once, then.

"He pretended it was okay if that's all the best she could do
it, but it was swell and she knew it just as well as he did. He
was just teasing her, I guess, sort of like he was her brother.
'Course, I never had a brother, but I wisht I had. A nice one,
I mean. A lots of brothers aren't too nice. But I had Daddy.
And . . . well, you don't know Daddy. But he's wonderful."

"I'm sure he is, Ginny. Just from what you've said about
him."

Her eyes were moist and she batted her lashes and looked
down at the floor. " 'Course, I guess I'm what you call prejudiced. But he's been wonderful to me. That's why it made
me sick when that old woman came down there. I stayed in
the house so she wouldn't see me, and we'd been having a lots
of fun, and then she came."

Her face settled sulky-mad like a child's and indignant too.

"She wouldn't come in the house. She said she was terribly
hurt, and terribly upset. She wasn't crying, but she was kind
of. She was more like somebody had done something awful
behind her back. And she took Molly right away . . . she
wouldn't even let her go say goodbye to the cook or anybody.
And Molly . . . she was just like a . . . a statue. She just
sort of stood. And she had a paint scraper in her hand, and
Marge had loaned me some overalls and we were all going
down to the boat, and Molly just went over and handed her
scraper to Archie, and just . . . just went and got in the car.
Her mother didn't like Archie at all. She said she just couldn't
believe Marge would keep her believing her daughter was sick
so she could . . . I don't remember how she said it, Mrs.
Latham, but it sounded like Marge was pulling a fast one to
get Molly for Archie, because she's so rich, and that made me

ever so mad. That just made me so mad, Mrs. Latham . . .
I never was so mad."

Her eyes were baby brimstone. The yellow chick really was
mad.

"And all Archie was doing was make her laugh and forget
she was scared of me, because I was a stranger. I just don't
think it's fair. I just wish Daddy had been there. I tell you.
And . . . I know whose fault it is. Because, this morning,
when I went over there, Forbes kept waiting for somebody,
and they came. I heard the car. And he had something in a
big envelope, and he said I didn't have to stay all day, I could
go before lunch. I told Archie when he called up I'd meet him
at half-past twelve, but their car came before noon and he
couldn't get me out fast enough, I tell you. I had to wait on
the corner for Archie for half an hour.

"And she didn't have any idea of going for Molly before
that, because her . . . her husband hadn't decided, and she
was supposed to wait for him."

Her face was set and her eyes still indignant. "—So that's
why I didn't go right downstairs at Marge's and just say to
her, 'I've quit.' I just don't dare quit now, because . . . well,
because it's sort of my fault. Because I helped build him up,
for Politics. And now I don't know what he's got in mind. I
ackshually don't."

XVII

"Do you think he wants to marry Molly?" I asked.

She looked at me a long time. "He's kin of Satan," she said.
"He could."

"He's what?"

"I said 'He's kin of Satan, he could.' Because, just think.
Money's what he wants, and he'd have the works. And I
know Daddy wouldn't like that creep running Taber City. But
you think of Molly. Don't always just think of money."

She was so serious that I thought I should perhaps apologize.

"Just think of Molly. If she's scared of me, she'd be in a
straightjacket first you know, with him. He's awful. Daddy
told me the kind of women he likes . . . you just don't know
the sort of things that go on, Mrs. Latham. But you don't have
to worry. I'm not going to let him do that. I know he's going
to try to get rid of me, too, just like he did this noon. But I'll
fix him."

She got up, a small erect nemesis, rather too like a flower, I thought, to undertake a job of these proportions.

"You just wait," she said staunchly. "I've . . . I've changed a lots of my ideas, the last few days. You take people like Marge and Archie. I didn't know people could be so nice. And they weren't being nice because they had to . . . why, they never even heard of Daddy. It was just me myself. And you didn't have to let me stay here, if you didn't want to. And even Mrs.—this woman, I mean—she's bats, really bats, or she wouldn't believe all the stuff, it just makes you sick at your stummick, but *she's* really nice. I feel sorry for her. And *he's* nice. But you take this other lady. Ham's lady friend. Don't you trust her for a minute, Mrs. Latham."

She said that quite severely indeed.

"And Ham. Why, when I came here I thought he was smart. But Daddy'd be surprised if he knew what I know."

She got up and looked at her watch, and I still didn't know whether she'd seen Vair or hadn't seen him.

"What does Mr. Vair think about——" I began.

"He doesn't," she said promptly. "Period. He's dumb, Mrs. Latham. He listens to all the wrong people. He doesn't listen to. . . . Why, do you know I haven't even seen him once? What do you think of that?"

"Not much," I said.

"Me neither. You hire somebody, and then you give 'em the big brush-off. But anyway, I've got to go, and I've got to get back. Uncle Phinney's taking me to dinner."

She opened the door and started out, and returned, standard order of procedure. "Oh, Mrs. Latham," she said, "I don't like to change my mind, but I guess I'll take my two hundred dollars, if that's all right with you."

She didn't actually say she didn't think the money was safe with me, but it was certainly implied. I got up to go get it, and remembered I'd left it in the bathroom when I went down to see Colonel Primrose. I knew it wasn't in there now, because the door was open and I could see the top of the john in the mirror, and it wasn't on it. Lilac must have moved it.

"I forgot," I said. "I put it away. Do you want it now?"

"When I come back will do." She was looking at me rather anxiously, I thought. "I've just decided to put it in the bank. Daddy says money's the only thing you can't insure and only ignorant people keep it in the sock. He says if the income tax man finds out you've got cash in the house he'll be hot on your trail, and Daddy says it's easier to steer clear of trouble than get out of it. What time will you be in, Mrs. Latham?"

"I'm staying in," I said.

"Okay, I'll be here at ten sharp. You know Uncle Phinney."

I went along the hall to her room and looked out the window, and saw her wave back to Lilac and step out into the street and hail a taxi, and saw one stop and the driver brighten as he reached back to open the door for her. She had on her blue off-the-face hat with the white rose nestled under her ear, and she looked less like a nemesis than an errant sunbeam. I was smiling unconsciously as I watched her go. The smile faded then and I saw an anxious face in the mirror that I hardly recognized as my own. I brushed that off too and went back to speak to Lilac, stopping to close the door at the foot of the third floor stairs. I did it automatically, never wondering why it was open in the first place, and took up the phone and pushed the bell for Lilac.

"Where's the blue silk envelope I left in the bathroom this morning?" I asked. "It's Ginny's, and it's got two hundred dollars in it."

With people using her kitchen as a means of ingress and egress, flouting all standards of propriety and decorum, I might have known she was spoiling for a row.

"Ain' nobody accusin' me of stealin'. Ain' nobody say I'm a thief——"

"Lilac!" I practically shouted it at her. "If you don't stop that *I'm* going to leave the house. Nobody's accusing you of anything. Where is the blue envelope?"

"Efn you mean that zippered case you lef' in the bathroom all covered with toothpaste, it's right in the closet, right in front of your own eyes."

"That's it," I said. "Thank you." We both banged down the phone, I expect. And it was there, in the bathroom closet, and a matter of relief to me and of greater relief to Ginny when I gave it to her when Sergeant Buck came to take her out to dinner.

I didn't see the Sergeant then, but I did see another friend of Ginny's that evening. He came a little after nine o'clock. I hadn't put the chain on the door when she went out to meet Uncle Phinney, and I didn't put it on when I opened the door then, confident it would be either Colonel Primrose or Archie. I didn't, in the lost world, expect it to be the noted columnist Edson Field. He wouldn't have got in if the chain had been up or if I'd been a little less surprised. As it was, he was across the threshold and inside before I could do much about it, except ask him to leave, which I did at once.

"Don't be that way, Grace," he said.

His eyes were too glittery and his long gangly figure too unsteady, and if he wasn't leering he came so close to it that I could have slapped him if I hadn't been so sure he'd have slapped me back. A strong wave of second-hand martinis made him even less attractive than he normally was.

"Mrs. Latham's my name, Mr. Field," I said. "And I'd be very glad if you'd go immediately."

"Well, I'm not going," he said. I realized he'd had even more to drink than I'd thought. "I didn't come to see you anyway. Where's Dolan?"

"She's gone out."

"Who with?"

"None of your business."

He looked at me offensively. "You're not bad, you know, when you're mad. I like women with spirit."

"Having none of your own, I should think you might," I said.

For a moment he wavered, his mouth coming out like a goldfish's trying to breathe in stale water. He shrugged his lank shoulders, turned and went down the hall to the living room. Someone had brought him to a party a couple of times, and forgetfulness isn't one of his failings.

"What about a drink?"

"Sorry."

"You don't mind if I get it myself, do you? I don't need ice."

He crossed the room to the dining-room door. When he barged against the desk chair I knew he was really basically intoxicated, not just tight. The stony sobriety of the very drunk was carrying him. I didn't know what another drink would do to him, and when I glanced at the phone I saw he had the craftiness of the very drunk, too.

"Don't bother to call the estimable Colonel, lady," he said. "I just saw him leave with Captain Lamb. Who's the homicide?"

My heart sank a little.

"Don't answer, then."

He came back with enough bourbon in his glass to fell a stone sober ox.

"You'd better let me get you some ice and water," I said. I went out to the hall pantry, and knocked on the dumb-waiter to tell Lilac to stand by, which was brutal considering it was her first night to sleep since Ginny Dolan had come to Washington.

"Look, lady," Edson Field said, when I put the water and ice on the table by him. "What about a deal, you and me?"

He lighted a cigarette and spat the loose tobacco out. His mouth was thin and nervous and had been sensitive once, I suppose, but it looked cruel to me, with the cruelty of a weak man confident of his power to suggest deals and make them.

"What kind of deal?" I asked.

He poured water in his drink, splashing the table as he dropped a lump of ice in.

"It's about some friends of yours."

"And a visit to their farm the other night?"

He splashed himself then. A lot of white showed in his eyes, or what would have been white if it hadn't been bleary yellow. "What do you mean by——"

"I was there," I said. "So was Colonel Primrose, if it interests you."

He put his glass down, his face yellower and gaunter. There are ethics even in his trade, and it doesn't do to get too bad a name.

"It was a coward's trick, wasn't it," I said.

He picked his glass up and took a large swig. "Okay," he said. "What did you do to old Brent, to give him a heart attack here in this room today . . . or was it in this room?" He raised his brows and sniggered. "How do you think Loopy Lena's going to like that when she hears it?"

"If that's your deal, don't bother," I said. "You haven't got Vair's Congressional immunity. Write anything you like. I'd love to sue you."

His shoulders slumped flaccidly. He pulled himself up sharply, slopping his drink, and tried to focus across the table.

"——You're trying to get me tight."

"You'd better go before I do."

"I know you're trying to get me out." He sagged down again and pulled himself up, leering at me craftily. "You're all alike. I hate the living hell out of all of you. I'll show you. I'll show up the whole rotten system. You're trying to be nice to me because you know what I can do to you. I know you. You're just playing me for that son of a bitch Vair. You think I don't know it."

I stared at him then. I didn't know whether he'd got me mixed up with Sybil Thorn, or what. He was moving his shoulders sideways and back, swinging in his chair, as if he was trying to make a lunge at me. It would have been alarming if I hadn't been close to the poker and a lot steadier on my underpinning than he was. He dropped his glass and watched it roll under his chair. I looked at the clock. It was twenty-five minutes to ten.

"Well, I'll tell you. You don't know all I know. You're two-timing me with that bastard that *I* made. *I* made him." He put his hand up and patted his wet coat front. "*Me.* I made him. I made him on your account and that's the kind of fool you made of me. That's what you did to me. You prostituted my pen . . . for that low-down two-timing——"

The tears had started to roll down his cheeks and now he held his face up and wept like a woman.

"That's what you did. You'd marry me. Sure, you'd marry me. You wouldn't marry me and you knew it. You're just

waiting for me to make him a big shot. I know you. That's
you. That's what I'm going to tell her. I'm going to tell it right
to her two-timing little face. But I'm not going to tell her till I
get all of 'em. Every. . . ."

He went on in a maudlin monotone, slumping down in his
chair and jerking up, in a fantastic half-stupor. He sat up then
with a final jerk, focussed on me again and blinked at me.
"What was I saying?"

"I don't know," I said.

He stared moodily across the table at me. "Deal," he said.
"We're going to make deal. She's going to get Dolan out of
here."

I waited, trying not to let him see how intensely interested I
was.

"Where's Dolan?"

"She isn't here."

"You told me that. Don't repeat."

"Sorry," I said.

"Okay. You think I'm tight. Well, I'm not. Am I?"

"I'm sure you're not."

"That's better. You keep a civil tongue in your head. I
know I'm a bastard, but that's the way I make my living and I
like it, see? This is the deal. You get me what she's got and
it's a deal. See?"

"You mean Ginny?" I said. "What's she got?"

"You're tight." He spat the words at me and pulled himself
up again. "Or maybe it's me."

He raised his hand and stabbed at me again with his long
thin forefinger. "Don't pretend you don't know what I mean.
You know damn well what I mean. Okay, it's deal. You get
'em and I'll use 'em. If you don't you know what's going to
happen? My wife's going divorce me. That's what's going to
happen." The tears rolled down his face again. "But I don't
care what happened to any of 'em. Okay. I'll tell you. What
do I get? That Allerdyce . . . he walks off with
millions. . . and me, that made that bastard. . . . He gets
my woman and her paltry half-million and what do I get out
of it? I don't want their filthy money, I want justice. . . ."

He swung forward and jabbed his finger at me again.
"Deal. I'll show 'em up . . . and if they want to buy us off,
we'll split. Fifty-fifty. Okay? We'll——"

I turned as the door bell rang. It was still ten minutes to
ten. In ten minutes I might really have heard what the deal
was.

"Who's that?"

"Ginny, I imagine."

"I want to see her." He managed to get to his feet.
"Where's the bathroom?"

I pointed across the hall, and he made it. I don't know how. I went quickly to the front door. It was Ginny, and Sergeant Buck was a dark figure down on the sidewalk. I dragged Ginny inside and went past her down the steps.

"Look, Sergeant. Go downstairs. There's a man here. I want Ginny to talk to him. But you wait on the stairs, will you? Don't come in till I call you."

He gave me a skeptical and frigid look, but he turned and headed down.

Ginny looked really scared.

"It's Edson Field," I said.

"Oh. *That* jerk. He came to see me, didn't he?"

She seemed relieved, and she was certainly matter-of-fact about it.

I nodded.

"I thought so. Well, I'm not afraid of him."

She started in and stopped. "Ham Vair didn't come, did he? He's the one I want to see. I told *her,* but she sends this . . . jerk, instead."

She marched on down the hall. In the living room I thought she looked more wary and not quite as confident as she'd been out there. Field was returning. I was astonished at the change in him. He had some technique for partly sobering up that was extraordinary, or if not for sobering up at least simulating it. I wondered if he hadn't probably been off and on in this way for several days. In any case, he was no more agreeable.

XVIII

"I want to talk to you, Dolan," he said. "Get lost, will you?" That was to me.

"She stays or I don't," Ginny Dolan said. "I don't like people that drink too much. If you want to talk to me you can talk right now."

"You want her spilling everything she knows about you all over town?" Edson Field looked her up and down. "She'll kick you out when she finds out you're a crook, Dolan."

"I am not a crook."

He put his hand out, palm up. "Kick in." You so seldom see people really sneer that it sounds melodramatic to say it, but that's what Edson Field was doing then. "Turn 'em over, and it's a trade."

"I don't know what you mean."

She said it so quickly that I saw she evidently did know. I saw the wary flicker in her eyes as he laughed. The little color she had left in her face had disappeared and the pulse in her throat was beating a blue-tinted tattoo it hadn't beat before, but she stood her ground.

"Give 'em to me and I call off Sybil. That's a trade for you, Dolan. Take it or go to jail. I advise you to take it."

Ginny's eyes widened. The white silk rose behind her ear was trembling. "You can't send me to jail."

"Sybil can and she's going to. Remember all the stuff you charged to her account? Remember that, Dolan?"

"She told me to buy it." The color flashed back into her cheeks and her eyes brightened. "It was her idea, not mine. The store called her up. I was right there and heard them talk to her."

"Not to her, Dolan. That was Saturday noon, wasn't it? She wasn't home Saturday."

"That's a lie. She was too home."

"No. She let the servants go and you knew it. Who did you ring in in her place, Dolan? Sybil wasn't there. She was having lunch with me at the Mayflower."

Ginny stared at him, the organdie frill at the throat of her blouse quivering as it moved up and down with the sharp rhythm of her breathing. "What's the trade?" she asked abruptly. "What does she want?"

"That's better." Field smiled. "I knew you were a smart girl. You hand 'em over, and go back to Taber City. She won't tell the store, and you're okay."

Ginny Dolan's eyes brightened. "—But if I hand them over to you. Not her. Then . . . could I stay in Washington? What about that, Mr. Field? You don't care about her."

He looked at her, and laughed shortly. "That's deal. Go get 'em. I'll wait."

She'd straightened up, the white rose and the organdie frills as steady as her blue eyes. "—Listen, Mr. Edson Field . . . you're just a dirty double-crosser, and I'm not scared of you and I'm not scared of Sybil Thorn, and I wouldn't give either of you anything! You make me sick at my stummick, and you can just get out of here! *Uncle Phinney!*"

It was Ginny who flashed over and picked up the poker and Ginny who called Uncle Phinney, and Ginny's blue eyes that were blazing with anger and contempt. But I was glad indeed Sergeant Buck was there. I was only frightened about one thing, then. I didn't want Buck to hurt the man. But there was something so awful in the pusillanimous, almost gibbering way Edson Field collapsed then that I knew Buck couldn't bring himself really to do anything to him.

He stood looking down at him with indescribable disgust. "He's drunk, ma'am," he said stonily.

"I know. Just get him out, please. Thank you, Sergeant."

I looked at Ginny when the door closed.

"They're just trying to scare me," she said, very calmly. "I'm going straight down to the store tomorrow and tell the man, and we'll see who goes to jail." There was blue brimstone then behind the curling lashes she batted at me. "Because, if she didn't give me permission, how would she know I'd bought the stuff? She doesn't get her bill till next month. That makes me mad. I'm not that dumb."

"You certainly aren't," I said, and meant it.

She'd been frightened nevertheless. She glanced at the French windows, and went over to test the lock on the screen.

"I shouldn't have told anybody your dog was deaf," she said soberly. "And I wouldn't . . . I'd just hate Daddy to find out I'd used anybody's charge account. He wouldn't like that."

She reached down, picked up the glass on the floor and put it carefully on the table.

"Ginny," I said. "It isn't any of my business, but if you've got something they want this badly, it isn't very safe for you, is it? Don't you——"

She shook her head, very soberly again. "It's safer for me to have it than not to have it, Mrs. Latham. But I . . . I haven't got it, really. But he knows it's gone, that's what scares me. Because I don't see why he'd tell them. Forbes Allerdyce, I mean. Because they'd call Ham Vair, and he wouldn't go for that stuff." Her eyes warmed indignantly. "That's dirty. Daddy wouldn't stand for that. I know he wouldn't."

Then she came over and patted my arm. "You just let me worry about this, Mrs. Latham," she said kindly. "We'll know in the morning."

We didn't know till the morning after, as it turned out, and it could hardly have been worse. But at the time, my confidence in Ginny Dolan was rather blinding.

"And I'm going to bed," she said decisively. "The lady at my school said you ought to go to bed early at least two nights every week or you look *haggard*." She bent her blue eyes on me. "You ought to remember that too," she said. "You *never* get any sleep."

And I didn't get much that night either, though I did have one good hour before Colonel Primrose called me. It was at half-past one. I hadn't tried to get in touch with him because I knew Uncle Phinney would report. When he called me, at that hour, I was too astonished to think whether he had or not.

"Look, Colonel," I said, when I'd looked at my clock. "You're sure *you're* sober?"

It was the first time in all my experience with him that he'd ever called me up at that time of the night and asked me to come anywhere—least of all his own house.

"Is there somebody who isn't?" he asked shortly. "Tell me when you get here. I'll be glad if you'll hurry as fast as you can. You can leave your door off the chain. The police are on the job."

I didn't see them when I went out, but I was glad to know they were there, and glad to see Colonel Primrose waiting for me at the corner, which was as far as he could come and still keep an eye on his own front door.

"Who isn't sober?" he asked at once.

"Edson Field. Hasn't Buck been home?"

"No, damn it."

"Oh, dear," I said. I told him quickly as we went on. And I should have waited for his sergeant to do it, I expect, for his black eyes fixed on me across the big flat desk in his living room weren't friendly.

"Why didn't you call me? You know Buck better than to give him a chance to. . . ." He came to a stop and drew a deep breath. "Where does Field live?"

"I don't know where he lives and I don't care," I said. "I didn't call you because Field said he saw you leave with Captain Lamb. He wouldn't have let me use the phone anyway."

"I didn't leave the house." He was looking up Field's name in the telephone book. "I need Field. If I could have got hold of him tonight, instead of you two——"

He broke off, listening intently, and peered out into the hall.

"Who's coming?"

I was a little angry myself. How was I to know he wanted Edson Field. He settled back in his chair as the sound in the street moved on.

"—If you'd just tell me things," I said. "I thought you were phoning Boston about Rufie Brent's tutor."

He took another deep breath. "If I could only get you to stick to known facts. . . . My dear Mrs. Latham, he never had a tutor. You ought to have seen that, from the first. He was a bright lad. He didn't need a tutor to get him a Low in English. Any normally——"

He broke off again, listening, pushed his chair back and got up quickly, his face clearing. I saw then that while he was irritated, at me and Buck, he was much more disturbed and genuinely anxious. He started for the door before the bell rang. "I was just afraid Archie was going to muck things up too," he said back over his shoulder. If it was an apology, it was well concealed. I wasn't concerned about that, however. I'd thought at first he was relieved now because this was Buck coming in . . . but of course Buck wouldn't have rung, and then I heard Archie's voice.

"—Got her," he said.

"Good man," Colonel Primrose said quietly.

"Hello, Colonel Primrose."

"Brave girl," Colonel Primrose said, and I knew it was Molly Brent.

"Come in. Mrs. Latham's here. Straight back."

She came in then. She was breathless but her eyes were shining, the yellow flecks bright gold in the warm lively velvet brown. She had a white coat on, but under it were the same paint-daubed blue jeans, with added streaks of powdery white on them. Her bare feet were in her old blue sneakers. Her cheeks were flushed, and if she'd had stardust sprinkled all over her she couldn't have been lovelier, or more finely drawn and radiantly alive.

"I was scared till Archie came," she said quickly. "I had to get out. I was afraid to try to phone anybody. I was afraid to tell Daddy . . . I didn't know what it would do to him."

She looked up at Archie. He was right behind her. He was wearing his stars with a difference, but their light was there too.

"Don't babble, Ragweed," he said. "Sit down. You don't have too much time. If you're going back. You don't have to."

"Yes, I do. On account of Daddy. But I'm not afraid, not now. I was just afraid I couldn't find you people, because I've never been in Washington before."

She sat down on the big old leather sofa, and Archie sat on the arm of it beside her. She looked down and hastily brushed off the powdery white dust from her blue jeans. "I climbed over the balcony rail and Archie caught me." She was still excited, but it couldn't have been a more healthy kind of excitement.

"Oh, golly," she said. "I . . . I didn't know what to do, when I walked in the house and Mother said . . . 'Forbes Allerdyce.' "

She was talking to Colonel Primrose now, and he sat there in his fireside chair, monumentally calm, watching her with that wonderfully wise and kindly air he has, letting her alone, letting her tell it her own way, when I knew what he wanted was one question answered and quickly answered.

"I . . . you see, I thought I'd lost my mind," she said. She put her hand up and smoothed back her copper hair. "It's an awful feeling. I could just hear Mother, and I couldn't see anything but him. And I . . . I didn't *know*, I really didn't know, for a minute. I though I must be crazy."

"You're not crazy, Ragweed."

"I know I'm not. But I didn't know it until . . . until I looked over and saw Mrs. Latham. I knew she was real, and I knew if I knew her I wasn't just making things up. But I knew before that. . . . I mean, when Mother said it was him, of course I . . . I knew it wasn't. But . . . that frightened me worse than anything. I thought *Rufie never told her* . . . and then I looked at her and I thought *she believes it.* . . . That was the horrible thing . . . because that's when I thought *maybe it's me. Maybe he is here. Maybe he came back. Maybe I am seeing him, really.*"

"Take it easy, Ragweed."

Archie pulled at that absurd donkey-tail of copper-colored hair, and she relaxed and shook her head.

"You . . . you just don't know what it was like. Until I saw Mrs. Latham . . . she moved, or maybe I wouldn't have believed she was real either."

Archie patted her shoulder. "But tell 'em, Ragweed. They don't know. Tell 'em who he was . . . Forbes Allerdyce. You knew him, didn't you, Ragweed?"

"Of course I knew him. I've known him all my life. We all knew him. But he was Rufie's, really."

I saw Colonel Primrose looking at her, gravely and intently, and then a light dawning in his face. He leaned forward in his chair, as if a weight had lifted suddenly from his shoulders.

"I mean, he belonged to Rufie, Colonel Primrose. It was Rufie who . . . who *invented* him. Because, you see, he never was *real*, Colonel Primrose. Rufie *imagined* him. That's why I was afraid I'd lost my mind. Because, there he was, but he couldn't be, because he . . . he'd never been. Don't you see? He was a name, just a name Rufie made up. 'Forbes Allerdyce.' He was a horrible little boy, at first, who always did the proper thing. We . . . we had so much fun with him!"

She raised her face, the tears welling up, flooding her eyes.

"Don't you see? We always used him. What would Forbes do? At dancing class, and all the other places we were supposed to go and didn't, we'd say 'What would Forbes Allerdyce do on this occasion?' And we'd say 'Forbes Allerdyce wouldn't do that.' Forbes wouldn't leave dirty towels around. Forbes wouldn't flunk his Latin. Then Rufie would write to Mother and say Forbes Allerdyce was some place. It was just for me. It meant somebody that was a drip, or somebody who wasn't there, like the time she wanted him to get a tutor, and he didn't want to be bothered, he knew he didn't need one, so he . . . he hired Forbes Allerdyce. She never knew. Just us. That's why I was so . . . so frightened, today. I . . . I had the horrible idea that maybe . . . maybe we'd really *created* him. Rufie was dead, but his Forbes Allerdyce was . . . still here. Really, for a minute I . . . I didn't know. And . . . I can't tell Mother! She'd *never* believe me . . . and I wouldn't want her to believe me. It would break her heart, to think Rufie's fooled her! She just never knew what stinkers we were! And it was just a joke. . . ."

She stopped and wiped her eyes with her shirt sleeves. "But . . . it isn't a joke, now. Because I'm afraid, Colonel Primrose. I'm afraid for Mother. He's real to her. But if you and Mrs. Latham could come, I could *catch* him. I could show her that this Forbes Allerdyce isn't our Forbes Allerdyce. Our Forbes is dead, the Forbes that had 20-20 vision and couldn't swim because his mother wouldn't let him. I can catch him if you'll help me. But . . . it's got to be soon, Colonel Primrose . . . because he's persuading Mother that Washington's bad for me . . . and bad for Daddy. Don't let him make her take me away, Colonel Primrose! I . . . I'm afraid of him. . . ."

"No, you're not, Ragweed," Archie said quietly. "Remember? You're not afraid of anybody, any more."

She looked up at him, her eyes blank for a moment. Then they lighted like stars again.

"No," she said. "Of course not. I'm not afraid . . . unless I'm alone."

"You won't be alone, Molly," Colonel Primrose said. "If you should seem to be, remember it's just another trap he's set. If you don't believe the trap, you can walk right through it. That's the faith you've got to keep."

He'd already seen the trap. Its outlines were so plain he'd have been stupid not to, I suppose. What he didn't see was how neat a trap it was, and how decisively it could spring.

XIX

Colonel Primrose got his hat and walked up the empty street to my house with me. He looked around, as he got to the steps, and the parking lights of a nearby car blinked twice.

"We don't need a guard any longer," I volunteered.

"You don't. Ginny does." Then, as I turned in surprise to look at him, he said, "Are those letters she's got here in the house, or is she telling the truth when she says they're not?"

"What letters, for heaven's sake?" I said. "Mr. Brent said he'd destroyed——"

He shook his head impatiently. "You're being wilfully obtuse now. There have to be letters. Rufie's 'Forbes Allerdyce' existed in two places: in the minds of three kids and in the letters Rufie wrote home. Mr. Brent says he destroyed the boys' letters. It's impossible. It's obvious he didn't destroy all of them. Allerdyce is minutely briefed, in the first place . . . and how else could he have heard about 'Forbes Allerdyce'? And now Field turns up. He's out to knife the whole bunch of them, and Ginny's got what he needs to do it with. What kind of thing would Field be able to use? It wouldn't be the first time he's used letters people didn't know he had access to. He wants them, Sybil and Vair want them, and you can be damned sure Allerdyce wants them. If Field knows Ginny's got them, Allerdyce knew it first. And with Buck in this besotted frustrated fatherhood rigamarole this kid's got him into, he isn't fit for anything but a padded cell. I hope that's where I find him and not in the lockup at the Seventh Precinct where I'm headed now if he's not at Field's. If he is, by God, he can stay there till he rots."

"Iron rusts," I said.

" 'Socializing,' " he said irascibly. "I can't make him see Allerdyce isn't socializing with anybody. You'd better persuade her to tell him so."

"And he'd break every bone in Allerdyce's body and be in the lockup at the Seventh Precinct," I said. "Or is that different?"

"It's a solution," he said. "That's the damnable thing about any case of this kind. Allerdyce'll go scot free. Brent won't drag his wife and Molly through the courts to prosecute. That's the special immunity of nearly all confidence men. Their victims are helpless."

I hadn't thought of that.

"You do what you can about the letters," he said. "You don't want that girl to end up in the Potomac. She's likely to if you and Buck don't quit regarding her as a blithe spirit. You don't think Allerdyce is going to let her stand in his way to millions? Now go in and go to bed and start making sense tomorrow . . . will you?"

I closed the door and put the chain across. That in itself was a gesture of submission, because I did it without thinking. Then I stood there, considerably more worried than I'd been at any point in the whole business. Of course, if Ginny landed in the Potomac, Allerdyce wouldn't get off scot free . . . but I'm glad that didn't occur to me, really. Or maybe I was just too stupefied. That was unfortunate too, because I needed to be able—I won't say to think—but to function, and chiefly to remember. What he'd said was true, of course. The Allerdyce on my front porch and the one rigidly infuriated at the table in the Brent library with the Manhattans for Mrs. Brent on the tray wasn't anybody for Ginny Dolan to fool with. And I did regard her as a blithe spirit . . . or maybe she'd convinced me, as she was herself convinced, that Daddy wouldn't let anything happen to her. I don't know. And she was out of the house at the crack of dawn the next morning.

"I want to see Ginny, Lilac," I said when she brought my tray with the three morning papers stuffed into the end compartment.

"She gone. She wrap up all her shopping and took it downtown."

"Oh no," I said. That was going to upset Mrs. Thorn. She'd never intended that.

"An' the Colonel been here. He came to see *me*, not you."

There was a suspicious smugness about her, but she was gone before I could make anything out of it. I picked up the paper and opened it to Edson Field's column, reminded of it, I suppose, by Ginny's response to his last night's visit. Maybe it could have been worse, but I wasn't sure.

"Watch for fireworks," it said, "when a Certain Rich Man finds out the hay his Local Legal Talent has been making under the pretense of shielding the Rich Man's invalid (?) daughter from unwanted publicity. Legal Talent has a charming wife and a secluded country estate. Also an unmarried brother, a well-known figure in Society stag lines, reputed to have a long string of broken hearts behind him. Add moonlight and apple blossoms and it's a perfect set-up. Washington is beginning to wonder if the rumors of the daughter's nervous invalidism weren't started with an eye to keeping out other competition. Nice work if you can get it."

All I hoped was that Molly wouldn't see it. The balance between faith and insecurity in the early stages of love is so delicately sensitive at best that it seemed cruel to weight it when Archie had no way to defend himself. But no doubt she'd see it. Allerdyce would tend to that.

I turned back to the front page. There was a paragraph saying that Mr. Rufus Brent was reported to have suffered a mild heart attack at the home of a friend, but the report had not been confirmed and members of the family were unavailable. I didn't have to wonder very long how quickly two and two would get together and make a mess of sixes and sevens, because my phone rang almost immediately and it was the woman who'd given the garden party. By dinner, everybody in Washington who was interested would know that Mr. Brent had learned that Archie was seducing his daughter and had a heart attack as a result. The damage of course had been done the day before, when Forbes Allerdyce's version of the story, with a photograph of Molly in Archie's arms, rage and guilt written on his face, to prove it, had sent Mrs. Brent, hurt and indignant, down to snatch Molly away from him. How Mr. Brent or anybody would react was secondary at this point.

And at ten o'clock, with what Edson Field, ranting about the rotten system, would undoubtedly have regarded as bourgeois respectability, but was sheer innocence plus complete stupidity on my part, I took the first happy step into Forbes Allerdyce's neatly arranged trap. Ginny called up. She was at the Brents' and she was really pleased with herself.

"Mrs. Latham," she said. "I took the stuff back, and guess what's happened?" The whole line from Nunnery Lane to P Street was strung with laughing silver bells as her voice skipped across it. "Well!" she said. "I'll *tell* you! He called me up. I *knew* he would."

"Who's 'he,' Ginny?" I asked.

"I can't tell you, but *you* know. *Him.* He called me. He invited me to dinner. *You* know. I *knew* he'd be mad as hops. But Mrs. Latham——"

Her tone changed, not wheedling exactly but darned near it. "I know you don't like him, but could he come to the house after me? It's much more *respectful.* I don't want him to think he can just snap his fingers and make me jump. I told him to come for me at seven. Was that all right, Mrs. Latham?"

I knew then who he was, of course. It was Hamilton Vair. My heart sank. It didn't sink far enough. If she was going out with him, I thought, it was just as well for him to be "respectful."

"Surely," I said, without a qualm of any kind. "That's quite all right."

Then I got another call from Nunnery Lane. It was Mrs. Brent.

"Mrs. Latham," she said. She sounded so happy that it almost broke my heart . . . and exasperated me intensely, may I say. "My dear, you can't believe the change that Forbes has made in Molly. She's gay, and she's not nervous at all. It's wonderful!"

"Good," I said.

"And I'm so pleased she wants to see people," she went on. "She asked me herself to ask you and Colonel Primrose to dinner tomorrow. Can you come?"

I didn't look at my book. If anything was in it, I'd have canceled it at once.

"I'd love to," I said.

"At eight o'clock, black tie. We'll make it a real party."

But it wasn't a dinner and it wasn't at eight o'clock the next night, and it was a real party only in the most fantastic sense of the word. I put down the phone however with no misgivings, nothing but exhilaration at the prospect of Molly's defeat of Forbes Allerdyce. She was keeping faith with a vengeance. If she was gay and happy and not nervous at all, it was wonderful. I only breathed a small prayer that Allerdyce was as convinced that his own charm was in part responsible as Mrs. Brent was convinced it was entirely so. But when things go too well it's the time to trust them least. . . .

Ginny Dolan came home to lunch, a really blithe spirit. She danced down the hall and stuck her sunlit little head in at my door.

"Hello, Mrs. Latham!"

And suddenly there for an instant the waters of the Potomac swirled darkly in my ears and I could see her in them. I suppose it was a mild attack of vertigo, but it was very vivid to me.

"Ginny," I said, "sit down. I've got to talk to you."

Her face went blank and she sort of plopped down in the nearest chair. "Have I . . . have I done something wrong, Mrs. Latham?" she asked anxiously, contrite at once.

"I don't know, Ginny. Colonel Primrose is alarmed about you, and so am I. It's this Allerdyce. . . ."

"Oh, you don't have to worry——"

"But we are worried, Ginny. You're out of your class——"

Her cheeks went a bright rose and her blue eyes snapped. "My class is lots higher than his."

"That's not what I meant, Ginny," I said hastily. "I meant your weight, or league, or something. I mean, he's playing for stakes that are so high that if you're in his way he won't——"

"Oh, I know that," she said. "That's the whole problem."

"Look, Ginny. You've got something Edson Field wants."

" 'Course I have. Because you know Daddy. Daddy says, never get yourself tied up with a certain kind of character without you take along a pair of wirecutters to cut yourself loose with, and that . . . that's what I've got. And that's what I'm going to do tonight. Because, you don't like Mr. Vair, but he won't stand for anything like this. Do you know

Forbes never lets me get alone with Molly one minute? Do you know that?"

"I'm not surprised."

"Well, it's true. And Mr. Brent. He tried to just say hello to me, before he went to the office, and that jerk was right in between us. And nobody wants to talk to Mrs. Brent. She doesn't even hear what anybody says but Forbes. She's hypmatized. She's really hypmatized."

"Ginny," I said, "have you got some of Rufie Brent's letters?"

I asked it so unexpectedly even to myself that if the charm school had some prescribed proof against shock it hadn't gone into sufficient laboratory experiment. Her face went blank, her eyes opened full width and her jaw dropped.

"Why . . . why, Mrs. Latham! I . . . I don't know what you mean."

"Yes you do, Ginny," I said. "Look, darling. You don't want anything to happen to Molly Brent——"

"No, and I don't want anything to happen to me either," she said promptly. "That's why I'm going to see Ham Vair. He wouldn't dare let anything happen to me, and he wouldn't want to, Mrs. Latham. Daddy says you be loyal to your friends and they'll be loyal to you. He just wants to be senator. Forbes and I were supposed to 'investigate,' that's all. We weren't supposed to hurt anybody. So he'll stop it. He really will, Mrs. Latham."

"Ginny, Ham Vair's just as bad as——"

"You haven't any right to say that, Mrs. Latham," Ginny said earnestly. "That's interfering with Politics in our State, and that's not right. I *know* Ham Vair. It's just these other people keeping him in the dark. That's all it is. When I give him those let——"

She swallowed the last half of it and stared at me.

"Ginny," I said. "Please. . . . Give those letters to Colonel Primrose."

"I can't."

Her little jaw was stubborn and her lips tight.

"That would be *disloyal*. I'm getting paid to help Ham Vair. You just have to trust me, Mrs. Latham. I'll take care of Molly Brent. I'll just *explain* to Ham Vair." She got up and went to the door and turned again. "Anyway, Mrs. Latham, you're just making a big mistake. I don't have Rufie Brent's letters. If you think that, you're absolutely wrong." She turned again, and again turned back. "Mrs. Latham, don't you worry. I'm going back over there. Forbes told me I didn't have to, but I'm going anyway. He's being very nice to me, I'll tell you, because I told him about last night, and I told him he needn't try to get what I've got, because I don't have it. And he doesn't know I'm going to see Mr. Vair."

"Are you sure about that, Ginny?"

She hesitated an instant. "I don't *think* he does, I mean."

She wiped her forehead then. "—Is it always this hot here?"

I looked out of the window. It was cool inside, but it wasn't out.

"Mostly," I said. "But we'll have a thunderstorm to clear it." It usually doesn't clear it, of course.

"Oh, no!" she said. I looked at her quickly. "It can't! It just *can't* thunder! I . . . I hate it!"

She wasn't afraid of Forbes Allerdyce, but she was definitely afraid of thunder and lightning. Her face was pale.

"I'm afraid there's not much you çan do about it, sweetie," I said. "Did you tell Lilac you'd be in for lunch?"

"I ate a sandwich on my way home. I . . . I just wanted to . . . to come and check." She looked out of the window. "Archie . . . Archie hasn't called me, has he?"

"Not this morning."

She looked pretty depressed, but it seemed to have been the thunderstorm that started it, Archie being an added straw.

"Mrs. Latham," she said, still not looking at me, "do you . . . do you think he *likes* Molly Brent?"

"Very much."

"Then . . . did you see that thing Edson Field wrote about him, in the paper?"

I nodded.

"That was mean, wasn't it? He wasn't trying to marry her. Just . . . just help her."

"Did she see it?"

Ginny looked away and nodded. "She was . . . sort of hurt, I guess. I tried to tell her, but Forbes got in the way and Mrs. Brent was crying. She's the limit. But I've got to go now. I've got to take a shower. I didn't go swimming. I wouldn't be caught dead in that suit I bought on Sybil's account."

She went upstairs. Her depression must have been fairly superficial, or perhaps she turned her radio on automatically. It was going full blast. She couldn't hear it in the bathroom with the water running and I closed the hall door so I couldn't. Then after she'd said " 'Byenow," smiling, as fresh as a dewdrop again, a very small glow-worm of an idea emerged from the cloudy chrysalis buried in my mind.

" 'I just came to check.' " Check on what? I got up from the lunch table, the glow-worm suddenly a full-fledged light. The radio, too loud, the water, running too long. The radio yesterday, and her not hearing me at the front door. The bolt drawn on the door at the foot of the steps to the third floor. I hadn't been up there for a couple of weeks. And I expect the letter I had from my younger son in the morning's mail helped the whole connecting process along. I'd opened it but I hadn't read it all, because it was very long and done with a typewriter ribbon so ancient that I needed Braille to figure it out. It was about four summer jobs available in industrial plants and their advantages and disadvantages, but academic in the extreme, because he'd take the one he wanted and asking my advice was a slight touch of Rufie's "Forbes Allerdyce," I thought with some amusement as I put it by the inkwell to read later when my mind was less trammelled and a little more patient.

" '—Come home to check.' " What she was checking was on my third floor. An intuitive flash, or just a continuation of half-forgotten details, abruptly remembered . . . whichever it was, the conclusion was implicit and I jumped at it, or hurried up to it, rather, and I was sure of it the instant I saw the bolt on the door. I'd pushed it clear home to hold it. Now it was only part way in. The letters, I thought. . . .

I must have looked pretty silly, the next half hour, searching my sons' rooms and closets and bathrooms with nothing but a pile of their old clothes and stuff in my hands when I came downstairs because Colonel Primrose had come and I heard him in the downstairs hall, the glow-worm of my idea very dead indeed.

"Rummage sale?"

I shook my head and told him. He gave me a sardonic and curiously bleak smile.

"You should have started your intuitions earlier, Mrs. Latham," he said. "You had the letters. You're curious at the wrong time."

"*I* had the letters?"

"In that blue silk envelope she gave you to keep and took away because you let it lie around. That's what you two were talking about the night Allerdyce eavesdropped. Do you remember?"

"Oh, no," I said blankly.

"Oh, yes. Lilac found it, in your bathroom."

"—That's why she bridled when I said it had two hundred dollars in it." I looked at him. "Is that what you came to see her about this morning?"

He smiled. "She knows a great deal more about what goes on in this house than you do, my dear." Which is true, of course. The times she's quit I haven't even been able to find a frying pan.

"Then Buck's got them."

I wished I hadn't said it, because I saw the exasperated

flush that mounted the back of his neck as he went over to the French window and threw his cigar out, for me to pick up. "—Or has she got them back?" I asked. "She's seeing Vair tonight."

"She's seeing Vair?"

I told him about that too. "He's calling for her here at seven o'cl——"

I don't know what happened to the rest of the word. I guess it's still unfinished, trailing unhappily somewhere in the air waves, with all the other broken words people have been too stricken to complete. Because he was looking at me . . . I don't know how to describe it. Just looking, I guess, and for a very long time, it seemed to me.

XX

"So it was that simple," he said. I don't know how to describe the way he said that either. It was the way you'd say it about something so irreparable there was no use being surprised or angry or shocked or have any emotion about it.

"What . . . do you mean? Have I done . . . ?" I found myself repeating Ginny's own question to me.

"My dear Grace," he said quietly, "don't you see what getting Vair here at your house, where"—he was about to say something else but changed it—"where Mr. Brent had his heart attack yesterday is going to mean to Allerdyce? I've had an idea it was what he'd try to do. I didn't think it was going to be . . . quite so simple. That's all."

"But look. . . ."

He shook his head. "Don't try to escape. It's all right, my dear. If he hadn't done it one way he would have another. At least this gives us a chance to do a little something on our own."

He looked at his watch. "Fortunately most of the newspaper and radio people in Washington are on to Vair. If he's fool enough to let Allerdyce ruin him that's up to him. The only trouble is who else it'll ruin at the same time. I must go now. I have an appointment with Edson Field at three o'clock. That's what I came by to tell you."

He came over and lifted my chin in his hand and smiled, and shook his head slowly. "You're very sweet, and I love you very much. But you're certainly a child at heart. When you didn't like Ginny you saw her very clearly. Now you like her, you're just like Mrs. Brent with Allerdyce. You swallow everything she says."

He took a deep, patient breath. "I don't know for what sins I end up an orderly life stuck with a couple of schizoid poltergeists like you and Buck.—I'll try to get here a few minutes before seven. Don't feel too badly."

He kissed me, but his heart wasn't in it, and if the Prodigal Son was also feeble-minded I was feeling a strong sense of personal identity with him.

And Congressman Hamilton Vair also turned up a few minutes before seven. I'd like to have found it amusing, but it wasn't, I'm afraid.

Ginny got there at six. Trying to guard myself and not be like Mrs. Brent with Allerdyce, I almost hoped she wouldn't come out into the garden to talk to me. But she did.

"Mrs. Latham," she said, "do you know where Archie is?"

"I've no idea, Ginny. Why?"

"Because Forbes Allerdyce told Molly he'd seen him having a . . . a very lively lunch with . . . with another girl, and I don't believe it. I told her so. I got a chance because her mother was inside and I just got up and said I was going to the bathroom and she said she'd come too and so even he couldn't stop us that time. But she's scared, Mrs. Latham. Do you know what?"

I didn't know what, so I just shook my head and waited.

"He knows he's not fooling her. She's overplaying it. He was talking about dancing class and she said, 'Rufie must have been pulling your leg, because we always ducked dancing class, but don't tell Mother.'"

She swallowed, a little paler.

"I saw him look at her after that just like she was a . . . a bug. And something else happened. He didn't know I was there yet. The maid let me in the kitchen door—she's nice, she's a friend of Lilac's—and he was talking to Mrs. Brent. He was talking to her about the . . . the will to death, he called it. He said, 'You've never noticed any tendencies, except the automobile accident?' He . . . he's trying to make her think the accident was her sub-conscious mind, like in a movie I saw.—And I told Molly to keep away from that swimming pool and keep her door locked and not take any pills or anything."

It was like a bad dream, or listening to a child describe a scene that had real horror because it had no real meaning.

"And Mr. Brent came home early. He doesn't feel too well, I guess, and I'm going to tell Ham that too. He better be real careful or he might be responsible. But that Allerdyce. I told you, he's kin of Satan."

She stood a moment with her teeth caught over her rose-colored lower lip, staring down at the basket of tulips I'd cut, not seeing them at all. Suddenly she looked up at the sky and broke into a peal of her delighted laughter.

"You were just trying to scare me," she said. "You see, it didn't thunder after all. You knew I didn't like it, didn't you? I've got to get dressed. Would my navy blue lace with a jacket be all right, do you think, Mrs. Latham? I don't have to wear a hat, do I?"

She wasn't down when the door bell rang and Lilac answered it. I was back in the living room. It was a quarter to seven, and half a second later Ginny was coming down the stairs, not swooping but very charm school.

"Oh, good evening, Mr. Vair."

"My, you look pretty, Ginny, and don't give me that Mr. Vair stuff. How's the girl?"

I heard Ginny burble, "You come on in, I want you to meet Mrs. Latham. Mrs. Latham?"

I came out into the hall, not wanting Mr. Vair any deeper in my precincts than he already was.

"How do you do, Mr. Vair?"

"Why, bless me! Ginny, you didn't tell me! Why, I know Mrs. Latham."

I didn't like him, so I had no difficulty telling the phony heartiness of that when I heard it. Ginny was smiling proudly at him. And there's no doubt he's pretty handsome, in a bluff blond broad-shouldered way. And he'd dressed for the occasion. He didn't have on his white silk, but he was impeccably garbed in a summer weight worsted with shadow stripes, beautifully tailored.

"Well, we're not going to keep you, Mrs. Latham. I'll get our little girl back to get her beauty sleep. . . ."

That wasn't all the conversation but it was the type and level and it took four minutes. It was one minute too long. Just as they opened the door and stepped out onto the porch Colonel Primrose arrived. I didn't, fortunately, see it, but I heard Ginny. "Oh, Colonel Primrose, I want you to meet a friend of Daddy's and mine. Mr. Hamilton Vair."

"I don't know whether the flash of light from behind a car parked at the curb was simultaneous with that or an instant after it, but Ham Vair's face was shining and his hand was held out to Colonel Primrose. My door was still open but I wasn't visible. I know that, because I saw a print of the photograph, with the house numbers across the whole white pilaster behind Ginny Dolan's angelic head, Vair greeting an old and valued friend, and the courteous mask that was Colonel Primrose's face.

All I did was stay back by the living room door waiting for Colonel Primrose to come in, after he'd had his picture taken with Mr. Brent's arch-enemy on my front porch. I saw then what he'd meant, but I didn't see all of it. I didn't see the rest till the ten o'clock news broadcast. What sticks in my mind, of the scene on the porch, is not the blinding flash of the photographer's bulb or Vair's broad back in my open door but Ginny's delighted laughter. "Did you *see*, Mrs. Latham? They took our picture, with me *right* beside him!"

That was only two hours later.

"He sent me home because he had to be on the floor of the House." She sounded like an old Capitol Hill girl and her face was beaming with pride and pleasure. "He's ever so sorry he hasn't had a chance to come see me, but he's been awfully busy," she explained.

Colonel Primrose had left, but he was coming back at ten. He'd taken the flash-bulb incident philosophically, if that's what you could call a grim silence, and I saw even then that it meant more to him than it did to me.

"I wanted to go with Ham, but I thought I better not. And he's very upset about Forbes Allerdyce, Mrs. Latham. Truly he is. And he doesn't know a thing about those . . . letters."

My heart really sank then. "Did you give them to him, Ginny?"

She looked at me cautiously and moistened her lips. "Well . . . not exactly," she said. "But I . . . told him where he could . . . could get them."

"Where?"

She looked squarely at me, and I swear Colonel Primrose was right. I could no longer tell when she was telling me the truth and when she wasn't.

"Edson Field," she said.

"Did you give them———"

"I just told *him* where he could get them," she said calmly. "He wanted to get even with Sybil Thorn. Why shouldn't I help him? He'd get even with Allerdyce at the same time. He'll open Mrs. Brent's eyes and everybody else's too. Isn't that what Colonel Primrose wanted to see him for? He was going to see him, why shouldn't I? Daddy says you've got to take the bad with the good, you can't pick and choose."

A kind of pall seemed to be hanging over the room, as if I were waiting for an axe to fall without knowing where or when, or as Ginny would feel if she knew a thunderstorm were coming. I didn't even try to look at her.

"Anyway, Mrs. Latham. Ham's just as mad as I am. Really he is. He made Sybil apologize to me. But it wasn't her fault. She *told* me. She didn't have anything to do with that charge account stuff. That was all Edson Field. She didn't know a thing about it till the store called her up this morning. She called Ham right away."

"I'll bet she did."

"You're just prejudiced, Mrs. Latham. You're trying to make out Ham's a skunk. But that's wrong. And you know!" She really brightened then, the original high-class yellow chick, eyes dancing, confidence shining like her yellow hair, a perfect nimbus around her, as it was around her lovely little face. "You should have heard him apologize to me about the job. But it wasn't his fault. He thought the girl in his office was leaving when she got married but she didn't. So he'll explain to Daddy and people. And he's going to fire Allerdyce."

I'd got up and turned on the radio, a little tardily, because I'd expected Colonel Primrose and he hadn't come. He'd told me what station to listen to. He'd also told me one other thing, when I'd relayed to him about the girl Archie was said to have had a lively lunch with.

"Molly knows that's a lie," he said. "Archie's been in sight all day . . . he gave himself a job working in the Elliotts' grounds. All she has to do is look over there. In fact she talked to him, for about an hour when Allerdyce was out of the house somewhere.—Don't tell Ginny Archie's over there," he added, and listening then to her gilding the lily that Allerdyce had once called Ham Vair, I had neither reason nor desire to tell her. She was a loyal supporter of the Hot Rod of the Marsh Marigold State, nothing I could say was anything but prejudice.

—Until the ten o'clock newscast came on and she heard it herself, there in my living room, with her own staggered and unbelieving little ears. It's one of the most vivid pictures I have left of that fantastic week in Washington, D.C. One minute she was sitting there on the sofa looking like an angel floating on golden clouds, no hands, and the next she was a blank white-faced child, her eyes drained utterly grey, her mouth open, so breathless and so still I might have wondered if she was alive—if I'd really cared just then about anybody or anything, I was myself so appalled at what we both were hearing.

It was so clearly and so bitterly etched in my mind that I can repeat it almost verbatim. I was tardy at turning it on, and the voice of the newscaster didn't swell fully on until the first words were lost, so that Vair's own name itself was the first word we caught.

". . . Vair introduced on the floor of the House at nine o'clock this evening. His manner fitted the grave charge he said he was, and from the Press Gallery looked genuinely, reluctant, to make. 'This man Rufus Brent can threaten to kill me,' he said. 'I'm not afraid of Rufus Brent. Let him come, or let him send his hirelings to do the deed for him. I won't be the first patriot who's fallen, brought down by the bloody hands of men who sell their country for their own filthy purposes.' Congressman Vair went on to say that he had been shocked, unbelievably shocked, at hearing, shortly after dinner that evening, that a man of Rufus Brent's supposed stature would descend to such a level, but while he could not reveal the source of his information, there was no doubt in his mind that the truth had been told him. No wife, he said, would go to another woman and tell her that her husband planned to kill any man, who did not herself have the most solid reasons for believing the truth of her statement. It may be, Vair said, she was trying to keep her husband from carrying out his bloody purposes. That, he said, he did not know and would not presume to judge.

" 'I am told that Rufus Brent had a heart attack yesterday at a certain house in Georgetown,' Vair said. 'I am told he had it when he learned that his wife had revealed his murderous intent and that it would not be concealed. I am not asking for a bodyguard,' he continued. 'I refuse to be intimidated by threats to my very life, just as I've refused to be intimidated when I've demanded, nay implored, this great body of public servants to rise up and in the name of the country you all love cast the gabardine swine from the public trough they've too long polluted and too long drained of the life blood of the great nation. I demand Mr. Rufus Brent's resignation. If I fall, my blood will be on his head . . . but it will be on yours too, my friends.'

"Mr. Vair was deeply moved and had to be assisted to the cloak room, but was able to leave shortly afterwards. He refused to see the Press. Well, that, ladies and gentlemen, writes a curious chapter ending to the bitter single-handed battle Ham Vair has waged against the head of the Industrial Techniques Commission the last three months in Washington. Stay tuned in to 'Songs of the Cotton and the Cane. . . .' "

The banjo striking up a nostalgic melody was no less macabre in that silent room than any other music would have been. I turned it off.

It was Ginny Dolan who spoke first.

". . . He . . . he's talking about you."

She was looking down at her hands lying in her lap, as if she'd never paid any attention to them before and didn't recognize them as hers.

"—He is, isn't he?"

"I'm afraid so."

I was so stunned I didn't recognize my own voice any more than she did her hands.

"It's . . . my fault, isn't it?"

Stunned as I was, her small bedraggled voice was still moving.

"No," I said. "It's . . . it's *Politics.*"

It was her own word, and she recognized it. She got slowly to her feet. And paradoxical as it was, I found myself waiting, hoping there was some verbal prescription of Daddy's that she could bring out to cover her spiritual as well as political catastrophe. I'm still sure he had one, but perhaps no occasion had ever risen for him to tell her. She went silently to the door.

"I guess I . . . I'd just better . . . better get out of the way," she said unhappily. "Do . . . do you want me to go somewhere else . . . to stay?"

"No, sweetie."

I thought with a perverse lump in my throat that if I wasn't careful I was going to be stuck with her the rest of my life. But it was a time for tears, not laughter, certainly.

I could hear the dejected whisper of her feet on the stairs and her door creak. It was the first time she'd closed it and the first time she didn't turn on the radio. Then Colonel Primrose came. He came up through the kitchen and into the living room. I closed my eyes because I didn't want to look at him. He came over and patted my shoulder.

"I'm sorry," he said. He was very angry, with that frustrated anger he'd been talking about that's the stigma of Washington these days, so much that there's no use tearing anybody to pieces if there's to be any sanity left at all. "Where's Ginny Dolan? I want to see that girl."

"Let her alone," I said. "She's taken it on the chin already. She's seen Vair's clay feet. I'm just hoping desperately she never sees they're partly Daddy's too."

"Get your coat," he said. "And send her down here nevertheless."

"Get my coat for what?"

"You're going over to the Brents' with me."

"I am not," I said. I got up instantly. "Look, Colonel Primrose. If that woman, or Mr. Brent, or anybody else wants to think I told Hamilton Vair this obscene nonsense, they can damned well think it and the hell with them. I'm not going to crawl on my knees to Mrs. Brent or anybody else. And Ginny's had plenty. Just get that. *We're through.* Both of us."

He smiled a little grimly. "You're far from it, Mrs. Latham. Both of you. In five minutes your phone's going to start ringing. There'll be reporters swarming all over here. Within twenty minutes Captain Lamb will be here, or somebody else from Homicide not as gentle as Lamb. They'll be here to see Ginny Dolan, and they'll see her whether you like it or whether you don't like it. Get her down here, at once."

I stared at him, as blank then as I'd been infuriated before.

"Edson Field was killed some time this evening. That's why I'm late. Lamb called me in. They found him two hours ago, strangled with a Venetian blind cord. Buck was damned near an eye-witness. He's been riding herd on Field for twenty-four hours to make sure he doesn't bother Ginny Dolan again.— Bother Ginny Dolan, for God's sake. He saw a man there, and he swears up and down it wasn't Allerdyce. While Ginny Dolan double-crosses him and sneaks in Field's back door and the maid next door sees her and gives an unmistakable description."

"When was———"

"This afternoon at half-past four when she left the Brents'."

"But she couldn't have killed———"

"She could and apparently did give him what he wanted."

"—The letters," I said. He looked at me frowning. "She said she told him where he could get them, anyway."

He shrugged his shoulders. "At three o'clock, when I talked to him, Field was ready to cut Vair's throat, if he could cut Thorn's and Allerdyce's at the same time. He knew Vair was making this speech and he'd arranged to go on the air at ten-thirty, and take Vair apart. At seven, he called the station and cancelled. Something happened . . . Ginny knows what it is. At five, Field went to Sybil Thorn's, for a drink, she says."

"He must have decided to settle for some of the millions then, instead of the justice he was weeping over here," I said.

"It was something offensive to Allerdyce, at any rate."

He smiled faintly at the look on my face.

"My dear Grace, it *has* to be Allerdyce. Ninety-nine times out of a hundred, murder's as plain as the nose on your face. I've got to see this girl. You send her down here, and you get your coat. We're going to the Brents'. *Not* on your account. On Molly's."

Ginny'd been out in the hall. She was moving into her room when I got to the head of the stairs, and when I went along the hall she turned and sat down on the foot of her bed.

"I heard him." She blinked her eyes down at the floor. "Mr. Field's dead." She twisted her hands together and swallowed. "But that's not all my fault." She had the sober impassivity of a child stunned by the outrage of some monstrously dirty trick it had been decoyed into being a part of. "I guess he wanted to live, the same as anybody else," she said. "It . . . it's not right."

She folded her hands in her lap. "But it . . . it was his fault. I didn't tell Forbes anything but that I was *going* to give him the letters. I told Mr. Field to pretend I was just . . . you know, sort of leading him on. And he promised. I made him promise he wouldn't use them, except to help Molly. And he did. He *promised*."

She drew her breath in deeply and let it go as if she hadn't been breathing for several moments.

"I guess . . . I guess he figured they'd pay him anything he wanted to get them back. Or maybe he just wanted to let them see who was boss after all, they'd made such a fool of him. You can tell Colonel Primrose that. Because I'm not going downstairs. He doesn't like me and I'm not going to talk to him. If the police come let them come. I've talked to lots of policemen. Daddy's the sheriff at Taber. I know how to talk to policemen better than I know how to talk to people like Colonel Primrose. You just tell him that. I don't care."

"He's just trying to help Molly, Ginny."

"So am I. But he can't push me around the way he does you and Uncle Phinney. You're just putty. He could even push Daddy, but I wasn't in the Army. And anyway. . . ."

She got up. "Look, Mrs. Latham." She went to the closet and pulled out her suitcase. "Would you . . . would you like to have a . . . a picture of me?"

XXI

I expect I'm not so resilient as I once was. I wasn't even sure I was hearing as clearly as I once was able to. She was stooping down and taking some handsome cabinet-size portrait folders out of her suitcase.

"I know you're surprised," she said. "But . . . well, Daddy says we all make mistakes. He says the thing to do isn't to brood over them. He says you try to mend them, and if you can't, you just have to forget. I know I . . . I've been a nuisance. And I don't have much I can give you . . . but if you'd like to have. . . ."

"Oh, Ginny, I'd love to have one," I said. I was really almost in tears.

"Would you really?" The first frail gleam of a smile I'd seen in her eyes since I turned on the radio was there. She gave me a really grateful and shy sideways glance, and put three pictures of herself out on the bed. Downstairs, Colonel Primrose wasn't exactly raging, but I could feel atmospheric pressure.

"I've got to hurry, Ginny," I said.

"Well, you can take your pick."

And that was easy. One of the three was the original of the demurely sweet and charmingly pretty girl I'd seen on Page One of the Taber City *Gazette*. The other two were Ginny in her ballet costume. One was enchanting, the other wasn't, very. It showed Ginny balanced on her toes and not too gracefully.

"I'm not really a terribly good dancer," she said frankly. She closed the cover of that one.

"Then may I take this?"

I don't know what it was, but I had, just that moment, some idea that there was more to this than met the eye. But I made my choice. It wasn't the one in the ballet costume.

She didn't just smile then, she laughed happily. "I knew you'd take that," she said. "That's Daddy's favorite too. Then she sobered quickly. "You better hurry. Don't tell him, will you. He'd think I was . . . I was trivial. Did . . . did he say reporters are going to call you up?"

I nodded.

She seemed to be thinking soberly, for an instant. "If they call, what should I say?"

"Just don't say anything. Say I'm not here. Be sure, won't you."

"Yes, ma'am."

I hurried down the hall, put Ginny's picture on my bed and got my coat. The phone rang while I was doing it, but only once and I knew Colonel Primrose was answering it.

When I got down he was glaring at me from the foot of the stairs.

"That was Agnes Manners of Northern Belt News Service. Where's Ginny?"

"She's stubborn," I said. "She'd rather talk to the police. If we're going we'd better go.—She's used to the police."

He hesitated a moment, and followed me out then. "What's happened to you?" he demanded. "There's nothing amusing about all this."

"I know there's not. I'm just a little groggy, I guess. Ginny gave me her picture. I wasn't to tell you. But it was so . . . so irrelevant."

"Her picture?" I was switching the car lights on. "What for?"

He asked it very seriously.

"Oh, just an act of contrition," I said. He was still looking oddly at me. "For mercy sake, give the kid a break, Colonel. You act as if she's Machiavelli or somebody. Don't be so relentless. She heard what you said about Field."

I told him about the letters, and what Field had promised. "She was just trying to play him and Allerdyce off against each other."

"And *I* act as if she's Machiavelli," he said sardonically.

We drove in silence across Wisconsin Avenue to Foxhall Road. I thought he was merely irritated, at me and Ginny, but he was much more than that.

"It's nice you can be so light-hearted about Ginny's picture," he said. "It's hardly a fair trade for Field's life and the destruction of the only evidence we had to support Molly Brent's fastastic story. If we have nothing to show as a source of all the intimate knowledge this Allerdyce has, don't you see even Mr. Brent won't believe her? Your young Machiavelli, my dear, may have destroyed a great deal more than a simple packet of letters."

"Destroyed . . . ?"

"The letters are burned. The police figure Field had them somewhere in plain sight . . . there's no evidence of any ransacking. They can tell the ashes of folded airmail paper when they see them. I'm not being foul about Ginny. I'm just desperately anxious that her bizarre mixture of astuteness and naïveté doesn't kill off a few more people here. You don't see what this thing tonight really means."

If I didn't know then, I knew a moment later, or began to know. There were police at the entrance of Nunnery Lane, with a rope stretched across between the concrete pillars, and half a dozen reporters there. One of the officers stopped the car, recognized Colonel Primrose and nodded us on through. There was something a little ominous in the atmosphere that was emphasized by the closed gate at the Brent house and the policemen there too.

I looked anxiously at Colonel Primrose. "Look . . . they certainly don't believe that stuff of Vair's, for heaven's sake, do they? Or do they?"

He shook his head quickly and pointed to the car a little ahead of me around the circle of the drive, and he was out and up the marble steps to the front door before I could adjust myself to the appalling impact of the insigne on the car's rear bumper. It was the one thing I should have been prepared for, and it had never remotely entered my mind . . . the blue cross above the license plate that meant there was a doctor there.

I could see Colonel Primrose's face in the light from over

the door. It hardened curiously as he waited for the door to open. My legs seemed numb and everything in slow motion as ominous as the silence that was like a pall over the whole Lane.

"Maybe I'd better not come in," I said. He shook his head, listening intently. I could hear steps on the marble pavement inside then. Someone was coming. The knob turned, and the door opened, not far, just enough to give me the illusion of a chain holding it secure against us. The illusion was sharpened the instant I saw it was Forbes Allerdyce who was there, a barrier far more effective than any chain would be . . . I saw that strange inert pause of his as he recognized us, and the sharp reflexive movement of the door in his hand, as if his unconscious impulse was to shut it immediately in our faces.

"I'd like to see Miss Brent, please," Colonel Primrose said.

And then a very strange and terrifying thing happened. Neither of us expected him to let us in, and he hadn't for a split second intended to do it. But the split second passed. There was a sharp flicker of almost satanic light in his eyes, and an electric tensing of excitement too dynamic not to communicate itself. It was a flash quicker than light, and in it, brilliantly illuminated for one hair's breadth of an instant, was the design. It was a design for the murder of Rufus Brent. It was almost like a high voltage fuse blowing, its acrid reek as sharp, it seemed, as the light gleaming in his eyes in that bare split instant of its conception. It had a kind of satanic logic too, that granted the devil's promise was brilliant in the extreme. I was the cause of Mr. Brent's heart attack. Seeing me would be an acute and terrible shock again.

I saw it too and it terrified me.

"Why, come in, Colonel Primrose. Come in, Mrs. Latham."

Controlled as he was after that fraction of an instant, he couldn't keep the faint glint of triumphant malice out of his voice as he swung the door open.

"Go right along. They're in the library. I can't imagine anyone they'd be happier to see."

He wasn't the smiler with the knife under the cloak. He was the smiler with the pole axe swung up over his head.

From somewhere in the distance came the long low banshee wail of a siren.

"You'll excuse me," Allerdyce said courteously. "I have to wait for the ambulance."

—He wasn't going to be there and be responsible for letting us in. ". . . They pushed their way past. I couldn't stop them. . . ." His version of it to Mrs. Brent was implicit in his easy smile as he moved to the door again.

I touched Colonel Primrose's arm. "Please, let's not."

He shook his head and went rapidly along the black-and-white chessboard hall to the library door. It seemed such incredible folly to me. I looked back. Forbes Allerdyce was laughing . . . not aloud, but it seemed to me I could hear him, hideously, and I drew back again.

Colonel Primrose took my elbow, opened the library door without hesitation and gave me a forward push into the room.

XXII

The doctor's curt professional voice clipped across the room: "You'll have to be quiet, Mr. Brent can't be disturbed," and Colonel Primrose brushed past him, with a callousness, as it seemed to me, that was shocking. He went directly to Mr. Brent on the sofa.

"I came as soon as I could," he said.

Mr. Brent looked ghastly. He was conscious, resting there . . . or not resting, I saw then, because there was a kind of awful tension in every muscle of his body, his face grim, one hand half-raised, like a great claw, as if some kind of compulsion held it there, removed from any volitional control he himself exerted.

"Is it Colonel Primrose?"

"—You must be quiet. You must be quiet, sir."

The doctor's voice was like a Greek chorus. Heaven knows everything else was quiet in that room. Mrs. Brent, her cheeks stained with tears, was motionless. Her eyes had fixed on me just once, so full of pain, so betrayed, that even though I hadn't betrayed her I felt as if I had and looked quickly away. Molly Brent was as still as death, like a flame-tipped arrow caught and imprisoned in a block of crystal. It was the first time I'd seen her not in white shirt and blue jeans and daubed with paint, and she was lovely. Only her eyes moved, with a haunting flash of relief, as she saw Colonel Primrose and me, and even then they darted warily to the hall where Allerdyce was.

And then the most extraordinary thing happened. Mr. Brent's hand, the tense cataleptic claw, suddenly relaxed and dropped to his side, the rigidity drained from it as it was drained from his rugged and care-tortured face, and his eyes, resting on his wife, glazed peacefully over.

He's dead. It was like the wind whispering through a broken shutter in my mind. Mrs. Brent gave a low heart-broken moan and Molly Brent took a quick step toward her.

"No, no." The doctor was at his side, fingers on his pulse. "Fine. Splendid. He's relaxed." He nodded encouragingly to Mrs. Brent.

Mr. Brent's eyes had closed. He flicked them open then, looked at Colonel Primrose for an instant, moved his head in some kind of sign, breathed gently and closed his eyes. Colonel Primrose took his hand, Mr. Brent's fingers closed on his.

I heard Allerdyce at the front door. ". . . Straight along." The tone of it like the words was as brutally callous as if the ambulance aides were disposal agents come to cart off a dead horse. Mrs. Brent showed no sign of having heard it, and Molly stiffened, her dark eyes suddenly alive with fear, as if she were seeing the great emptiness of the house and herself alone in it, her father gone, her mother blind. I thought for an instant she was going to turn and streak off, the way she'd done at the farm, and God knows this time with reason to do it. But she stood fast.

"Mother!" she said. Allerdyce was in the hall, Colonel Primrose had followed the white-coated litter-bearers to the library door and stopped there. "Mother! Send him away . . . Allerdyce. Please, Mother! Don't let him stay here tonight!"

"—You would be very wise, Mrs. Brent," Colonel Primrose said.

· Perhaps if I hadn't been there, she might have listened to them . . . or if the picture of Ham Vair shaking Colonel Primrose's hand with Ginny Dolan, proud and happy, and with my house number plainly visible behind her curly head, hadn't been right there on Mr. Brent's desk. In spite of her distress, her eyes moved to it.

"—How could you have done it. . . ."

It was me she was talking to.

"I didn't, Mrs. Brent," I said. "I had nothing to do with it."

"Please. . . ."

Colonel Primrose shook his head at me.

"Where is Forbes?"

"I'm right here, Mrs. Brent."

He came in and went directly to her.

"Go to your room, please, Molly. This has been a hard day. You aren't really well."

"I'm perfectly well, Mother. He's lying to you. I didn't imagine anything of what I said. You've *got* to believe me."

"Please, Molly."

For an instant Molly was a flame newly lighted. The light

died out of her face and eyes then and she crossed the room silently and went out. Mrs. Brent closed her eyes.

"I'm very tired, Colonel Primrose."

"We're going, Mrs. Brent. I want to tell you that Molly is not ill. She is not imagining these things. She is deeply devoted to you and her father."

"I . . . I don't want her to be unhappy," Mrs. Brent whispered. "I . . . I've never understood her. . . ." She got up heavily. "Forbes will see you to the door. You'll excuse me, won't you."

She went past me without a word, and I heard her going up the stairs.

What if he is really a murderer? I thought. *They're alone with him in this house.*

A cold hand fastened itself on my heart. I started as Colonel Primrose took my arm. "Come along," he said. "They'll be all right. Nothing will happen here tonight."

"—I don't know why you're so down on me, Colonel," Allerdyce said coolly. He was the cultured young man again. I hadn't been aware till that instant how far he'd been different from it those past few moments, as if his triumph of that night had got the best of him.

As he opened the door for us, I could almost have believed for an instant that one of the concrete pillars at the end of Nunnery Lane had moved and planted itself firmly there at the foot of the marble steps. It was Sergeant Buck, his fish-grey eyes fixed on Allerdyce, politely holding the door for us. If he had any idea of what was behind that congealed dead pan searching him from tip to toe, he was a superb actor and a man of steel finely tempered.

"I don't understand?" he said, very Ivy League indeed. "What's the idea of this . . . ?"

Buck looked at Colonel Primrose, turned and spat, a visible period, and strode across the cobblestones to the gate.

Colonel Primrose looked back at Allerdyce, standing at casual ease there in the doorway. "For your information, Mr. Allerdyce," he said, urbanely and very Ivy League himself, "Sergeant Buck came to have a look at you. He was very nearly an eyewitness of the murder of Edson Field this afternoon. His testimony will convict the murderer. Come along, Mrs. Latham."

Then, as we turned, I heard a frantic voice, Mrs. Brent's, calling from the stairs across the hall behind us. "Forbes! Forbes! Molly's gone!" and Colonel Primrose turned, pulled the door calmly shut there and went down the steps. I thought he was mad, stark staring mad, or I was.

"Let's get out, quick," he said. "—Archie's got her away."

But that was a mistake, as it turned out. Archie hadn't got her. He'd waited there, for hours, by the terrace, but Molly Brent didn't come. I was out in the car, waiting for Colonel Primrose to get through his long talk with Sergeant Buck, when Archie came running around the end of the house and up to them. Colonel Primrose stood for an instant listening and came running to the car. "Get home quickly," he said. "She may remember your house number from the picture. Remember these things: call Marjorie as soon as you get there. She may try to get to the farm. Call my house and tell Lafayette to get up and let her in if she comes, and call Lamb and tell him to send a man to Archie's apartment. Describe her to him. If there's a policeman out here at the gate tell him I say to stay there."

He was back in the house then. Sergeant Buck stood by the steps. It took me a minute to get myself together.

"The Colonel said to get going, ma'am."

That voice was like a garbage can dragged over a steel grating, except for the monstrous immobility of the face it issued from. I got going, and stopped at the other concrete pillars. There was a policeman there. The reporters had gone.

"Nobody's come in since the ambulance left, except the big guy to see the Colonel, and nobody's left, lady. No red-headed girls."

"Well, watch, anyway," I said.

Two squad cars, red lights blinking and a touch of the siren at the intersection, zipped past me half-way down Foxhall Road. And at my door I had to bang against that blasted chain for hours, it seemed like, before Ginny came down, her hair in pin curls, barefooted, in her bathrobe and nothing on under it.

"I was taking a show—" She stopped in the middle of the word as she had in the shower and stared at me. "What . . . what's the matter, Mrs. Latham?"

"Has Molly Brent been here?"

She was following me back to the phone in the living room and she stopped dead.

"Molly? What's . . . what happened?"

"Molly's gone."

"But Allerdyce . . . where's he?"

"He's there."

She plopped down on the sofa. "Oh, that's all right, then," she said. "Why didn't you tell me, and then I wouldn't have worried." She folded her bathrobe around her knees and re-garded me calmly and with great detachment. "Don't you worry," she said. "She's not dumb. That's the trouble with all you people. She's not a baby. She's got some money—I gave her some this afternoon. Because we knew she might have to get out of there." She looked at me again. "But you'd better call Marge, I guess."

"It's getting out of that place, Ginny," I said. "It's dark, and if she's frightened. . . . But there are police there."

"Oh, well."

She pulled the robe around her knees again. "She'll . . . she'll be all right. She'll call up."

I didn't know whether she was as confident as she pretended, but she was in my room like a flash when the phone rang at midnight. It was Colonel Primrose. They hadn't found her but she'd called the hospital and told the nurse to tell her father she was all right and not to worry. The call had come in within half an hour of the time she'd left, so the hunt through the slopes around Nunnery Lane was called off. And Archie Seaton was searching the roads leading to the farm, so nobody could call him to tell him she was safe.

And the next morning my phone started ringing at eight o'clock. I'd glanced at the papers, but there was nothing in them I hadn't heard on the broadcast. Ham Vair couldn't elaborate until he was safely cloaked with Congressional immunity, and I wasn't at home to the reporters who started calling me for comment on his night's speech and Mr. Brent's new attack. There was no mention of Molly Brent, and with Ginny following me around like a hungry puppy and diving for the phone every time it rang, and Lilac taking that day of all days to start washing the ruffled curtains, muttering and grumbling, I was glad to escape the house even for the dentist at eleven o'clock. I was just getting my bag off my bedside table when the phone rang, and I beat Ginny to it by a hair's breadth, as she was clear across the room and I was right on top of it.

It was a very crisp, very efficient female voice.

"Miss Virginia Dolan, please. Congressman Hamilton Vair is calling."

"Just a moment," I said.

Ginny already knew.

"That's Ham Vair, isn't it?" she demanded eagerly. Her eyes were sparkling. I stared at the child, really aghast. "I *knew* he'd call me," she said, and took the phone, batting her eyes excitedly as she waited for his booming voice. I didn't hear it, because she held the phone tight against her ear. All I heard was the yellow chick in full charm school form.

"Oh, hello, Ham! How are you?"

She listened then, her eyes widening, smiling like an angel. "Mad? Me? What would I be mad about, Ham? Goodness, no. Hones'ly, Ham."

She paused again. Then she said, "Why, Ham, aren't you sweet? I'd love to have lunch with you . . . but not today. That wouldn't be too good, would it . . . so close after your speech. Next week, what about that, Ham? Okay. Thanks a lots. 'Bye now."

She put the phone down, the charm school smile still on her face till she turned her head and saw whatever it was on mine. Then she broke into a peal of the merriest lilting laughter I've ever heard.

"I wish you could see your face, Mrs. Latham," she said. "You look just like my mother."

Then she sobered abruptly, and put her hands on her hips and squinted her eyes together.

"Look here, Mrs. Latham," she demanded. "You didn't believe *that,* did you? You didn't think all he had to do was whistle and I'd come, did you? Well, you ought to be ashamed. *Hones'ly.*"

Her eyes were molten sapphire. "I don't know what you think I am, Mrs. Latham. Daddy says if you're a sucker once, it's not too bad, but if you're a sucker twice, you *are* a sucker. I just said that to him to keep him quiet till I'm ready for him. Daddy says if you keep 'em on your side and keep 'em guessing, they fall like rotten apples and you don't get hit. You just wait. You don't think we want *him* for our senator, do you, Mrs. Latham? You don't think *I'd* eat lunch with him! Because now I know. I thought Forbes had stolen those letters from him, but he didn't. Ham Vair gave them to him. That's why Allerdyce took them back to Sybil."

When the phone rang again then, Ginny answered it. "It's another reporter," she said over her shoulder. "—I'm sorry, Mrs. Latham isn't here." She slapped the phone down. "Why don't you go? They'll drive you crazy."

I was going as soon as I got my strength.

XXIII

It was a foul day, simmering hot with that metallic overcast that means a thunderstorm in the making, and I'd have run into another one if I'd gone home to lunch when Lilac was doing curtains. It was about three o'clock when I walked back across the P Street Bridge and saw Archie's car in front of Colonel Primrose's. He was there in the back room, and he looked awful. He hadn't shaved, he hadn't slept and he was as gaunt as if he hadn't eaten for days.

"She called Marge," he said. He put his head down on his hands and kneaded his stubbly pink skull as he'd done at the farm. "I'll kill that devil if he scares her again."

Colonel Primrose had both his telephones, listed and unlisted, out in front of him on his big flat desk and the extension from Detective Headquarters in an open drawer at his side.

"If you'd stayed at your own place she'd have called you too," he said brusquely.

"I'd go crazy. The boy'll tell her where I am."

I couldn't tell from Colonel Primrose's irascible glance whether he was angry or disgusted.

"Well, snap out of it and get started," he said. "And watch yourself. Leave things to Buck. It's his business. If Buck doesn't show, you know Captain Lamb's man. But stay put. I could be wrong, but you'll get your girl."

He looked at me then, said "Sit down," and waited till the front door closed on Archie. "The damned young fool," he said. "He can't see this is the one place she won't call."

"Why not?" I demanded. "And where's he going?"

"He's going where I expect Allerdyce to turn up," he said shortly. "And 'why not' is what I've been trying to get hold of you all afternoon to tell me."

He looked at me very oddly, I thought.

"It's time to quit playing games," he said deliberately. "Do you know where Molly is? Or don't you?"

"Of course I don't. How should I know? Or should I?" He was beyond me. "Do you know?"

"I have a damned good idea. It's the sort of childish conspiracy I expected you to be in on. If I'm wrong, I apologize."

I was already sitting down, so there was nothing left for me to do but take my hat off and mop the perspiration off my forehead and look as thoroughly blank as I was. I quit mopping my face then as an obvious question occurred to me.

"If you know where she is, why don't you go get her?"

"I'm waiting for Allerdyce to move," he said quietly. "As long as I can. I underestimated him. I figured he'd be out by now. That was the whole point of that business at the front door. But he's a real gambler. He's not getting out as long as he's got a gambler's chance. That's why I haven't 'found' Molly Brent. And he's still got a gambler's chance. It all depends on Mr. Brent."

He sat there thinking for a moment.

"Allerdyce outsmarted himself, last night. He's hanging on at the house because he thinks Brent's a far sicker man than he is. He ushered us into the library last night, of course, so when you appeared Mr. Brent would have another attack. That was a mistake. He knew it was Vair's broadcast that gave Mr. Brent this attack. He still doesn't know he had the attack not because he believed Vair but because he saw at once Vair was lying. If Vair hadn't gilded the lily, Brent would still have been on Allerdyce's side when we got there. As it was, he was waiting for us, holding on to himself desperately."

What part of that broadcast could be called gilding the lily, when the whole lily was false, I couldn't see.

"Look, my dear," he said. "I was in touch with Brent all day yesterday and got to see him a minute or two this morning. He's a realist. He knows all women talk. I told him what his wife had told you, and what Field told me at three. He knew about the speech Vair was going to make. He wasn't surprised at the picture of Vair and Ginny and me on your porch . . . though Allerdyce got hold of it too quickly. But when we heard the broadcast, he saw what was up, and he knew for a fact you hadn't told Vair."

I might have been acting in a wilfully obtuse way again, but I didn't understand.

"For the simple reason," he went on, a little more patiently, "that Vair didn't know what had given Mr. Brent that first attack, at your house yesterday. If you'd told Vair any of it, you'd have told him that. There's nothing he'd have liked to use better than the picture of Molly. Vair's assuming it was your telling Brent his wife had told you about the threat showed the whole thing was phony."

I said "Oh."

"Up to then Brent had believed, in spite of everything, that Molly was making up a story and you and Marge were hysterics. I was serious when I said the loss of the letters appeared a bad blow. I couldn't prove they were burned. So Brent regarded all of us as fugitives from the pulps. Last night he suddenly realized that if anything happened to him, Molly and her mother were in terrible danger. That, of course, is why he relaxed when he saw me . . . up to then, he'd been in hell's own agony at what Molly and Mrs. Brent could be in for if he died.

"If Allerdyce finds out Brent's not as sick as he thought and he's going to recover, he'll clear out, fast. Buck's out there, waiting. If little Miss Dolan hadn't been so *Machiavellian*, with her politics. . . ."

He broke off and looked out the window.

"This weather worries me. I don't want it to break."

I looked out too. There didn't seem a chance of its breaking before the usual late afternoon. There weren't any black clouds that I could see. What the weather had to do with it anyway I didn't see.

He sat there drumming on his desk for a minute, looked outside again, reached for his phone and dialled. "Busy," he said. "What's Brent's private number?" When I shook my head he got his notebook out of his pocket and dialled again. When that was busy too he frowned and pushed his chair back.

"I can't wait any longer. We'd better get out there. Where's your car?"

"At home."

He dialled again. "There'll be a taxi here in a minute. You'd better come along. I'm afraid Mrs. Brent's going to need a friend."

He pulled open the center drawer in his desk. I'd started to put my hat on and stopped. He was taking out the blue silk envelope with my milk of magnesia toothpaste on it, that Ginny had taken from my casual hands to give to Buck.

He smiled, not without a certain embittered amusement, at the look on my face. "At least Lilac and Buck had sense enough to look and see what was in it. After the business of Edson Field at your house, and when the police found letters burned in his fireplace, Buck thought he'd better clarify his and Ginny's skirts, as he puts it. He came through this morning. Wire-cutters, I think you said. Ginny took six, out of the original packet, and a covering letter to Vair, and she kept them. Vair was sent the batch by a marine, a constituent of his, who'd got hold of them, thought the Brents lived in Vair's district because there's a Brentool Plant there and sent them to him to deliver. Ginny must have got hold of them at Allerdyce's hotel, and if she hadn't told Vair, Field and Allerdyce that Field had got all of them, she might be where he is now. She was also risking your neck, as well as her own."

When the doorbell rang he got his hat and raincoat and followed me out to the taxi. I was still a little groggy.

"—Wire-cutters," I said. "You were right, then, about the letters. Mr. Brent was wrong."

There was some genuine amusement in his smile then. "I was right. For the wrong reason. Two of these have a detailed description of 'Forbes Allerdyce.' "

We rattled across the street car tracks on Wisconsin Avenue, and I thought of something else then. "Why didn't you tell Archie? If you know where Molly is?"

"I was stupid enough not to think of it till ten minutes before he came, and I needed him then."

We slowed around the curve and up the hill to Nunnery Lane.

"Stop at the left-hand gate. Turn around and wait," Colonel Primrose told the driver. We got out and hurried across the cobblestones to the front door. The courtyard was as empty as the Lane had been. Neither Buck's car nor Archie's was in sight. Allerdyce's was. The door of the garage was open and I could see it in there, the University of Maryland sticker on the window giving it an almost obscene air of spurious youth.

"He's still here," I said. He was a gambler and a killer and still here. "For heaven's sake, be careful," I said. "You haven't got a gun."

He rang the bell and then reached out and turned the knob. The door opened, we stepped inside. I've never been in so silent a place. Colonel Primrose stood there for an instant.

"—Mrs. Brent?" he called.

It was still silent there. He went rapidly along the hall to the library door and I followed. Mrs. Brent was there. She was sitting in the needlepoint armchair near her husband's desk, his private telephone zinging rhythmically away in the open drawer. Her face was ghastly, her blue eyes drained, her lips as flaccid as her hands lying uselessly in her lap.

She raised her eyes slowly to Colonel Primrose.

"He's . . . gone," she said.

I thought for a moment that this was the despair that Mr. Brent had foreseen, the anguish at the bitter loss of another idol wrenched from her heart. But I was wrong.

"How could I have been so blind?" she said. "How could anyone have been so cruel, Colonel Primrose? All day I've been waiting to hear from my husband, and from Molly. They told me not to come to the hospital, and I knew Molly would call me if she could. But he . . . he's had the telephones out of use. Molly had to . . . to send me a telegram. I had to telephone the doctor myself. He told me my husband was better and they'd been trying to call me. And I . . . I looked up at Forbes, and I . . . saw him looking at me. I was afraid. I was desperately afraid, Colonel Primrose. And he saw I was, and he said . . . he said horrible things to me. He was furious. He was like . . . like an animal. I was sick. . . ."

She put her head down in her hands. "But how . . . how did he know? How did he know all. . . ."

Colonel Primrose took the blue silk envelope out of his pocket, opened it and took out the letters.

"This is how he knew, Mrs. Brent. These are all that are left."

She looked at them.,

"But, my husband destroyed all their letters. . . ."

"Not these," Colonel Primrose said gently. "These are not your boy's letters to you, Mrs. Brent. They are your letters to him. The ones he cared about so much that he saved them. They were found after he was killed, and they came into the possession of this man. It was your own words, and your own memories, that he gave back to you. You believed them because they came from your own experience and your own heart. It was your account of the 'tutor' Forbes Allerdyce that gave him that name and that character."

He put the letters in her hand. She let them lie there, her eyes slowly filling with tears. "Rufie kept them," she said softly. She looked up then. "You know, I'd . . . I'd begun to wonder," she said, to my surprise. "Because they were little imps, really, so much of the time, and it . . . it didn't sound like Rufie to pretend to a tutor that he was always such an angel!"

She was silent for a moment. Then she said, "Thank you, Colonel Primrose. I never knew they . . . they'd keep what I wrote. I just wrote the things I wanted them to remember . . . to tell them both how much we loved them. Thank you . . . so much."

He was at the telephone before she'd finished. "—Help Mrs. Brent get her things, Grace, and wait for me in the taxi."

We went out into the hall. "You'd better get a raincoat," I said. The first rumbles of outlying thunder had begun ominously to roll. I didn't go upstairs with her but back through the drawing room to the service wing. The maid was huddled out there, waiting for the storm.

"Did Allerdyce have a car?"

She got up and nodded. "He took Mrs. Brent's."

"Was Sergeant Buck here? Do you know him?"

"Yes, ma'am. I saw him. He was right behind."

I went back to the hall. "—Baggage room or check room," I heard Colonel Primrose saying.

His face was grave as he got in the taxi with us. He rolled down the window and looked up at the sky. It was so dark already that the driver switched on his parking lights and by the time we were crossing Wisconsin Avenue he had full lights on.

"It's going to be a stinker," he said. "What's the address again, Mister?"

When Colonel Primrose gave him mine I looked at him questioningly.

"Archie's meeting us there. I got hold of him."

He was very grave, and I didn't know then that the fear he had was for something more terrible than Allerdyce, or that Allerdyce had already been trapped at the Penn View Hotel, where he came to collect his luggage and his maroon convertible, and that he was already under arrest and charged with the murder of Edson Field. He didn't want to tell Mrs. Brent, and he didn't want to tell her, or me, what the danger was that he feared worse, as the storm was coming, literally and figuratively, piling up and bearing down with a speed and violence he couldn't have foreseen.

It was literally true, certainly, because normally we'd have had at least another hour, the way it looked when we left his house. It had darkened as abruptly as if a sable pall had been suddenly wrenched loose and thrown out to cover the world. I had my key out. The first wide flat drops had begun to spatter the windshield when the taxi stopped and Mrs. Brent and I hurried across the walk and up the steps. I looked back for Colonel Primrose, but he'd stopped, and then I caught a glimpse of Archie getting out of his car. He was half-way down the block and the curb was solidly lined. The wind was whipping the trees, tearing loose the leaves and hurling them like black snow against the shutters. I tried to wait for the two of them, but I couldn't because the wind was tearing the door from my hand. I'd expected the chain would be on, but it wasn't, and the door crashed full open then, the wind funnelling through the hall. Mrs. Brent got in, and I caught the door and had to use all the force in my body to crash it shut.

Then the flashes of heat lightning playing around the ends of the earth leaped across the sky, and a great jagged spear of lightning, with the thunder simultaneously, shattered the universe and blazed white in my hall, and millions of gallons of rain let loose and poured down, beating at the windows.— Coming inside, I thought as I saw the wall above the staircase. Water was dripping down it. Then I saw it was black instead of blue and I knew it wasn't rain water but tap water because it's happened before, when the bathroom taps are left open when the pressure's off and start quietly running, still open when the pressure's on again. And I didn't stop to bother about Mrs. Brent. I dashed up the stairs around the newel post. It was the third floor bathroom, not mine and not Ginny's . . . and just then another streak of lightning ripped out, lighting the hall. On its heels, as if all the horsemen of hell were loose tearing over the field of heaven, came another rending crash, and in the light or in the after-image searing my mind I saw Ginny Dolan.

She was crouched at the foot of her bed, hanging on to it, her bright spun-sugar head buried in her arms, in such a frenzy of terror that I forgot the pouring taps on the third floor.

"Ginny!"

I ran to her. Her body writhed, her arms were pressed hard against her ears.

"It won't hurt you, darling!" I shouted above the crash-bang that shivered the figures on the mantel and shook the windows like a bomb blast. But then I saw the water coming down her wall too, and I ran toward the stairs.

"Don't! Don't!"

She tore herself away from the bed and beat her fists on the floor.

"Don't go up there! Get Archie! Get Archie! Don't go up there . . . please don't!"

Then I knew where Molly Brent was, and I knew more than that . . . I knew what Colonel Primrose's fear was, for Molly Brent, and I ran back to the stairs and called for Archie, because I knew only he could go up those stairs to the girl up there, with hell's monstrous cameras lighted with every searing flash out of the black night in her tortured mind.

Then he was there, coming up the steps four at a time and around the newel post, and Ginny Dolan was beating the floor with her little fists. "Don't scare her! Don't scare her! In back! Oh, Archie, I've tried *all day* to get you!"

She buried her face in the bed then as another flash and another resounding crash came and the ornaments on the mantel and the bottles on the dressing table reverberated like tiny cymbals, grace notes trembling above that orchestration of the universe.

Then, as I reached the door at the foot of the third floor stairs to open it for Archie, it burst open, and the stairs were blue-white with the glare through the skylight. Upstairs, a door crashed open, and crashed shut again.

"Quick, Archie . . . she's opened a window!"

He went on up four at a time, but silently, and I hurried up behind him. The water was pouring in quiet rivulets all down the baseboard. He'd quit going swiftly then, and was going slowly, desperately slowly, feeling his way on the stairs lighted only when another flash came above the skylight. I could see the rigid line of his head and shoulders. The wind caught the door to the back room and ripped it open again and he sprang forward to catch it, to keep it from crashing shut then. He braced himself against it for an instant then. We could see her, caught then in another of those monstrous flashes epitomizing all her terror—the night and the huge camera flashes, the rending crash of the thunder like the crash of her own car against the tree—as she stood at the opened window, the rain and wind beating in on her, trying blindly to run. . . . Another door slamming downstairs sent a swift shudder through her body pressed close to the window, her hand out, and Archie raised his voice, to get through the deafening impact of wind and rain and thunder and her own terror. His voice was vibrant and clear and alive as the love it carried across the room to her.

"Ragweed . . . it's Archie. Ragweed!"

She moved her head, her eyes blindly staring, but she'd heard.

"Hey, Ragweed, get away from that bloody window. It's wet out there."

She turned then and he was across the room. "It's Archie, Ragweed." He caught her in his arms and she clung to him. He held her one moment with both arms, and reached out then for the window. "Let's close this thing. We don't want to get drowned."

And I suppose that's what I was waiting for. Sticks and stones and good wet plaster were nothing to them but a lot to me, and I slipped into the bathroom and turned off the water that must have been quietly running for hours.

XXIV

They were still there when I went back and closed the door, Archie still holding her tight, and talking to her in words that were pretty silly, I suppose, but that had all the tender balm of Gilead in them. And at some point it must have quit being brotherly, because when they came downstairs and Molly rushed to her mother's arms her eyes were flecked with gold as burnished as her hair, and she was a starlit girl, as radiant as the sun that was shining now on the Silver Moon roses on the garden wall.

They were considerably improved too, when I saw them, because Archie'd shaved and Molly was dry, in one of Ginny Dolan's blue dresses, her donkey's-tail groomed in proper place again. They hadn't even seen my sodden walls. But Mrs. Dolan's daughter had, I tell you. She was down on her knees when I came down from the third floor, desperately trying to sop up the pool of water collecting at the foot of the stairs with a bath towel, so scared and so white-faced that the tail end of the storm had no more fears for her. The poor kid was sobbing, trying her best, and when she saw me it was like seeing doom itself.

"Oh, Mrs. Latham . . . it's my fault! She didn't know, it's all my fault! I was just trying to get her some place *he* couldn't find her. Uncle Phinney took me out, and the cook's husband got us away. Because we couldn't tell Colonel Primrose. We tried to get Archie, and then Lilac said you wouldn't care. But she said if we told you, Colonel Primrose would be sure to find it out, and Uncle Phinney said he couldn't tell him, official-wise, because . . . because he'd have to tell Mrs. Brent, because if he didn't he'd . . . he'd be accessible after the fact and abduction's against the law. That's why we couldn't tell anybody. . . ."

She caught her breath, and looked down at the soaking bath towel and up at the wall still quietly dripping. "I . . . I'll do anything, Mrs. Latham. Mother would . . . she'd kill me, if she knew."

"Don't worry," I said, happy for once not to be told I looked just like that woman . . . except, of course, I do feel like killing my own young when they've flooded me out. It seemed so minor, however, after the catharsis of the unleashed elements and the relief of Molly Brent's salvation that it really didn't matter much. "It'll dry out," I said.

Of course I'd seen what it was that Colonel Primrose meant by his "conspiracy of children," and I should have known it, I expect, over at the Brents' when Sergeant Buck had stuck, with his monumental immovability, there in the courtyard, disturbing it only to tell me to get going, instead of lighting out with all the rest of them to search the grounds for Molly. He was the maverick, accessible before and after the fact and also during it.

But Ginny Dolan was still a miserably unhappy little girl. "I . . . I just thought if I . . . if I could fix Ham Vair," she said dolefully, "he'd turn on that Allerdyce, and everything'd be all right. But that Allerdyce, he's kin of Satan, but Ham Vair . . . he's really Satan."

She took the towel into the bathroom and wrung it out and brought it back for another mopping up.

"Just leave it, sweetie. Lilac'll get the rest of it."

That was malice for you. It would be the one time a mess was of her own making, not mine.

It was that evening, after Mrs. Brent and Molly and Archie and Uncle Phinney and Ginny had gone over to the Brents', and Colonel Primrose and I had gone to the Army and Navy Club for dinner and to get away from it all, that I told him what Ginny had said. And it was then he told me that Allerdyce was under arrest and would be charged with the murder of Edson Field.

"It's unbelievable," he said, "how that one thing changed his whole appearance. I remembered what you'd told me, about how he looked on your front porch without his spectacles on. When he let us out at the Brents', I got a good look at him from one side. You could see they magnified a pair of pig eyes. When Buck saw him at the Penn View, when he and Archie cornered him, he'd taken them off, and Buck recognized him at once. He'd seen him coming out of Field's."

"It seems pretty grim to me," I said, bitterly, "that Ham Vair, who really is the Satan behind all this hell's broth, just gets out of everything scot free. He can mourn for his good friend Edson Field, he can deny Forbes Allerdyce and be terribly shocked and wholly innocent. His trusted investigator double-crossed him. He started out to wreck Mr. Brent, and he's done it, as far as ITC's concerned. Mr. Brent'll have to go home and rest. Ham'll go to the United States Senate. The homespun David who brought down Goliath."

Colonel Primrose was smiling placidly.

"You've got the right comparison," he said. "Your identities aren't quite right. You haven't seen the evening papers. I brought one along.—David used a slingshot, I believe. Didn't you tell me Ginny Dolan prefers wire-cutters?"

On the front page of the paper he handed me was a picture, a whole three columns wide, of a girl in a ballet costume, and about the prettiest girl who ever wore one and still managed to look so sweet and so demure that it was cheesecake in crinoline if ever I saw it.

TALENT SHOW WINNER NEVER GOT JOB VAIR PROMISED

the caption over it read. Under it, with a promise of the whole exclusive story of the Life and Times of Miss Ginny Dolan in next Sunday's and following issues, was an interview in which, under a distinguished woman reporter's by-line, a little David from Taber City had really laid a Hot Rod Goliath in the dust.

I could see those morning-glory blue eyes wide and innocent as a charm-school rose as Ginny Dolan struck Congressman Hamilton (Call Me Ham) Vair to the heart with Daddy's wire-cutters and twisted them, time after time.

It wasn't—the twinkling-toed, keenly disappointed little winner of the much-touted contest Mr. Vair had conducted in the Ninth District of the Marsh Marigold State told the reporter—that there wasn't a job open when she got to Washington. She knew Mr. Vair had a very large staff and if he enlarged it people would begin to wonder where the money came from. He should have told her parents, she thought, because they'd be worried about her alone in Washington, especially when Mr. Vair had promised to meet her at the train, and indeed if it hadn't been for a very kind older man getting a taxi for her, and another friend of her father's getting her a nice place to stay, she didn't know what she'd have done, in a great big city all by herself, that first night she arrived.

I looked at Colonel Primrose. Archie as a very kind older man was a particularly nice touch.

After the way everybody, parents and high school students alike, had worked to make the contest a success, Miss Dolan hated to have to go back home and have everybody laugh at her. "It makes us all look sort of like suckers," she said. "But I guess we are," she added. She went on to say that it had surprised her very much to see Mr. Vair drinking cocktails, because she'd heard him herself make a speech about cocktail parties in Washington, and promise people who'd vote for him that he'd keep his nose to the grindstone and never let himself be lured by the false blandishments of Washington Society that drained the manhood from the representatives of honest hardworking people. No siren song in his ears, he'd said, and that's what surprised Ginny Dolan so much when he took her to dinner at his lady friend's home that had the biggest bar Miss Dolan had ever seen outside a hotel. She supposed he had to go there, of course, because she understood his lady friend was putting up a lot of money for his campaign.

And while people in Taber City weren't what you'd call straight-laced, Ginny didn't think they'd like their representative in Congress married to a lady who'd been divorced two times and called Taber City a hick town. She didn't, she said, think it was right for Mr. Vair to laugh at things like that. She was also surprised at the clothes he wore. In Taber, she said, he went around like everybody else, but at his lady friend's house he took off his regular coat and put on a silk coat she'd bought as a present in New York. Miss Dolan just didn't know what the men of Taber City would think of that.

But the thing that shocked her most, she said, was that a soldier in Korea had sent him some letters belonging to a boy who was killed, and he was supposed to send them to the boy's bereaved parents, but he hadn't done it. He'd kept them and used them for his own campaign, and Ginny didn't think the mothers of boys who were fighting in Korea would like that sort of thing very much. In fact, Ginny was terribly afraid that Hamilton (Call Me Ham) Vair wasn't the high-class man she and everybody in Taber City had once thought he was. And anyway, Miss Dolan said, "If he's going to get married, I don't think he ought to wait just because he's afraid we won't elect him if he married a very rich lady who thinks we're hicks. Because we don't like 'foreigners' running our business. We don't like divorce, and men in fancy clothes and stuff . . . but if that makes us hicks, we like that, and I guess we'd better get another hick to send to Congress. And I'm not saying I've never seen my father take a drink," Miss Dolan finished that day's interview, "but he doesn't lap it up and wink and say don't tell the folks back home. I'm real disappointed in Mr. Vair," Miss Dolan said.

I put the paper down and looked at Colonel Primrose again. He was considerably happier about it than I was . . . for if this was how Ginny had been keeping Ham Vair guessing till she was ready to shake the bough, it didn't take three guesses to see who the rotten apple was going to land on—if Daddy was the hand and Vair the glove.

She came into my room to answer the phone the next morning.

"Is it long distance?" she asked. It was the only time she hadn't made a dive for it.

I nodded, and Ginny swallowed. I saw the swallow start, and go clear down until it disappeared under the small round collar of her blue print rayon pajamas. Then she approached and took the phone out of my hand, very reluctantly indeed.

"—He's going to be awful mad at me," she said, and braced herself. Then she said, "Oh, hello there, Daddy! How are you?" It was a stout effort, and I left her to it and went into the bathroom to finish dressing. When I came back, she was propped against my bed, her bare feet flat on the floor. She was still white around the gills.

"Oh, brother," she said. "Is he mad at me."

I guessed the rotten apple had hit harder than I'd thought. She was the soberest little girl I've ever seen.

"Well, what did you expect, Ginny?" I asked. "After all, if he's Vair's chief——"

"Oh," she said. "Oh, I don't mean that." She brushed that off like a dog hair off the sofa. "He doesn't care about that. Ham's sunk. You should have heard what Daddy called him. I guess Mother's not home, because she doesn't let him use that kind of language, not in the house. That's all right. Ham's sunk and the sooner he knows it the better off he'll be. I know Daddy. Daddy says never hang on to a liability politi-cal-wise—or otherwise, unless you're married to it, Daddy says—and brother, that's what Ham Vair is right now. And I'm not through with him and his lady friend and her charge account, I tell you. No, *sir*. It's not Ham he's mad about. It's me."

"You?"

"My picture," she said. She stared down at her pink toes. "He says it's in the papers all over every place. That's what he's mad about.—Not enough clothes on."

She was still very sober-faced indeed.

"He's strict about some things. But I think I explained all right."

A mischievous smile danced suddenly in her sidelong glance at me.

"I told him I *had* to use it, it was all I had. I told him I'd given you the good one I really wanted to use, and I couldn't take it back, could I? Daddy wouldn't want me to be an Indian giver, would he? I asked him and he had to say no, of course."

All the silver bells were laughing then.

"Of course, I knew which one you'd take, when I offered one to you, and you don't have to keep it. You can give it to Molly. She'd like to have it and they're terribly expensive."

She giggled, and sobered up again. "But he says I've got to come home. He's going to phone Uncle Phinney to bring me. I guess I shouldn't have said that about the older man in the Station. But he'll be so glad to see me he won't care. That's Daddy. And anyway, the Brents are going to Taber, and I want them to meet him. Because the doctor called up last night while we were there. He has to take a little care of himself. But Molly's going to get married—I'm going to be bridesmaid—and with Ham Vair off his neck and Mrs. Brent acting like a civilized white woman, like Lilac said she ought to, I guess he won't have so much to worry him. So I guess it'll be all right, I guess."

She left the next morning. Uncle Phinney looked like a six-wheeler Diesel rig escorting a kitten, taking her out to the taxi that was taking them both to the Union Station, Ginny back to Daddy and Buck back to see his long lost, securely married love. Colonel Primrose could call his bursting pride frustrated fatherhood if he liked, but it was a pretty sight to see. And there'd be no pickups of older men, or beardless youths ei-ther, between P Street and Taber City.

It wasn't till she was safely gone that I really found I missed her. No chains on the door to bash it into, no pin curls, no radio, no midnight lectures on politics, no charm school, no creeps on the telephone, no Mrs. Dolan to haunt me in the shape of things to come. Peace, it's wonderful. Except Daddy. I missed Daddy.

The plaster dried and the ceiling fell and there was a major paint job to do. Colonel Primrose viewed the state of things placidly one morning late in June.

"There's a house just down the street," he said, smiling at me. "It's all painted. I told you it's very empty, Grace."

— It was time to consider the whole matter, and simpler now all my sticks and stones were a mess I'd be glad to leave. But the postman had handed me a letter, when I went to the door to let Colonel Primrose in, and I made the mistake of opening it on the way back to the living room. It was from my younger son. He'd got a new ribbon for his typewriter so I didn't need Braille to read it.

"Dear Ma," it said. "I don't know whether old Archie told you, but he got me a swell job out here at the Brentool Plant in Taber City. It was on that list I sent you"—that was in the letter still on my desk that I'd never really completely read— "but he's the one that really fixed it up for me. I guess you wouldn't know he's going to marry the Old Man's daughter. They're out here now, the Brents and old Archie, and they introduced me to a girl. She's bridesmaid and I'm going to be usher. Big deal. But sit tight, Ma. I'm going to bring her home, you'll be nuts about her. She's——"

That's all I read. I didn't read another word. I just brushed the dog hairs off the sofa and sat quietly down.

"Colonel Primrose," I said. "If there's a wedding, what relation is the mother of the bride to the mother of the groom?"

"None," he said, slightly puzzled.

"That's still too close."

"What are you talking about?"

"Mrs. Dolan . . ." I said. "And don't just stand there. If you love me, go. Go out to Taber City . . . and spring my son."

I told him, then, and he smiled and went placidly on lighting his cigar.

"The yellow chick's a very solid, very *high-class* little lady," he said. "We could do a lot worse . . . for a daughter-in-law, I mean."

"We could, indeed," I said. "A lots worse."

An ominous thought assailed me then.

"Look, Colonel," I said. "Do you happen to know? Does Uncle Phinney think my son's respectable?—Good enough for Ginny Dolan?"

Colonel Primrose smiled. "I was wondering," he said. "I was wondering if you'd forgotten your old friend Sergeant Buck."

CPSIA information can be obtained
at www.ICGtesting.com
Printed in the USA
LVOW08s0237210617
538825LV00001B/9/P